INTO THE FIRE

INTO THE FIRE

★ ★ ★

Bill Yenne

B
BERKLEY BOOKS, NEW YORK

THE BERKLEY PUBLISHING GROUP
Published by the Penguin Group
Penguin Group (USA) Inc.
375 Hudson Street, New York, New York 10014, USA
Penguin Group (Canada), 90 Eglinton Avenue East, Suite 700, Toronto, Ontario M4P 2Y3, Canada
(a division of Pearson Penguin Canada Inc.)
Penguin Books Ltd., 80 Strand, London WC2R 0RL, England
Penguin Group Ireland, 25 St. Stephen's Green, Dublin 2, Ireland (a division of Penguin Books Ltd.)
Penguin Group (Australia), 250 Camberwell Road, Camberwell, Victoria 3124, Australia
(a division of Pearson Australia Group Pty. Ltd.)
Penguin Books India Pvt. Ltd., 11 Community Centre, Panchsheel Park, New Delhi—110 017, India
Penguin Group (NZ), 67 Apollo Drive, Rosedale, North Shore, 0632, New Zealand
(a division of Pearson New Zealand Ltd.)
Penguin Books (South Africa) (Pty.) Ltd., 24 Sturdee Avenue, Rosebank, Johannesburg 2196,
South Africa

Penguin Books Ltd., Registered Offices: 80 Strand, London WC2R 0RL, England

This is a work of fiction. Names, characters, places, and incidents either are the product of the author's imagination or are used fictitiously, and any resemblance to actual persons, living or dead, business establishments, events, or locales, is entirely coincidental. The publisher does not have any control over and does not assume any responsibility for author or third-party websites or their content.

PRINTING HISTORY
Berkley trade paperback edition: December 2008

Library of Congress Cataloging-in-Publication Data

Yenne, Bill, 1949–
  Into the fire / Bill Yenne.
    p. cm.
  ISBN 978-0-425-22375-8
  1. Afghan War, 2001—Fiction. 2. United States—National Guard—Fiction.
I. Title.

  PS3625.E46I58 2008
  813'.6—dc22

                                                        2008019880

PRINTED IN THE UNITED STATES OF AMERICA

10 9 8 7 6 5 4 3 2 1

CONTENTS

★ ★ ★

Prologue

★

Inyo County, California
September 7

★ ★ ★

"We got a blowup on Juniper Ridge, people," the fire boss shouted to his command staff, trying to appear calm. "We gotta get boots on the ground up there."

The California Division of Forestry had its hands full, fighting two adjacent wildfires that were converging on the little town of Mitchell, located in the Inyo Mountain foothills west of U.S. Highway 395.

"We haven't got boots to *put* on the ground," a worried-looking man with a soot-smudged face said as he removed his yellow hard hat with the CDF logo on the front. As he brushed his hair back, rivulets of sweat trickled down his forehead. It was midmorning, and already the temperatures were in the high nineties.

"Why the hell *haven't* we got boots to put on the ground?" the fire boss asked angrily.

"The crews we were supposed to get from Tuolumne County had to be diverted up to the El Dorado National Forest," the other man explained with a cough. The smoke-filled air made it hard to breathe, not to mention hard to see farther than a quarter of a mile. "The fire they got up there just jumped to nine thousand acres overnight, and it's a half a mile from South Lake Tahoe in a couple of spots."

California east of the Sierra Nevada was engulfed in flames. It was the worst fire season in years. With five major fires—and nearly a dozen minor ones—going simultaneously, the CDF's resources were stretched to the breaking point. One of the fires, nicknamed Redwood Creek, was burning inside Sequoia National Park, so the National Park Service had its hands full trying to save the grove that included some of the park's oldest and largest redwoods, including the General Sherman, the largest tree in the world.

"Tell that to the sixty-three families we evacuated from Mitchell overnight," the fire boss said disgustedly. He knew that he was shooting the messenger, but he had gotten four hours of sleep in three nights and he was a bit cranky. "If we don't get a fire line across Juniper Ridge on the east side, that whole damned town is toast."

"What about the air tankers?" a third man asked.

"If they weren't already working the Redwood Creek Fire, there's nothing they could do up on Juniper Ridge," the fire boss explained. "We got fifty-mile-an-hour winds up there. That's why we got the blowup. You can't put a safely loaded air tanker or chopper up in gusts like that. Even if you could, the drop would get blown off away from the fire. That's why we gotta get *people* up there."

"We ain't got people," the second man said sadly, still mopping his brow. "Our crews are all up by the Lone Pine fire, trying to keep 395 open. I don't know if even that's possible."

"What's *that*?"

The others turned to look through the sooty air toward where the fire boss had suddenly pointed.

Four tan deuce-and-a-half army trucks were driving up the road toward the command post.

"What *is* that?" asked the third man. "Is that the cavalry?"

"That, my friend, is the National Guard." The fire boss smiled. "That's our boots on the ground."

Justin Anderson and other members of the 3rd Battalion of the 184th Regiment of the California Army National Guard had dropped everything to be on this hot and smoky hillside in the middle of a nowhere corner of California that none of them had ever visited. A week ago, Justin had been surfing at Huntington Beach, his only care being the size of the waves that thundered in from the Pacific. Mainly, his care was that they weren't thundering as they should. Sometimes, when there is an offshore wind, the waves are puny. He didn't realize it then, but the same offshore flow that makes the waves second rate also dries out the inland hills, turning them into a disaster waiting to happen, the disaster that Justin and his fellow Guardsmen now faced.

Like all the others, Justin was not a Guardsman most of the time. He was just another guy, living with some other dudes in a cheap bungalow out in Venice and working his way through his third year toward a Criminology degree at UCLA. But for one weekend every month, and for a two-week stretch each year, he was a soldier in the 184th Regiment of the Cal Guard.

When a disaster struck, the Guard was supposed to be ready to back up state and local agencies. That's why each of the states have the Guard. The Army National Guard is technically part of the United States Army, while the Air National Guard is part of the United States Air Force. Except when nationalized by the president in time of war, the National Guard is under the control of the governor of the state in which specific units are located. When mobilized for war, as had been the case frequently since 2001, Guard units came under the command structure of the U.S. Army or U.S. Air Force.

Disaster had struck, and the governor had mobilized the Cal Guard. Justin Anderson, surfing one day, in college the next, found himself hacking brush and digging a trench across a hill-side somewhere about an eight-hour drive by truck from Los Angeles.

He knew it was a hillside, because the ground at his feet wasn't level. He knew little else, because through the dense and smoky haze he could *see* little other than the ground on which he was standing. He could see the part of the fire break that he was work-ing on, and he could hear the other guys nearby as they hacked and scraped at the ditch that everyone hoped would be enough to keep the flames away from Mitchell, California.

"Never thought I'd be this hungry at a barbecue."

The voice was that of Chuck Ellis, the assistant manager of a copier place in Glendale.

Justin squinted through the bluish haze. He could barely make out Ellis's silhouette through the dirty blue curtain that hung in the air.

"Wish you'd remembered to turn on the air-conditioning," Justin joked back.

"I'm sorry," Ellis said. "I thought you said you wanted me to turn up the furnace."

It was midafternoon, and the temperature had topped the century mark. The humidity was so low that the guys on Juniper Ridge figured it to be in negative double digits.

"You can go ahead and turn the furnace down now," Justin said. "Dial it back to about seventy or so, okay?"

"You got it."

Justin paused to pull down his bandanna and take a sip of water. Even that tasted hotter than seventy degrees.

He soaked the bandanna, pulled it back up over his nose and mouth, and grabbed his shovel.

Helmand Province, Afghanistan
September 7 (One Year Later)

★ ★ ★

The hills were engulfed in flames.

A pair of F-16s thundered overhead at ear-splitting altitude, making the ground shake. The Mk 84 bombs that tumbled off their wings ripped into the hillside, impacted, and the earth shook some more. Justin Anderson took little notice. He was used to it. It seemed like a very long time since he had noticed that the impact of heavy ordnance was out of place. His eyes were on the opposite hillside, watching and waiting, looking through the haze of compromised visibility for the enemy he knew to be there.

The village of Khadwal-i-Barakzayi lay at the base of a burning ridge. The sheets of flame and the billowing pillars of black that were creeping ever closer to the structures reminded Justin of Juniper Ridge one year earlier.

So, too, did the smoky stench that hung in the air.

It seemed like a lifetime since Juniper Ridge.

Justin hadn't thought about it much after the Cal Guard had

come home from Inyo County. They were up there for just four days, but they had built the fire line, and they had saved the town of Mitchell. They had plenty to be proud of, but having saved a town seemed totally out of context with being a student running for classes on the UCLA campus. Juniper Ridge gradually became just a blue black, misty dream, a memory overshadowed by the here and now.

He remembered that last night up in the mountains of Inyo County, as they sat around eating their dinner and talking. By that time, they knew that they had saved Mitchell, and the fire was contained. They knew that they could relax. They knew that they were going home.

Someone had said that he hoped that this was the closest they would ever come to combat. Justin had forgotten that until now. He wondered what made him remember such a prophetic moment.

It seemed like a lifetime since Juniper Ridge, but in reality, it had been *two* lifetimes.

Justin had gone back to a life of surfboards and classrooms, of cool ocean water and droning professors. Then, suddenly, he was here. A new lifetime came to consume him. Everything about his lifetime in Los Angeles—the beach, the campus, and even his bungalow in Venice—had long ago become a blue black, misty dream, a memory overshadowed by the here and now.

"Here they come!"

As Justin turned, the ripping sound of automatic weapons filled the air. A large number of armed men in turbans were rushing the narrow defensive line where the men of the 3rd Battalion of the 184th Regiment of the California Army National Guard were dug in.

Through the haze, it was hard to tell how many there were.

They were like blue black shadows materializing out of the smoky air. They looked like ghosts—except for the bright yellow orange muzzle flashes of their AK-47s.

The muzzle flashes were the same color as the flames that engulfed the hills.

CHAPTER ONE

Old World

★

University of California at Los Angeles
February 3
(Five Months After the Juniper Ridge Fire)

★ ★ ★

Justin Anderson made a right turn off Sunset Boulevard and wheeled his Porsche 911 toward the big parking structure on Sycamore Court. The old Porsche had seen better days. It rattled a lot in lower gears, but that didn't matter. It was still a chick magnet. Chicks liked Porsches, and they knew nothing about model years. At least they didn't care. It was still a status symbol within chickdom to ride with a guy in a Porsche.

Justin checked his watch.

Dammit!

Eleven minutes. He had eleven friggin' minutes to park and get to class down at Haines Hall more or less on time. He was cutting it close, but if he could grab a slot near the stairs, he could do it. One good thing about having enlisted in the California National Guard was that it had gotten him into the best shape in his life. For him, sprinting over to Haines was a piece of cake, and he was proud of this fact.

The UCLA campus was more than two hundred miles due

south of that Inyo County tinderbox where Justin's Guard unit had battled the forest fires last fall, and about a million miles from Camp Roberts, up in San Luis Obispo County, where Justin and his fellow Guardsmen had just trained for two weeks in December. It wasn't *like* having two lives, it *was* two lives. He rarely thought about his Cal Guard life while he was on campus and vice vesa.

Like the Porsche, Justin wasn't the best car in the lot, but chicks found him easy on the eyes. He was tanned and fit, with the body of a surfer, not a football player. He was athletic without being a jock. UCLA had a lot of top-grade jocks on its Pac-10 football team and its world-class basketball team, but Justin wasn't one of them. He could hold his own in a pickup game, and he could probably outrun half the football team if it came to that, but it didn't. He really didn't care. When it came to that sort of jock posturing, he was too busy hanging loose. Most jocks on campus were just jock wannabes anyhow.

Today, Justin was running not for a touchdown but for Professor Heddin's Criminology 303 class over at Haines. Justin had decided to major in criminology so that he could join the FBI, like his father. When Justin was growing up, he was an okay student, but his father had always pushed him to do better. As with most boys in high school, Justin pushed back. He had taken an easygoing life for granted, but suddenly, things had changed. He was a senior in high school when his dad was badly injured while saving three people in a hostage situation at a bank in Detroit.

While his father was recuperating, the two had a number of long talks: the kind that fathers often have with sons about the meaning of life. Justin eventually learned from his father that it was important to give back to your country, and he decided to do so by joining the Guard. But for Justin, this was as much about gimme as giving back. The Guard would help with college tuition.

The recruiter smiled when he told Justin, "We'll put zero degrees of separation between you and your education." The guy told Justin that the National Guard had a program, an enlistment option, called College First. It allowed people to attend undergrad or graduate school full-time, with financial benefits that could potentially pay for someone's entire education.

Justin smiled when he asked, "Where do I sign?"

National Guard experience wouldn't look so bad on his résumé when the time came to apply to the Bureau.

"Mr. Anderson," Professor Heddin said as Justin barged through the door and tumbled into a seat near the back of the room. He was not smiling. "I don't care whether or not you want to be in this class, but I wish that you'd make your entrances a bit less disruptive for the rest of us on those frequent days when you're coming in late."

"Sorry, Professor," Justin said, trying not to smile. "But it's only six minutes."

"Mr. Anderson, this is not an entry-level course. This is upper-division forensics. The people who are sharing this classroom with you are not here taking Something 101 to get rid of their sociology requirement. I would assume by your being here that you are serious about the content of this course and about how that might pertain to a career."

"Yes," Justin acknowledged sheepishly. The old professor stared at him over the top of the glasses that perched on his narrow red nose. Heddin would have resembled a buzzard, if buzzards wore herringbone jackets and bow ties. Most professors didn't care whether you arrived late or whether you arrived at all, but this man was of a different generation.

"Those who go into careers where criminology is applicable

are entering jobs where timing and precision are of utmost importance. Being on time is the least that I would expect. See me after class."

See me after class! The cloud hung over Justin as the professor droned on and on about striations and gunshot residue. Justin took a few notes, but his mind wandered. The old man had scolded him for a reason. He wanted to jolt Justin into paying closer attention, but it had the opposite effect. His mind wandered. He'd much rather be at the beach. Better still, he'd much rather be *off* the beach on the face of a five-story wave.

Justin was crouching on his board, feeling the power of some minor monster, when suddenly the people around him started standing up. Shit! Class was over. He looked at his notebook. Three lines of notes and some scribbles. He'd lost track of the whole damned fifty minutes.

"You wanted to see me?" Justin said, approaching the professor. Might as well get it over with.

"Mr. Anderson, do you have any idea what sort of grade you're getting in this class this term?"

"I think I've got a pretty solid C, so far?" Justin ventured, phrasing his answer as a question.

"You *did* have a pretty solid C *minus*."

"Did have?"

"The midterms aren't due to be handed back until next week, but I've graded yours and thought I'd better give you a little preview."

"Okay..." Justin replied tentatively.

"You failed," the professor said succinctly. "You failed, and you failed miserably.

"How miserably? I figured that I ought to have gotten at least a D."

"A D? Hardly. You got eleven correct out of sixty-two. Even if

I were to cut you some slack on the essay question, you failed. Do you have any idea why you failed?"

"Not paying attention?"

"Why weren't you?"

"I dunno. I guess I just didn't get to all the reading?"

"Did I not make it clear that the midterm was a third of your grade?"

"Yes, you did make that clear."

"Then, Mr. Anderson, I'm afraid that you now have a failing grade in Criminology 303, and you had better do extremely well on the final."

"Yes, sir."

Since he'd been in the Guard, Justin has become accustomed to calling people *sir*. He couldn't tell whether the professor took it as a measure of respect or that Justin was mocking him. He just looked at Justin with an unsympathetic expression. Everything that needed to be said had been said.

Outside the austere redbrick walls of Haines Hall, it was just another perfect spring day in LA. Justin had an hour to kill before his sociology class, so he decided to go grab a latte. As he was making his way past the Shapiro Fountain, he heard someone call his name.

"Laurie," Justin said, glancing up at a young woman in faded jeans and a dark blue tank top lugging a pile of books. "How ya doin'?"

"I'm well." Laurie Hall smiled, tossing her head so that her long blonde hair shimmered in the sun. "How are you? I hadn't seen you around for a while."

"I've been studying pretty hard," Justin lied. "Gotta do good in these midterms so that I can keep the old GPA up."

"Yeah, I know," Laurie agreed, smiling at him in that almost shy way that women have of letting you know they're interested in you without actually saying they're interested in you. Like his Porsche, Justin was a chick magnet. Chicks liked surfers, with their easygoing grins, just as they feared jocks, with their angry sneers, and avoided nerds, with their detached self-absorption. And Justin had always liked Laurie, with her easygoing manner and her perfect smile. They had seen one other at parties quite a bit and had talked a lot. She was just a sophomore, so they didn't have any classes together, but they were both in the sociology department, so he often saw her around.

A couple of times, Justin had thought about asking Laurie out, but he never had. He looked at her now, admiring the contours of her body in the skimpy tank top and tight jeans, as they made small talk, and he wondered why he never got around to asking her out. It was a mystery. She was hot.

He needed to rectify his previous oversight.

"What are you doing tonight?" Justin asked, coming right to the point.

"Ummm..." she said nervously, taken aback at his suddenness and trying not to blush. "I was gonna study, but I don't really have to...guess I'm not doing anything."

"You wanna go have dinner somewhere?"

"Umm, sure." She smiled. "I'd like that."

"How about we go over to Nobu in Malibu?"

"Nobu?" Laurie smiled, her eyes lighting up. She was more than slightly stunned. Nobuyuki Matsuhisa's ultrapopular, hot-as-wasabi eatery was not just trendy, it was the kind of place that the glossy magazines called chic. "That sounds very nice."

They made plans for Justin to pick her up at her apartment in Santa Monica and parted company with the broad smiles of two people who were very excited about the evening to come.

After daydreaming his way through his sociology class, Justin headed home to shower, roust some clean slacks out of the back of his drawer, and put on that new Tommy Bahama shirt that he was saving for an occasion like this. He didn't bother to shave. Chicks liked that stubbly look.

When Laurie answered the door, Justin caught himself choking down a lump that surged into his throat. All afternoon, he'd pictured Laurie's perfect figure poured into those faded jeans. Now he was looking at her perfect figure poured into a satin, spaghetti-strap dress with a deep V-neck that perfectly accentuated her cleavage. Her wholesome face with the cheerful smile had looked good on campus that afternoon, but with just enough eye shadow, and with lipstick that matched the color of her dress, no word short of *gorgeous* described her. He cursed himself for never getting around to asking her out before.

"You sure look nice," he said in a tone that made up for the understatement in his choice of words.

"Thank you," she smiled, pleased to have an affirmation of her choice of wardrobe. When Justin had asked her out, Laurie had skipped her afternoon classes to race out to the mall and agonize for two hours at three dress shops before making her choice. If she was going to Nobu, she decided that she was going to Nobu *right*.

They made small talk as they headed up the Pacific Coast Highway. Justin told her that he knew of a party that night farther up the road in Malibu and suggested they might stop by after dinner. Laurie recognized the names when Justin mentioned two actors, both fellow surfers, who would be there, and Laurie said it sounded like fun. It was always fun to rub shoulders with Hollywood types. As they turned onto Cross Creek just before Malibu Canyon, Laurie asked him if he came to Nobu often.

"No, actually, I've never been here," Justin admitted. "I've just always wanted to try it and see what all the hype was about. Have you?"

"No, but I've sure heard about it," Laurie repled, surprised to be asked such a question. Nobu was way beyond her budget, and so far, none of the guys who'd asked her out had suggested anything in this neighborhood of the stratosphere. Nobuyuki Matsuhisa had come to California from Japan by way of Peru, where he invented his special style of Latin-Japanese fusion cuisine that had people talking—and using superlatives as they did. A-list celebrities came to Nobu for quiet dinners and dropped a thousand bucks on champagne.

With a perfunctory smile, the hostess showed them to a quiet table near a corner. Laurie thought she recognized Robert De Niro at a table across the room, but she couldn't tell. Justin was sure that there were more than a few pairs of male eyes on Laurie Hall as they walked through the crowded restaurant, and he *could* tell.

When she opened the menu, it was Laurie's turn to find herself choking down a lump that surged into her throat. The prices burned her eyes so badly that she could feel her mascara start to melt. For a girl from Manteca who had been to a city no more than a dozen times before she was accepted at UCLA, these were the kinds of numbers that made her instinctively want to order a salad and get the hell out of there.

"Lots of good-looking stuff here," Justin said, apparently unfazed by the numbers. Laurie wondered whether they were looking at the same menu. He didn't mention that he had his father's credit card. His mother had insisted that he have it as backup when he went to school—for "unavoidable expenses." Taking Laurie Hall to Nobu was, in Justin's mind, an unavoidable expense.

"The broiled black cod with miso sounds delectable. What looks good to you?" Justin observed.

"Well," Laurie said, noting the price of the broiled black cod and looking for something a *little* less pricey. The Kobe beef looked good, but you don't order the most expensive thing on the menu on a first date—especially *this* menu. "Well, I think that the rock shrimp tempura...with the ponzu sauce...would be good."

She was right; it was delicious. So, too, was the conversation. She had always thought of Justin as a "hang-loose" surfer dude, but the man who emerged as they talked was a lot more three-dimensional. She hadn't known that his father was an FBI agent, especially a decorated hero who had been wounded in the line of duty. She knew that Justin was in criminology, but she hadn't known nor grasped the depth of his commitment to the field and his desire to commit himself to all that "truth, justice, and the American way" stuff—like in the Superman stories. She understood him better now, and she could start to imagine him filling the role as *her* Superman.

Justin was also growing more fond of Laurie. She was hot. He knew that long before he asked her out, but a lot of chicks were hot. There was a lot more than hot to Laurie. She was more than just a small-town girl with a B average in the most challenging campus of the state university system. Like so many women pursuing sociology degrees, she had the trappings of a do-gooder, but when she talked about making the world a better place, she was a lot more articulate than most.

There were some surprises that cropped up as they poked at their dinners, not wanting the evening to end. Justin was surprised to learn that she spent her Saturdays teaching blind children to swim. Justin had never given it much thought, but Laurie explained that it gave them self-confidence when they overcame a fear of something as intimidating as a huge volume of water they could not see. Laurie was astonished when Justin told her that he was in the National Guard. That was the last thing she would have imagined.

After dinner, they decided that neither was in much of a mood for the party, but when Justin offered to show her one of his favorite surfing beaches, she readily agreed.

The weather was still warm, and they both laughed when Laurie's three-inch heels proved impractical for walking on sand. Justin held her hand while she removed her shoes, and she didn't let go as they started strolling toward the surf. The moon was full, and it made the waves almost phosphorescent.

Having discovered that she was a swimmer, Justin asked whether she had tried surfing.

"No, I guess I never really thought about it," Laurie said. "They don't really have big waves in Manteca."

"You want to try it?" Justin asked.

"Sure." Laurie smiled. "But I don't think I'm really dressed for it."

"I don't mean now." Justin laughed. "I mean sometime. I could take you out sometime. We could go down to Huntington or Doheny or someplace."

"Yeah, I'd like to do that." She smiled. "Sometime."

Justin marveled at how beautiful she looked in the moonlight. This was one of those situations that they must be thinking of when they used the word *romantic*.

In fact, such a word was almost on Laurie's lips when a wave abruptly surged upon them, splashing the two distracted twenty-somethings with its salty froth.

Seeing the water level surging suddenly to almost waist level, Justin instinctively grabbed Laurie and lifted her up in his arms. As Laurie felt herself being snatched from the surf, she immediately flashed back to her earlier fantasy about this big man with the scraggly whiskers being her Superman. It felt good. It was a little awkward to suddenly be grabbed up into someone's arms, but it was very romantic.

The wave receded almost as quickly as it arrived, followed by a successor so timid that it barely covered Justin's feet. Nevertheless, he carried Laurie up the beach away from the ocean. He was about to put her down when she reached her arms around his shoulders and pulled herself close to him.

Their first kiss happened so naturally that it was not in the least bit startling, as first kisses often are. The second was long and passionate. The third began and ended only when it was absolutely necessary to take a breath of air.

She felt his hand on her bare thigh, as she maneuvered her hand inside his Tommy Bahama shirt. He was surprised by her eagerness and the way she resisted as he tried to put her down. The fragrance of her perfume was intoxicating and her kisses succulent. At last, as she got her arms beneath his shirt, she allowed her feet to touch the ground.

"Aren't we a mess," Laurie giggled, stepping back and straightening her skirt. "You're soaked."

"You got a little splash of ocean on you, too, I noticed," he laughed. The lower part of her dress was wet, but she was right, his last pair of clean slacks was sopping wet.

"Well, I would have been *soaked*, too, if Superman hadn't come along and swooped me up." She smiled. "I guess we better get out of these wet clothes."

"Umm, we could go over to my place in Venice," he said. It wasn't often that a guy so easily gets handed an opportunity for such a line. "My roommates are down in Cabo for a week."

"That sounds like a good plan," Laurie said, taking his hand. "I don't think my girlfriends would be very receptive to me bringing home a big drowned rat."

Rochelle, Colorado
February 3

★ ★ ★

"*Soy cansado*," Felipe said, yawning and looking at the line of pick-ups pulling out of the sprawling parking lot at the huge home improvement warehouse. "*No deseo esperar al gringo rico.*"

"Speak English, man," Luis Carillo told him. "This is America. This isn't Mexico. If you're going to make it here, you gotta show them that you want to fit in. I don't like sitting around here in the cold, waiting for the rich gringos to hire me to do odd jobs any more than you, but these gringos pay you more in a day than you could make in a month back in Sonora."

Felipe just shrugged and spat a wad of spent chewing tobacco into the gutter.

It *was* humiliating. Luis hated sitting around here watching the contractors come and go in their warm pickups, waiting for someone to wave and say that he needed *dos hombres* to clean up scrap lumber at a construction site, or *tres hombres* to do demolition work on a remodel. He hated the way most of the gringo contractors treated you like a slave, and he hated the fact that even though he finally had his green card and a job stocking shelves at Target, he still had to spend his weekends doing this. As much as he disliked all of this, he liked the money. In America, money was the key.

Luis had come north as a teenager, splashing his way across the Rio Grande near El Paso long before the Border Patrol started taking this seriously. He worked in the melon fields for a while but continued to move north. He had been in eastern Colorado for a decade now, out here in the wide-open spaces far from the Rockies.

When Luis first came, Rochelle was just a dusty farming town, the hub for the farms and ranches that spread across Elbert County in a landscape that looked more like Kansas than the mountainous western part of Colorado that gringos think about when they think about going to Colorado for skiing. Today, Rochelle was turning into a suburb, not of Denver, but of Denver's eastern suburbs. This was where the gringos who worked in the office parks on the outskirts of Denver came to buy their "affordable" four-bedroom, three-bath homes. It was the construction of huge tracts of such houses that provided employment for countless—and uncounted—Hispanic men, both illegal and legal.

"*Soy cansado*," Felipe repeated disgustedly. "*No deseo esperar al gringo rico.*"

"Well, then go ahead and leave," Luis told him. "Go to the bar. Suck on Coronas all afternoon while I take the gringo's money."

"*Usted es est pido*," Felipe said, calling him stupid. "*Usted desea ser un gringo?*"

"No, I don't want to *be* a gringo. I just want to be able to have the money they have."

"*Conozco a un hombre… él puede hacerlo rico*," Felipe said slyly. "*Usted toma los paquetes para él.*"

"If this hombre you know can make you rich delivering packages, why aren't you rich? Why are you *here*?"

"*Rico, Luis,*" Felipe said. "*Usted toma los paquetes para él.*"

"No."

The word was the same in both languages. Luis was not interested in delivering packets of cocaine for the hombre who promised to make Felipe rich. Luis wanted to be an American. He wanted to marry Roxanna and bring her up from Chihuahua—legally—as his wife. He wanted to live with her in one of the homes in the housing tracts instead of in a one-room travel trailer. He wanted their children to grow up American.

Just as Felipe slouched down and pulled his dirty Colorado Rockies baseball cap over his eyes, a blue pickup slowed, and the man shouted at them.

"I need *uno hombre* to do some work, *pór favor*," he said, holding up one finger. His Spanish accent on *pór favor* was terrible, but even if Luis understood no English, the gringo's meaning would have been clear.

Luis sprinted toward the truck, prepared to vault himself into the bed. That was the usual drill. The hired help rode in the back with the lumber. This time, the gringo pointed to Luis and then to the door on the passenger side of the cab.

Felipe ambled across the pavement toward the truck, but the man held up his finger and repeated, "*Uno hombre.*" He only needed one man. Sometimes, if you pretended not to understand and just got into the truck, they'd let you go anyway. Not this time.

Luis grinned smugly at Felipe as he got into the truck, and Felipe replied with a single finger gesture of his own. Luis was glad that the gringo hadn't seen it.

"*Buenas días,*" the man said, "Speak English?"

Luis was about to reply, when he suddenly froze. He knew the man. He was a man from Luis's *other* life.

Luis Carillo lived three lives. There was his life as a Mexican, as part of the Hispanic culture below the border, where his family identity was rooted and where Roxanna waited. Second, there was his life as a green-card American, living and working as a stranger in a progressively less strange world. Third, there was his life as a member of the Colorado National Guard. When he got his green card, he figured that the best way to prove that he *really* wanted to be an American was to join the National Guard. The little bit of money he got for showing up every few weeks didn't hurt, either.

Now, his three worlds had suddenly collided.

The man driving the pickup, the man who had just picked up a casual laborer, was a sergeant in the 3rd Battalion of the 157th Field Artillery. Luis knew him well, and he knew Luis. The question of whether he would *recognize* Luis did not go long unanswered.

"Carillo? Luis Carillo? Is that you?"

"Yes," Luis said, hanging his head. He was embarrassed to be in this predicament. He had held his head high as a guardsman, but here he was, having been discovered to be the lowest of the low in American society: the shadow world of the casual laborer.

"What are you doing out here?" Sergeant Ben Meehan asked. "I thought you worked at Target or somewhere?"

"Yes, I do," Luis said, staring at the floor of the F150 as it idled at a traffic light. "I do this on weekends to make extra money. I'm trying to get enough money in the bank so that I can bring my girlfriend...her name is Roxanna...to bring Roxanna north...so we can get married."

"Shit, man," Meehan said, shaking his head. "I wish I would have known. You speak really good English. I could get you on part-time jobs that pay a helluva lot more than what you can get hanging out with casual labor. You're a smart guy. You should be working as a carpenter's helper, not dragging crap off of job sites."

"I just never knew how to get into that kind of work," Luis said, looking up.

"You have your green card, right?"

"Yes."

"Okay, when we get back from deployment, I'll make some calls," Meehan promised. "As soon as the 157th gets back from Afghanistan, I'll get you set up with a helluva lot better job. You can probably even quit your job at Target. The way they're building all these places out here, you oughta be able to get on with a good outfit."

"Thank you, Sergeant Meehan," Luis said, smiling. Like few times since he sloshed across the Rio Grande a dozen years ago, he felt as though he belonged in America.

Venice, California
February 4

★ ★ ★

"What the hell?"

Justin Anderson awoke to the sound of someone knocking on his door.

What the hell time is it?

Justin opened one eye to look at the clock radio on the dresser. As he watched the red LED turn from 8:22 to 8:23, he noticed the rumpled pile of peach-colored satin on his floor, and he remembered the night before. Laurie Hall had been like an animal last night. Justin had been badly mauled, enjoying every minute of it—correction, every hour. It had gone on until past midnight, when they took a break for cold pizza and went at it again. He had no idea when the mauling ended, but it was 8:24 now.

"Somebody is at the door," Laurie said groggily, sitting up in the bed and modestly pulling the sheet up to cover her exquisite breasts.

The knocking at the door repeated.

"I know," Justin said, rolling over and looking up at her.

Damn, she was sexy with her hair rumpled like that and traces of eye shadow still defining her eyes. He wanted to pick up where they left off, but someone *was* at the door.

"Justin, are you there?"

The voice was that of Chuck Ellis, and it was very out of context. Justin's Cal Guard life and his life in the Venice bungalow were worlds apart, and it was jarring when worlds collided.

"Yeah, I'm here," Justin shouted. "Gimme a minute, will ya?"

"Who is it?" Laurie asked, obviously concerned.

"Guy from my Cal Guard outfit."

"What does he want?"

"I'll find out," Justin said as he pulled on a pair of jeans and a T-shirt.

"Hi, Chuck," Justin said as he opened the door. "It's good to see you, too. What's happening?"

"It's the regiment, Justin," the other man said breathlessly. "Today is mobilization day. I didn't see you, and your cell phone was off. I didn't know if you had a landline."

"I don't," Justin answered. "Now, what's all this about a mobilization day?"

"Didn't you get the notice?" Ellis asked. "The notices went out more than a week ago. I got mine. Your name was on the list. You should have gotten yours."

"They sent it by friggin' *mail*?"

"That's how mine came."

Justin started digging through the pile of letters and junk mail that was lying on the table near the door. He usually opened his mail once a month to pay the bills. The rest was always just junk mail. Nobody important ever sent him any real mail. It was always just e-mail. Even his mother never even sent him a real birthday card anymore.

"Oh yeah, this," Justin said, and he located and ripped open an envelope with the blue and gold California National Guard logo.

"I can't believe this shit," he said. "This is *today's* date!"

"That's what I've been telling you," Ellis assured him. "We were supposed to muster at 0730. When you weren't there, I figured I'd better come get you. We're supposed to leave from the armory in Van Nuys at 1400 hours."

"This can't be real," Justin moaned. "That's five hours. I can't do that. This has to be a mistake. I have classes this afternoon. When I signed up, they said I wouldn't be mobilized. Not for years."

"If that's the case, then it's definitely a screwup," Ellis said, glancing at Laurie, who was standing in the bedroom doorway. She had commandeered Justin's bathrobe and was listening nervously to the men talking about a mobilization. "Why don't you call the registrar at the university? They can probably e-mail you a form or something."

"Good idea," Justin said, grabbing his cell phone.

Making herself at home, Laurie invited Chuck Ellis to come in and have a seat while Justin stabbed at the phone with an interminable number of extension numbers and numbers from his student ID card. As Laurie rooted around in the bungalow's tiny kitchen looking for a coffeepot, Justin finally got through to a live person. He identified himself, explained part of the problem, and was put on hold.

"Yes, this is Justin Anderson," he said, as the real person came back on the line after a minute or so of listening to more obnoxious on-hold music.

Laurie and Chuck paused to listen.

"That's damned right," Justin said. "I signed up under the College First enlistment opportunity. Yes, that's what they said...

they told me that my education is high on their priority list. They guaranteed no overseas deployment."

The person on the other end of the line said something about two years.

"Two years?" Justin replied. "Yeah, I guess so. Yeah, I guess it's been over two years. Two years seemed like a helluva long time, back then."

Laurie and Chuck could hear more chatter but couldn't tell what was being said.

"I know that my GPA is low," Justin said. "But I'll bring it up this quarter. Go ahead and check."

There was a pause as someone was checking something. Justin looked genuinely worried.

"Yeah, I'm still here. You checked? Flunking Criminology 303? But the quarter's not over, I *could* still get an A. What do you mean, you're sorry? This is my life here!"

"What did they say?" Laurie asked as Justin clicked off the phone. She could tell by what she'd overheard and by the pallid color of Justin's face that what they had said was not good.

"They said," Justin began, speaking as though he were in a state of shock, which for all intents and purposes, he was, "the guarantee of no overseas deployment was only for two years. This is my third year, and my GPA happens to be down this quarter, and I guess I'm flunking Criminology 303. I've been *had*."

"We've all been had, Justin," Ellis said, standing and patting him on the back. "All of us, the whole 3rd Battalion, ships out at 1400. I gotta get back. You want to ride back over there with me?"

"What if he doesn't show up?" Laurie asked.

"Well, that would make him technically AWOL," Chuck said. "Actually, he's been technically AWOL since 0730, but that would be overlooked if he's on the truck at 1400."

"What is AWOL?" Laurie asked.

"It means absent without leave," Justin explained. "It means that I'm subject to arrest. It means that they send the MPs after me, and if they catch me, I go into the stockade, and then if I'm lucky, they'll let me out to go wherever the 3rd Battalion is going, but with a black mark next to my name."

Laurie looked at Chuck, who nodded in agreement. Justin was right.

"Just where *is* the 3rd Battalion going?" Laurie asked.

"Afghanistan," Ellis said.

Waycross, Georgia
March 3

★ ★ ★

"Jimmy, where the hell you at?" Lennie Cahner shouted, walking through the service bay of Cahner's Quick Lube and Service. The boss man had a predilection for shouting before looking. If he would have taken two minutes to look, he would've seen that Jimmy Ray Flood was flat on his back under the partially disassembled transmission of a 1999 Dodge pickup.

"Y'all got that fuel pump replaced in Mr. Brewster's Toy-ota?" Lennie Cahner yelped, still not seeing or even bothering to look for Jimmy Ray.

Lennie was not the real boss man. He was actually the boss man's twenty-two-year-old son, but when his daddy wasn't around, that made *him* the boss man. Jimmy Ray didn't like that, but then there were a lot of things that he didn't like about Lennie, starting with his arrogant and condescending attitude. Jimmy especially didn't like that this punk was a dozen years his junior, and that he treated all his black employees as though the Confederacy had won the Civil War.

"You told me to get this transmission done before noon, and not to touch anything else till I was done with it," Jimmy Ray explained, not bothering to slide out from beneath the Dodge.

"Well, Ah'm tellin' you to get your ass outa there and back onto Mr. Brewster's Toy-ota," Lennie said, still talking louder than he needed to, and pronouncing Toyota as though it were two separate words. "Ah told him that y'all'd have it ready by noon."

"You never told *me* that," Jimmy snarled.

He tried to control his temper, but it wasn't easy. His mean streak was Jimmy's worst enemy, and keeping it under control was a constant battle. He had a lot to be angry about. He had a lot to be *very* pissed off about. Raised in Chicago by a hardworking single mother who had him when she was eighteen, Jimmy grew up in the projects and on the wrong side of every law that wasn't written in the streets. He was only sixteen when he was finally busted for car theft and aggravated assault.

The assault rap was legitimate, but with the car theft, he was taking the fall for a guy who was twenty-two and who would have done serious time. As it was, Jimmy did eighteen months because of a pretty long rap sheet. When he got out, the guy who had done the car theft was dead. Jimmy and his mother moved back to the rural South, where their family had lived for generations. That was sixteen years ago—a lifetime. Finally, Chicago and the projects were receding into the distant memory of bad dreams.

Jimmy was an angry guy, but he was also a smart guy. He knew what had gotten him locked up, and he was determined, at all costs, to keep his mean streak under control. It was easier said than done. Wherever he looked, some white trash cracker was pissing him off, and he ached to bust the asshole in the face. But he didn't. Or at least he hadn't so far. If he ever did, Lennie would probably be the first.

One of the only things that held Jimmy back from clobbering Lennie was that old man Cahner was always fair to him. He wasn't touchy-feely or all smiles, but he didn't go out of his way to be a jerk like his son. The thing that he liked *most* about the old man, though, was how he kept Lennie in line. Whenever he was around, Lennie cowered like a whipped dog.

For the past sixteen years, Jimmy had been taking deep breaths and gritting his teeth, imagining that for every white trash cracker he wanted to kill with his bare hands, there was another pissed-off black guy—or white guy—who would be pissed off enough to beat him to it.

At ten minutes to five, Jimmy Ray Flood walked into the office and slapped two sets of car keys down on the desk near where Lennie Cahner was resting his boots. The transmission in the Dodge pickup was reassembled and turning the way it did when it rolled off the line in Detroit back in 1998. The owner, who needed it by noon, had called at 1:30 to say that he wouldn't get by until around 6:00. The fuel pump was installed in Mr. Brewster's Toyota, and Jimmy had even hosed the bugs off the grille.

"Could y'all sweep up that mess over in the lube bay?" Lennie said, barely bothering to glance up from the fishing magazine that he was reading.

If the old man was here, he would've let Jimmy leave ten minutes early—since he had finished his work—but Lennie relished his role as the kind of slave master who treated all his black employees as though the Civil War hadn't happened. Someday, one of the guys was going to pop Lennie. Jimmy wished it would happen soon, but he wasn't going to be the one who made it happen.

At 5:01, Jimmy clocked out and left without saying anything more to Lennie and started walking the half mile to the little one-bedroom shack that he rented. The family on whose lot the shack was located called it a cottage, but everybody else called it a shack. To Jimmy, it was home, but not exactly the home of his choosing.

A half-dozen years ago, Jimmy had lived in a good house with a pickup in the driveway and a hatchback in the garage. He and Kadeefa had made it past the seven-year itch, and Cathy was in a pretty good kindergarten. Everything seemed as though it was perfect and going to stay that way. But there were demons in that house, and they were living inside Jimmy.

He tried hard to keep his anger in check, but sometimes it just boiled over. A couple of beers were often all it would take. He managed to be civil at work, and most of the time. He never laid his hands on anybody, but sometimes he would just break things to blow off steam. Kadeefa saw the worst of it, and she laid down some rules. Finally, when Jimmy crossed the line one too many times, she took Cathy and moved back to Atlanta.

They tried to reconcile, but in her head, Kadeefa had already moved on. Three years ago, Jimmy showed up at Kadeefa's place in Atlanta to take Cathy to the mall. Kadeefa wasn't there, but her boyfriend was there in the apartment when Jimmy arrived. Jimmy lost it. He flew into a blind rage. Cathy grabbed him to stop him from killing the man, and he nearly hit her.

When Jimmy realized that he could have hurt his only child, he was stunned. Cathy, meanwhile, was terrified of the madman she saw in her father. Jimmy knew he had a long way to go to undo this impression.

He had turned his life around when he left Chicago, but he hadn't turned it far enough. The second thing he did after he begged his eight-year-old daughter to forgive him was to promise himself that he'd give up drinking. Back in Waycross, he started going to the Baptist church that his mother attended, and he joined the gym. He also joined the Georgia National Guard. He decided that he needed discipline in his life, and he figured that if he didn't have self-discipline, he'd get himself some of the drill sergeant kind of discipline.

Jimmy Ray got his drill sergeant discipline all right, and two weeks ago, he got his marching orders—literally. The letter in his little tin mailbox informed him—it used the phrase "to inform you"—that the 33rd Battalion (Provisional) of the Georgia Guard's 122nd Regiment was being deployed—to Afghanistan.

Two days from now, Private First Class Jimmy Ray Flood would be at Charleston AFB, boarding a big, fat airplane with about six hundred guys who he knew from summer camp.

Old man Cahner had wished him well and had told him that he would hold a job for him. Lennie never said a word. For all his posturing and wearing of camouflage-colored clothes, he was a coward. He talked the tough-guy talk, but Lennie wasn't going to be putting *his* life on the line half a world away.

The night before last, the other guys at the garage offered to take Jimmy out to the Silver Bullet for a few beers to say good-bye. Jimmy had politely declined. The demons had to stay locked away.

Jimmy could hear Big D yelping as he approached his cottage. He would miss that dog. Sometimes, when he was feeling sorry for himself, it was as though Big D were the only friend Jimmy had left in the world. Then he thought of Cathy. Tomorrow, he'd be in Atlanta to spend his last day in America for *at least* the next six months with her. It might be six months, or it might be more. They had said that the tour was going to be only six months, but the other outfits over there were all getting their tours extended, so who knew what to think?

Jimmy scratched the mutt's belly as he rolled on the ground near the limit of his chain. As Big D grunted happily, his owner looked at his cottage. It was just a shack, but Jimmy would miss it. The landlady said that she could hold it for him for a month or so, but not for six, and certainly not for a year. He'd moved everything to his mother's garage over the weekend. Tonight, when he picked up his duffel bag and Big D, an era of his life would be over. He'd spend his last night in Waycross under his mother's roof. Big D would be there until he came back from his deployment—whenever that would be.

The dog was panting loudly, his tongue lolling out of his slobbering mouth as Jimmy turned his old Ford into the driveway. His mother lived in a neat little bungalow with a screened-in porch and some kind of flowers planted all across the front on either side of the front door. Her new Buick was in the carport. She had done well for herself since they came down from Chicago. She started out filing papers for two guys at a small insurance agency. Now it was more than a dozen guys in a pretty big insurance agency, and Jimmy's mom was the office manager. She ran the place. Even the partners did as she told them.

Big D hit the side door barking excitedly, standing on his hind legs and pushing at the screen with his front paws.

"Shut up, dammit," Jimmy shouted as he lifted his military-issue duffel bag out of the trunk. "Just a minute. I'll let you in."

He fully expected to hear his mother shouting at him from inside, telling him to keep Big D quiet. She liked the dog—which was a good thing, considering that the two would be roommates until Jimmy returned from Afghanistan—but the barking really did get old fast.

"All right, here you go," he said, unlatching the screen door. Inside, it was dark, but he could see a couple of people at his mother's kitchen table. He was just trying to process who this might be, when somebody turn on a light and a whole bunch of people screamed, "Surprise!"

It was a damned surprise party, and Jimmy realized it was for him. There were balloons and fried chicken. There was a hand-lettered banner with his name on it and more people that he knew than he could remember ever being in the same place at the same time. There were neighbors, guys from the gym, and people he recognized from the church. There were even two of the guys from Cahner's Quick Lube. The only person missing was Cathy.

Iowa City, Iowa
March 3

★ ★ ★

"My only regret...well, one of my *bigger* regrets...is that I won't be here for track season," Cindy Hunt joked as she stood at the microphone. She looked up at the packed bleachers in the Jackson County High School gym and at the banners that said things such as "Good Luck, Mrs. Hunt," and "See you in the Fall, Mrs. Hunt."

"I know that there are some state champion sprinters in this room. I'm not naming names, but I think when the trophies are handed out in May, there are going to be some college scouts in this room waiting to talk to certain juniors."

She smiled at the applause. When the principal insisted on this pep rally, she had said, "No, a thousand times no." He had overruled her, but at least she could make it *not* about her. Cindy was celebrating her tenth year as a history teacher here at JCHS, and her eighth as the girls' track coach. She hadn't planned to be leaving suddenly in the middle of the year, but duty called. Coach Hunt was *also* Second Lieutenant Hunt, a communications specialist with the 3rd Battalion of the 185th Regiment of the Iowa Army National Guard.

Two years ago, she had been at a teachers' conference where another attendee, a woman who was the principal at a school in Council Bluffs, told Cindy that the Guard needed more women who were teachers. Also a colonel in the guard, she told Cindy that a lot of young women were now joining the Guard right out of high school, and they needed women as role models. Cindy was reluctant, but she was promised that she could come in as an officer. Still, Cindy declined. However, when two girls who had been on the JCHS track team joined, so did Cindy.

At first, things went very well. Cindy felt as though she could truly make a difference. Getting tapped for an overseas deployment had been the farthest thing from her mind. She had a career and two kids under eight. They couldn't possibly ship *her* out. She was wrong.

"I also want you to know that I stayed up late last night, and all of that last round of college recommendation letters are in the mail," she announced. Again, there was a groundswell of applause, mainly from seniors who were late in making their applications to state schools.

Cindy looked at her husband, the usually unruffled Mr. Hunt, the sophomore English teacher better known as Mr. Dickens for his insistence on the study of the works of the nineteenth-century English author. He smiled and clapped, but beneath the facade, he was deeply disturbed about his wife going away. Like Cindy, he had never imagined that she would ever leave Iowa City for anything more complicated than two weeks of summer camp. Suddenly, his world, too, was turned upside down. He had never imagined himself as a sudden single father, but one day the deployment notice arrived, and everything changed. In his mind,

Peter Hunt paraphrased the opening sentence of *A Tale of Two Cities*: "It was the worst of times...period!"

The principal made a speech about duty and honor, Cindy smiled nervously, the band played "The Stars and Stripes Forever," and there was more applause.

At last, the ceremony that Cindy had dreaded drew to a close. The students poured out of the bleachers. Most headed for the doors and the fruits of an early dismissal, but the track team girls came down to give Cindy their last tearful hugs. Out of earshot, several of the boys were saying that they thought it weird for Mrs. Hunt to be going to war while her husband stayed behind.

When it was all over, Cindy was the last to leave the gym. Peter had gone to the lot to get the Xterra, while she stayed back to speak with the well-wishers. The sound of her footsteps made a hollow echoing sound as she walked toward the main door, above which the huge wildcat team logo was painted on the wall. Clutching an armful of bouquets, she paused and turned. So much of her life had been spent in this place. Most of her adult life, in fact. What was she getting herself into?

In the car on the way to pick up the Jessie and Isabelle from extended care, and over their dinner of frozen lasagna, Peter and Cindy said nothing about tomorrow and how their lives would change. They had said it all before—at least a hundred times. There was nothing left to say. They had rubbed their emotions raw.

Peter felt guilty that it was his wife going to war and not himself, he was fearful that she may not come home, and he resented the fact that he would have to be the nurturer until she was back. Cindy felt guilty about what she would miss by not being here. She would not be here for Jessie's and Isabelle's last day of school—nor their first day of the next year. She'd miss Isabelle's first day in the first grade. Cindy tried not to think about the birthdays that she would miss.

Cindy let the kids stay up past their bedtime, but not long after. "It's best not to break their routine," she had told Peter. She tried very hard not to cry as she tucked them into bed, but she failed.

Listening from the hallway, Peter Hunt heard a small voice ask, "Why are you crying, Mommy?"

At age seven, Jessie was old enough to understand conceptually that Mommy was going on a long trip, but five-year-old Isabelle was not.

Cindy blew her nose, wiped her tears, and looked at the woman in the master bedroom mirror. This was the first time since she had been in high school herself that she had cut her hair so short. It was the first time in years that her long blonde hair had not tumbled to the middle of her back. She thought that the short hair made her look older. Maybe it made her look more like an army officer. At least it would be easier to manage for someone who would be living in a tent for six months.

"Do you think my hair makes me look older?" Cindy asked as Peter came into the room.

"You look very nice," Peter said tactfully. He had always found her attractive. Indeed, she was. Because of the National Guard, and the need to keep up with a teenage track team, she was in excellent physical shape, and her face still radiated that youthful beauty that had turned Peter's head all those years ago.

Cindy looked at Peter in the mirror. He was nine years older and slightly balding, but she still thought of him as the younger man whose head she'd turned. He was her soul mate.

As he put his arms around her waist, she turned to hug him. He kissed her forehead and then her neck. She shivered slightly, as she usually did when she was aroused.

This involuntary reflex released a surge of contradictory emotions. On one hand, she wanted to smother herself in her husband, but another part of her wanted to push him away. In twenty-four hours, they would be separated by thousands of miles for thousands of times longer than they had ever been apart. On one hand, she wanted to cling to him and postpone the inevitable, but the other part of her wanted to push him away and get it over with.

His tongue found that special place beneath her ear, and she involuntarily responded. But consciously she did not.

"I'm sorry, babe," Cindy said, pushing him away gently. "I guess I'm not feeling so very sexy tonight."

She looked at him, trying not to cry. He looked back, not knowing what to think nor what to say. It was her call. If she wasn't in the mood, that was it. It was her world—more than his—that was about to be upended. Two days from now, and two weeks from now, he'd still be in this familiar room. He'd still be a few steps from their little girls and a few steps from his daily routine. He'd be tackling the day-to-day difficulties of single parenthood on his own, but it was a familiar routine. For Cindy, everything would be radically different. Just how different, neither of them could truly imagine.

He kissed her on the head and stepped away. She looked as though she were about to cry as she changed the subject.

"What time is June going to pick up the kids?"

They had arranged for a neighbor with kids at the same schools as Jessie and Isabelle to pick them up in the morning. Peter would drive Cindy to the airport for her flight to Charleston, where her battalion would transfer to a military aircraft for the long journey overseas.

"At about a quarter to six."

"That's too early," Cindy said. "They shouldn't have to get up that early."

"But we have to get out of here by six if I'm going to get you to the airport in time."

"I'm going to call June," Cindy said, digging through the pile of clothes on the dresser, looking for her cell phone. "I think I'll just take a cab to the airport."

"But...you...I mean...but you won't have a chance to say good-bye to the kids."

"I already have. I've already done it a hundred times in the past few weeks. I just want to get *gone*. I want to get it all done and get back *home*. I don't want all the tears. I know we're all going to be crying our heads off."

"But..."

"But that's how I want to do it," Cindy said firmly, thumbing the numbers on the key pad.

"That's how I've *got to* do it."

Waycross, Georgia
March 4

★ ★ ★

"What the hell?"

Jimmy Ray Flood woke up to the slippery sensation of a canine tongue licking his foot.

It took him a minute to remember where he was. As he rolled around and sat up on his mother's sofa, all the pieces fell together: the party, the music, the fried chicken, and all the people who wanted to wish him well as he went off to a place that was unimaginably far from Waycross, Georgia.

Big D wasn't himself today. Was it sleeping overnight on the floor at Jimmy's mother's place, or did he know that something much bigger was about to change? The way that Big D looked at him with those big, sorrowful, bloodshot eyes, Jimmy was sure that the dog knew that they were about to be separated for a very long time.

Jimmy stood up and headed toward the bathroom, surrounded by the quiet debris of last night's festivities. There were a few balloons, a bowl that still contained some coleslaw, and an uneaten ear of corn. Instinctively, Jimmy picked it up a chewed on it. His nephew, Lamar, who was still snoring in the spare bedroom, would go with him and drive the car back.

The empty beer cans in the bag near the door reminded Jimmy that he was glad that he'd stopped drinking. The good luck cards from the church ladies were on the mantel, where his mother had put them. He promised himself that he'd take time to look at them.

Normally, Jimmy didn't like surprises, but this had been okay. He was glad that everyone had come out to see him. Yesterday, as he was changing that fuel pump, he had actually started thinking about people he would miss. He had wondered whether anyone— other than his mother—would miss *him*.

He had stayed up late talking to her and to some of the others. Talk had turned to where he was going and what he was going to be doing. Eventually, his mother had gotten around to sharing a few ideas about soldiering. Jimmy's grandfather had gotten drafted a long time ago. They sent him to a faraway place that he used to call Nam. According to Jimmy's mother, that was about the only word he had to say on the subject. Jimmy never really knew him. He wasn't around much, and he died while Jimmy was doing time.

Now Jimmy was about to be doing another kind of time. His mother didn't seem too happy about this time, either, but she *did* tell him that she was proud of him. She even had a picture of Jimmy in his uniform on the wall.

The sun wasn't up yet, but Jimmy's mother was. She was frying her son some breakfast before he headed off to Atlanta to spend the day with Cathy.

"You stay safe over there, you hear," Jimmy's mother said as they sat down to ham and eggs. Normally, she didn't cook a big breakfast, but she wanted her son's last day to be special.

"They've got diseases over there that we haven't got over here. Like malaria and typhoid, and *my Lord* I've read about the dirty water they have in those kinds of places. You have to be really careful of that. It's not just drinking the stuff. If you get a cut and it gets infected, you could have yourself a mess of trouble."

"I'll be careful, I really will," he assured her. He knew, and so did she, that getting an infected cut was far from being the worst thing that could happen to Jimmy in Afghanistan. About a week ago, he had been over here watching television when a story came on about a soldier from Waycross who came back blind and missing an arm and a leg. Now this guy was planning to study for the ministry. Jimmy and his mother had just looked at one another. They didn't say anything. They didn't have to.

Today, she felt like she had to say *something*. What does a mother say to a son going someplace dangerous? She tells him to be careful, and she says it sternly, because ever since he's been able to walk, he's been a boy taking chances. In a mother's eyes, that's what boys do.

Finally, breakfast was over. The talking was over. It was time for hugs, but soon that time would be over, too. It was time for tears, but for Jimmy's mother, the time for tears would not be over until the day he walked *back* through that screen door.

Jimmy's nephew grabbed a slice of ham and a piece of toast and shoved it into his mouth as Jimmy handed him the car keys. The kid was only eighteen, the same age that Jimmy had been when he got out of jail. Lamar's life had been a lot easier in most ways. He would probably finish high school. He had a part-time job. And he had never been arrested. Aside from underage drinking and some minor traffic violations, Jimmy doubted that Lamar had ever *really* broken any laws.

They pulled out of the driveway just as the sun was coming

up. Jimmy waved to his mother. It felt lame just to wave, but what else could he do?

His mother waved and tried not to cry. Big D tried to run after the car, but he hit the end of his chain and tumbled to the ground. He barked excitedly, but Jimmy just watched him getting smaller and smaller in the rearview mirror. It felt really lame just to drive off, but what else could he do?

The image of Big D stayed with him most of the way to Atlanta.

"You're almost an hour and a half late." Kadeefa scowled, greeting her ex-husband as Lamar dropped him off at her suburban Atlanta town house. "I thought you outgrew that kind of punk ass shit."

"Don't give me attitude, girl, I'm not your husband anymore," Jimmy replied. "I wish I coulda been here sooner. There was a whole lot of road construction the other side of Macon. And I've got a lot going on this week."

"So you're getting all soldier-boy on me, now?" Kadeefa said, shaking her head. She still hadn't forgotten that Jimmy had broken a tooth out of her previous boyfriend's smile three years earlier. The only reason the guy hadn't filed charges was that he had several outstanding warrants. "Like I care. Like maybe this soldier shit is what you need to get all that aggressive shit out of your system."

"Daddy!" Cathy screamed from the other room. The sound of her voice made everything better. It made Kadeefa's attitude almost bearable.

He hugged her. He hadn't seen her in more than a month. He wished that he had come up two weeks ago when the deployment notice arrived, but things had gotten out of hand. Well, that was water under the Satilla River Bridge. He was here now.

Seeing her as irregularly as he did, he was always amazed by how much older she seemed each time. He still thought of her as the cute little kindergartner she was when they still lived in that long-distant happy home, but now she was eleven. When he got back from Afghanistan, she would almost be a teenager.

Cathy shrugged shyly when he asked whether she wanted to go over to the mall.

Kadeefa shrugged impatiently when he asked her whether he could leave his duffel bag at her town house until he and Cathy came back. He felt lost without his car, which was now cruising south toward Waycross with his nephew at the wheel. He didn't need it, because the mall was actually just across the parking lot from the complex where Kadeefa lived, and Jimmy knew that he was going to have to get used to being at the mercy of powers beyond his own control when it came to transportation.

Cathy was quiet and subdued as they walked across the vast parking lot that encircled the mall. It bothered Jimmy to see her this way. It used to be that he couldn't get a word in edgeways when he asked what she was doing in school. Today, the same question just elicited a "Nothin'."

As they walked through the food court, he asked her whether she wanted a milkshake. He knew she liked milkshakes.

"I guess so."

"Yeah, me, too," he said hopefully.

She was quiet as they waited for the shakes, but when they sat down near a large, noisy fountain, she looked at him as though she wanted to say something and couldn't find the words.

"Daddy…"

"Yeah, baby."

"Mama says you're going over there where the war is going on."

"Yeah, baby. I'm going to Afghanistan. I'm catching the bus to Charleston tonight. The plane leaves from there tomorrow."

"What you gonna be doing over there?"

"Well, y'know baby, I guess I'm gonna be doing pretty much whatever they tell me to do."

"Why do you keep callin' me baby? I'm eleven now."

"Well, I guess 'cause I always called you that and 'cause you're my baby."

"Uh-huh."

"Do you want me to stop callin' you that?"

"I dunno."

"Okay, I guess I'll call you Cathy from now on."

"They said…you know, people at school were talking…y' know, about the war and all."

"What about the war?"

"They said that people were gettin' hurt over there. Hurt real bad. There was a thing on television, y'know."

"I know it's pretty scary when y'all see it on television, but y'know it's not all that bad. They only show the really bad stuff on television 'cause, well, y'know, it isn't much news if it's just a guy comin' home like everything's okay."

"I sure do hope you'll be comin' home like everything's okay," Cathy said. A tear was now trickling down her cheek.

"Don't you go cryin' now, girl," Jimmy said, instinctively wiping the tear. "Ain't nothing gonna be happening to your daddy. Most of the folks we got over there just work in offices."

"Are you gonna be in an office, Daddy?"

"Yeah, sure, probably for sure," he said, failing to mention that he was just an infantry grunt, and they put infantry grunts out front with rifles, not back at a bombproof building with air-conditioning and paper to shuffle.

"Well, I sure hope so," Cathy said, trying hard to smile.

"Don't worry about it one bit. I'll be home before you know it."

"Promise?"

"Promise."

"I sure will miss you."

"I'll sure be missing you, too, Cathy."

She just hiccuped and sobbed. Another tear started trickling.

"Tell you what," Jimmy said, rolling up his left sleeve. "You know this wristwatch. The one you used to like to mess with when you was little? Well, why don't I just leave that with you for safekeeping? That way, you got somethin' to have that you know I'll be comin' back for. Here, lemme set the time, so you know what time it is where I'm gonna be at. It's almost four here, so it's a little after midnight over there right now."

She took the big silver-colored watch that she knew to be one of her dad's favorite possessions. Tears ran from both eyes as she looked at it and then at him.

"Don't cry, Cathy," I'll just be sittin' in an office somewhere, and I'll be back here in a few months."

"Ain't going to be needing your watch?"

"Naw. With the army, I don't need to know what time it is. One thing I know for sure about the army is that it isn't time to do something until they tell you it's time."

"I sure hope that you're going to be okay," Cathy said, smiling slightly at his joke. "I'm gonna miss you."

"Don't you worry about that. When you got my watch, it's gonna be like I'm right there next to you."

"Not exactly."

"But you know what I mean. You know that I'm gonna be missing you a whole lot too, right?"

"Yeah, I guess so. Really?"

"Really. Whadya mean, really? Of course I'm gonna miss you.

"Oh, Daddy," she said, hugging him more tightly than he had been hugged in a long time. The older she had gotten, the more perfunctory became her hugs.

"Oh, Cathy, I sure am gonna miss my little girl."

"Me, too," she said, looking up at her father with tears welling in her eyes again. "And one other thing."

"What's that?"

"You can still call me baby if you want. That's okay with me."

CHAPTER TWO

New World

★

Helmand Province, Afghanistan
March 15

★ ★ ★

"Heads up, people!" Master Sergeant Ricky Alvarez shouted from the lead Humvee. "There's a bunch of Toons on the right up here, coming up. Keep your eyes and ears open, boys and girls."

The sergeant used the nickname *Toon* to refer to the Afghan civilians, most of whom were Pashtun in this part of Helmand Province. Maybe it was derogatory, or maybe it was just short-hand. He called the women in the company *girls*, but only a few had complained, and then only at first. By now, the people of the California Army National Guard's 3rd Battalion had been in country long enough to know that they had far more important things to be concerned about—like staying alive.

At the moment, the biggest thing for the boys and girls of Alpha Company of the 3rd Battalion to worry about was, in fact, the group of Pashtuns along the side of the dusty, two-lane road. The Taliban often used groups of civilians to screen them as they attacked coalition convoys with IEDs. Anybody in this ragtag group up ahead might be a Taliban. The Americans couldn't tell. Probably most of the Afghans in the crowd couldn't, either. As Alvarez had ordered, they kept their heads up and their eyes peeled.

"What's up!" screamed a kid of about the age of nine as he waved at the Americans. The soldiers smiled and waved back. It might be the only English phrase he knew, something he picked up from being around the Americans, who had been coming and going in his country for as long as he could remember.

Private First Class Justin Anderson pulled down the bandanna that he wore over his face to keep out the dust and grinned at the kids. He tossed a couple of packs of Juicy Fruit to them, just as American GIs had been doing to kids in war-torn foreign lands for generations. Several kids scrambled for the gum. Justin watched to see whether the "What's up!" kid got any, but the small forms were obscured in the swirling dust cloud kicked up by the convoy, and Justin turned back to scanning the crowd.

He couldn't believe that it had been just a few weeks since he was cruising up the Pacific Coast Highway in his Porsche with Laurie Hall, dressed like a fashion model, at his side. As he looked down at the Afghans, dressed in their dusty rags with their dusty, unkempt hair, he couldn't believe that it had been less than two weeks since he was sitting at Nobu, surrounded by people who probably spent more on their last haircut than these people made in a year.

What a difference a few weeks could make. He contrasted the Malibu women, with bare legs up to their thighs and tops that barely covered their breasts, to the Afghan women, whose blue burkas didn't even have a slit so that you could see their eyes. Since 2001, it had been legal in Afghanistan for women to climb out of these sacks. In Kabul, most women had. Out here in the boonies, though, women who shed the burkas wound up getting their throats cut by the Taliban sympathizers. Justin returned a smile to a little girl, who was not yet old enough to be "bagged," and wondered what her future held. This was sure as hell a very long way from Malibu.

"Wanna break?" Chuck Ellis called from inside the Humvee.

"Sure," Justin replied. He'd been topside manning the M240 heavy machine gun, and he was glad to trade places with Ellis and get out of the dust.

As he climbed down into the armored interior, a corporal from Red Bluff handed him a bottle of water. It was stuffy inside the Humvee, and it smelled like stale sweat, but at least the light armor provided a modicum of protection if the bad guys started to shoot up the convoy.

With Ellis manning the machine gun, there were two guys in the back of the Humvee, plus the two up front. There used to be one more, but he went home early. He took a really bad mess of shrapnel in his leg on the second day after the 3rd Battalion arrived in Helmand. They hardly got to know him. Steve from Van Nuys is what they still called him. They never got to know his last name, and he wasn't in country long enough to get a nickname.

Soldiers in combat had always given each other nicknames. It helped to both personalize someone and to depersonalize yourself. "I'm not here," you say. "The guy with the weird nickname is."

Justin's nickname was Dude, because they thought he looked like a surfer, which he did. They called Ellis SpongeBob, because his blond, flattop haircut made him look like the cartoon character. The guy from Red Bluff was known to his mother as Raymond, but here in country, they had called him Spider ever since they saw how nimbly he could crawl through the hatch of a Humvee.

"What time we supposed to be there?" Justin asked as he took a slug of tepid water.

"About an hour, I guess," Spider replied, looking at his watch.

"There" was a small town in the mountains of southern Helmand Province, due south of the provincial capital at Lashkar Gah. Neither Justin nor Spider could remember the name. Ever since they landed, the 3rd Battalion's job had been to patrol, which meant deploying to various remote towns and villages for varying lengths of time to show the locals that the coalition was present in their little corner of Helmand.

The Cal Guard arrived at Lashkar Gah in the middle of the night and in the midst of chaos. The town's name in Pashtun means "the place of the soldiers," and that was what it was: American troops, British troops, a few Canadians, and even fewer Afghan National Army. They were coming and going at the airport and on the narrow roads around it. The multinational troops of the International Security Assistance Force, ISAF, were stepping on each other's toes, yelling at each other's vehicles that were blocking their way, and generally trying to get the hell out of the mess around the airport.

The California battalion had deployed from March Field in Riverside with four companies, and they were split up almost immediately when they landed. Lieutenant Colonel Deacon, the battalion commander, and his staff had a long talk with a couple of colonels, looked at a map, and pointed. Alpha and Bravo went south. Echo and Foxtrot went somewhere else. Justin wasn't sure where they went. He wasn't even sure exactly where his own Alpha Company was going. The guy who seemed to be in charge just got them assigned to vehicles, told the lead driver something, and pointed into the darkness. Justin crawled into the back of the Humvee and fell asleep.

When he woke up, it was daylight, and the convoy had pulled into a primitive-looking village in a cultivated valley. Somebody said something about a tenth of the world's opium coming out of this valley.

It turned out that they were at a forward operating base of the British 16th Air Assault Brigade. Captain Van Dyke, Alpha Company's boss, held a briefing for the two hundred or so guys in the company and explained that the Brits had been assigned overall command of ISAF ops in this part of the country, but they'd run into trouble. Lieutenant Sloan, Justin's platoon commander, added that Helmand had been a mess ever since Operation Mountain Thrust, the combined NATO-Afghan mission targeted at Taliban fighters in the south of the country. All they knew was that all the briefers kept harping on the 160-kilometer border between Helmand and the Pakistani province of Baluchistan. The British and Afghan troops had been forced to take increasingly defensive positions under heavy insurgent pressure, and it had been a muddle ever since. The Brits finally had called for help, and Uncle Sam sent the Cal Guard.

Somebody said something about kicking some Taliban butt, and almost on cue, the base came under mortar attack. The chaos at the airport the night before was nothing compared to what ensued.

He had heard mortar rounds explode before at summer camp up at Camp Roberts, but Justin now realized that this was for real. Somebody was trying to kill him *for real*.

This was where Steve from Van Nuys got hit. One minute, he was just another kid from the San Fernando Valley who drove a truck for a tape duplication service. The next, he was a bloody mess, lying on the ground with eyes as big as DVDs. Steve was lucky. They got him stabilized and called for medevac. Four other guys whom Justin had recalled seeing on the plane were being bagged—as in body bags.

Holy shit, this is war, Justin had thought. Watching Steve and those four other guys was a wake-up call. It was his rude welcome to a world very unlike anything he had known.

Now, after less than two months in country, Justin was start-ing to find it hard to remember what his *other* world was like. He could remember what LA looked like, but he found it hard to remember what it smelled like to be in a room full of people who bathed regularly. He remembered what the drone of Professor Heddin's voice sounded like, but he found it hard to remember what a beef enchilada with cilantro *tasted* like.

Justin was lost in thought, trying to recapture the smell of Laurie Hall's hair, when the Humvee suddenly jerked to a stop.

"What the fuck?" Spider snarled. He had dozed off and was now suddenly awake.

"We're there," Chuck Ellis shouted down from his perch.

"We're where?" Spider asked, looking out the window.

"We're in beautiful downtown somewhere."

"Good, I gotta go take a leak," Spider said, popping open the door.

Justin followed him out and stretched. After sitting in the back of the cramped vehicle for hours in his full combat gear, he was stiff as hell. He surveyed the scene. His outfit kept getting smaller and smaller. He had arrived with the full battalion, and two of its four companies peeled off right away. Then Alpha and Bravo went their separate ways. Next, Alpha was subdivided further. Here Jus-tin was with the 3rd Platoon, just thirty-one guys in five Humvees. Justin realized it was exactly the same number of people there had been in Heddin's Criminology 303. Well, *now* there were thirty. Justin had dropped the class. In Crim 303, half the people had been female. In the 3rd Platoon, there were only six women.

Justin could see Lieutenant Sloan and Sergeant Alvarez talk-ing with a British officer and a couple of bearded guys in Afghan National Army uniforms, and he decided to stroll over and eaves-drop. One of the Afghans was explaining a diagram of the vil-lage in passable English. The Brit, who was a *left*-tenant as they call their lieutenants, told the Americans where his unit had been in relation to this village and where the bad guys had liked to rig ambushes. Justin wondered whether Alvarez would call the Afghans Toons to their faces. He knew that the Afghans also had some choice nicknames for Americans, but he guessed they'd all probably keep it civil for the time being.

Sloan looked up from the diagrams and scanned the view. It was a pathetic little town consisting entirely of single-story buildings. There were a few cars on the single paved street. A line of trucks with European license plates rumbled past, kicking up the inevitable dust cloud as the paved street ended and the dirt road began. These were NGOs bringing relief supplies into Afghanistan from somewhere across the Pakistan border. After decades of war, this poor country depended on outside help to survive.

"Sergeant Alvarez, now that we're here, we need to get that fact established," Sloan announced. "I'd like to have you take some men and make an initial foot patrol out to the south side of town and swing back around the perimeter to here. I want us to get a feel for the place, and I want the people here to know we're here and see us on foot patrol. It's real important that they see us."

"Yes sir," the platoon sergeant said, looking at Justin. "Anderson, you look ready to go. Why don't you tell Bob and Spider that we're goin' for a walk."

Alvarez grabbed three other guys, and the seven-man patrol set out to see and be seen. Alvarez said something about Justin being eager, and he put him on point.

Walking the alleys off the main street was like stepping back into the Middle Ages. The poverty was unlike anything that Justin had seen, even in the worst parts of East LA. There, the ramshackle buildings are spattered with graffiti, and the streets are filled with garbage. Here, nobody had anything to use for writing on walls, and, except for a few chicken bones, no garbage was on the streets because the people were too poor to even *have* garbage.

The people stared warily at these men with their M16A4 rifles and night-vision gear on their heads. The Americans all looked overweight because of the body armor beneath their uniforms. The body armor didn't help Steve from Van Nuys. The mortar hit his leg. A few inches higher, and he might have walked away. As it was, he would never walk again.

Off in the back of the group, the men were talking.

"What do they call this place, Sarge?"

"The name of the town is Sherishk," Alvarez answered.

"Sure stinks is right," someone else laughed, making a play on the phonetic sound of Sherishk.

Nobody else laughed, because it was so very true. The place really did smell terrible. Justin wished that he could remember the smell of Laurie Hall's hair.

The patrol left the back street, circling toward a crowded market. There were a lot more people here, and more activity. Alvarez ordered the men to lower their weapons.

"Fan out and try not to look like we're here to serve a fuckin' arrest warrant," Alvarez said. "Smile at the Toons. Don't let your guard down, but try to be friendly."

On the back street, it was mainly old people and kids. Here, Justin saw people his own age. They were still a world apart, but there were some in their twenties. Then he saw a young couple dressed defiantly in Western clothing. It was strange to see a woman without a burka strolling through the market. The girl was pretty, with long, dark hair and deep, black eyes. Justin wondered whether she and the guy with her were Afghan, or whether they worked for one of the NGOs that seemed to be running all over Afghanistan.

Justin said hello, and the girl smiled bashfully and nodded. Her

companion just looked surprised to have been greeted by one of
the heavily armed Americans. Even if most people were grateful
for the overthrow of the Taliban, there was still an innate tension
and a nervousness about talking to coalition troops. The people
knew that the Taliban were not really gone, and they knew that
ISAF and the Americans would not be here forever.

"How you doin'?" Justin asked, wondering if they spoke
English.

"Fine. How are you?"

The accent was thick, but the girl understood.

"Where are you from in America?" she asked.

"LA," Justin answered. "Do you know where that is?"

"Of course." She smiled. "My uncle owns a shop for food in
Gardena. Do you know where *that* is?"

"Sure," Justin said, laughing. She was playing with him. He
relaxed a little bit.

"I was in Gardena when I was a girl. I like California very
much. Palm trees."

"What do you do here in…?" Justin asked. He couldn't
remember the name of the town. All he could think of is "sure
stinks," but he didn't want to say that.

"Sherishk," she said, finishing his sentence. "I hope you will
be in Sherishk long enough to know its name. I am from Kabul,
but I went to university in France. I am, we are, here with Alli-
ance pour des Familles. We are NGO based in Paris. We come to
help reunite family members in the middle of war."

"I see," Justin nodded. He liked the way she pronounced Sherishk. The melody of her accent made it sound almost as though
it didn't stink. As Justin parted company with the NGO girl and
her friend, they all smiled.

In the background, Justin heard the sound of a muezzin
beginning his call to prayer over the tinny PA system. One of the

soldiers was dickering with a merchant at one of the stalls in the market, and Alvarez stopped the transaction to allow the retailer to pray.

The Americans continued walking as the faithful faced toward Mecca to answer the call to pray. In the distance, there was a loud, dull thud.

"What the hell was that?" Spider asked.

"Sounded like it might have been an explosion," Ellis answered.

"Bomb went off," the sergeant announced. He'd been on the radio with Lieutenant Sloan's command post.

"Did they hit our guys?" Justin asked urgently.

"No, it was a good, solid five hundred meters from where they were," Alvarez said, seeming a bit nervous. "They saw it, though. They're responding. They want us to start double-timing it back there, now."

"Look," Spider said, pointing toward a column of black smoke rising into the cold, blue sky. "What would make some sunuv-abitch set off a bomb just as these people are starting to pray?"

Taking a shortcut, Justin's patrol reached the scene a few minutes later. Flames were pouring from a small storefront, and a car was on fire. It might have been a suicide car bomb, the kind of thing that Justin had seen before only on television. There were dead and wounded Afghans everywhere. People wailed and sobbed. Blood and bits of flesh were on the ground and the walls of the buildings. Justin realized that nothing on television could prepare him for having the sounds of pain and death all around him. Certainly, nothing on television could prepare him for the *smell*: burning gasoline and burning flesh.

Justin realized that he was a long way from Westwood Boulevard—a very long way.

Alvarez ordered the patrol to set up a perimeter. The platoon's medics were already pitching in to help the Afghan medical personnel who had come to the scene.

Justin started to turn away from the carnage when he heard the sound of screeching tires and a gunning engine. The incoming car, an old white Nissan, was coming fast. Justin and Spider signaled him to slow down, but he accelerated. The Americans knew from their training that it is an insurgent tactic to detonate a bomb and wait for rescuers to converge on the scene, then attack with a second bomb to take out maximum casualties.

They had to react.

Justin shouldered his M16A4 and centered the sights on the windshield. There was one man behind the wheel. Justin had never aimed his weapon at a human being before, but he squeezed the trigger.

Things went into slow motion. The windshield shattered in a hail of 5.56 mm rounds. Justin thought that he had hit the guy. He was sure he had, but the car kept coming. As Justin and Spider took evasive action to get out of the way, the speeding car swerved violently, impacting a low stone fence.

A split second later, the car bomb detonated, sending flimsy, twisted, Japanese steel flying. Justin could feel the searing heat on his face as the shock wave knocked him off his feet.

Justin and Spider managed to get to their feet quickly, but a couple of Afghan civilians were not so lucky. As bad as it was, though, the car bomb would have done a lot more damage if it would have hit the scene of the first explosion. Justin had killed his first human being, but he had saved many more.

As he and Spider raced to the scene of the second crash to render aid, Justin noticed that one of the bodies nearby was moving. He turned. It was the young woman from the NGO, the one who had an uncle in California, the one with the dark hair and the beautiful dark eyes. Her khaki pants were torn and drenched in blood. She had taken a terrible injury to both legs above her knees. Justin flashed back to Steve from Van Nuys. Steve had survived. Justin would make sure that the NGO girl did as well.

As Justin reached her, the girl was trying to get up. She was leaning on one elbow and scratching at the dirt. No doubt she was willing her unresponsive legs to move.

She looked up at him with instant recognition and grabbed his hand. She squeezed it tightly as Justin tried to open his first aid kit with the other hand. He could see the bone and smell the sickening, ferrous stench of the blood. He had to get something into the wound to stop the bleeding. He tried to free his hand, but she would not let go. At last, he pulled off his bandanna and shoved it into the wound, pushing through the thick, sticky blood, squeezing the pulsing artery as hard as he could.

The NGO girl realized what he was doing. He could see this in the big, dark eyes. Even with the expression of terror on her face, she still looked beautiful. As she started to open her mouth, he saw that her lips were trembling. Her whole body quivered as the chills of the shock started to set in. She coughed slightly, and blood spewed from her mouth. This was not a good sign. Coughing up blood meant internal injuries. Coughing up this much blood meant really serious internal injuries.

Justin reached down and took her into his arms to comfort her, and to try to make her warmer because of the shock. For a moment, she clung to him, her whole body shivering uncontrollably, but at last, the shaking stopped, and her hold on him relaxed. Her hand went slack and tumbled out of his grasp. He grabbed it, but it remained limp.

He looked into her face. The trembling had stopped, and her unblinking eyes stared straight at him. Her pain was gone. Her agony was over.

Khost Province, Afghanistan
March 15

★ ★ ★

"Does this remind you of the Rockies?" Buddy Sorrell asked, squinting through his binoculars.

"Could be," Luis Carillo told him as they gazed southward into the rugged jumble of mountains that separated Afghanistan from Pakistan. "I don't get up into the Rockies much. I don't go to that part of the state. I've seen places that look like this down in Chihuahua."

"More trees in the Rockies," Buddy said. "A whole lot more trees."

"Not so many trees in Chihuahua."

"Hard to know what we're supposed to be shooting at without any roads or anything," Sorrell said, putting down his binoculars and shaking his head.

"It's like the border country where the coyotes bring people into New Mexico or Arizona," Luis said. "Not so many roads there, either…more like none…but there's trails. If you want to know where they're coming across, you look for trails. See that place to the left of the big rock that looks like a piece of cornbread?"

"Yeah, kinda," Buddy said tentatively. There was a spark of recognition. "Oh yeah. I see it now. It goes this way and a little bit that. Yeah, okay, I see it now. How did you spot that?"

"You have to know where to look, amigo." Luis grinned.

It was *ironía grande*—great irony—for Luis. A dozen years after he headed north to illegally cross a border, he was on the other side of the world guarding a border that he hadn't known existed, and he was guarding it from *others* who were headed north to cross illegally. Back then, he had come looking to build a life. Today, he was looking down into a rugged landscape for people who planned to destroy lives.

Ironía grande.

For political reasons that Luis and the other Guardsmen could not understand, the Taliban and Al-Qaeda enjoyed a safe and secure haven within the borders of Pakistan, an American ally. The coalition troops could not go there to hunt them, but the Taliban and Al-Qaeda could come north to hunt Americans or anyone they felt like killing.

Ironía grande.

The coalition troops could not go down there into Pakistan to hunt them, but if they were caught on the Afghanistan side, the coalition could blast them.

If the bad guys did get caught in coalition crosshairs—and that was always a big *if*—the coalition had plenty of firepower to bring to bear. They had airpower. They had A-10 Warthogs and AH-64 Apache helicopter gunships with Gatling guns, air-to-surface missiles, or all kinds of bombs. The coalition also had "steel rain." The Colorado Army National Guard's 157th Field Artillery had recently changed over from M109A5 howitzers to the M270 MLRS, or Multiple Launch Rocket System.

The M270 was a twenty-seven-ton tracked vehicle that was built on the chassis of a Bradley Fighting Vehicle. It looked like a tank, except instead of a turret, it had a huge box the shape of a cereal box lying on its top. Inside the box were a dozen thirteen-foot, seven-hundred-pound M26 solid-fuel missiles. Each one was loaded with hundreds of little bombs—the manual called them "submunitions"—that were more or less like hand grenades. That's how the bad guys in Gulf War I had gotten started calling the MLRS "steel rain."

The "gun bunnies," as the M270 gunners were called, could throw these missiles up to twenty or thirty miles. Any bunch of Taliban who got pelted with steel rain would have a hard time getting away. In the meantime, though, the gun bunnies had to get the MLRS to within twenty or thirty miles of the bad guys. That was easier said than done.

Echo Battery of the 3rd Battalion, Luis's outfit, had been the last Colorado Guard unit to get steel rain, and they had six of the big, clumsy-looking vehicles lumbering around in Khost Province. In the regular army, an MLRS battery had up to ten M270 launcher vehicles, but Echo Battery was a little shorthanded.

Because they really were clumsy—and slow—especially in this terrain, the M270s needed to be protected. This was Luis's job. While the gun bunnies, the three-man crew of the M270, shot the big stuff, Luis and his platoon just lugged around their M16A4 rifles and protected them from getting ambushed.

So far, nobody had shot at anything. When they were bringing the M270s down on flatbed trucks from Bagram Air Base, there were rumors of a possible Taliban attempt to ambush the convoy. Steel rain's babysitters were ready for action, but nothing materialized.

"I see somebody coming through right down there," Sorrell whispered excitedly, pointing and handing the binoculars to

Luis. About ten guys on foot were making their way down the same trail that Luis had just pointed out.

"Echo one, this is Echo four," Buddy said, whispering into his PRC-148 MBITR, or multiband intrateam radio. "Do you copy?"

Luis thought that Buddy was being overly dramatic the way he whispered into the MBITR. At this distance, he figured that the guys in turbans could have barely heard them if he had shouted, but Luis guessed it was better to be safe than sorry.

"Copy you, Echo four. What's happnin', Buddy?"

"Listen, Sarge, we got a dozen guys coming down outa the mountains on this trail over here. They're armed."

"Shit man, all these clowns over in this part of the world are armed. Can you see if they're carrying anything that looks like heavy weapons?"

"No, I don't think so. Some packs and stuff, but nothing too big."

"Lemme talk to the lieutenant and get back at you," First Sergeant Charlie Schlatter replied. "Echo one out for now."

"What's up?" Luis asked.

"He's gonna talk to the battery CO and decide what to do."

"Better decide quick," Luis said, pointing across the canyon to the place that rounded the rock that Luis thought looked like a piece of cornbread. "Look at that shit."

"Fuckin' A, man," Buddy said, looking through his binoculars. "We done hit the jackpot today."

"Echo one, this is Echo four. Do you copy again, Sarge?"

"Yeah Buddy, the lieutenant said we ought to let them go. He thinks they might even be on our side."

"Things have changed over here, Sarge. You asked about heavy shit? Well, they got a whole string of packmules comin' through now. They're packed with all sorts of shit. Man, I'm seeing what looks like RPG tubes and everything. Correction, they got friggin' tubes there with RPG rounds attached. These punks are Al-Qaeda for sure."

"Roger all that, Buddy," Schlatter replied. "Can you give me the coordinates?"

"On the map that we're using, I'd say that it runs from Hotel-Hotel-fourteen to Hotel-Hotel-seventeen," Sorrell said, using the military phonetic alphabet. Add Hotel-Lauriet-fourteen to that, 'cause that's where they're coming out of the pass."

"Are they still coming?"

"Can't tell, they're coming around this hill. No, wait a minute, I think they're all down in the valley now. A bunch like the first bunch just came through. They must be bringing up the rear. You can strike Hotel-Lauriet-fourteen and maybe add Hotel-Hotel-eighteen, because that's farther down the valley."

"Good deal, Buddy. Cover your ears. This is Echo one out."

For a moment, Luis and Buddy watched the men and pack animals picking their way down the rocky trail that paralleled the streambed in the bottom of the V-shaped canyon. An occasional squeal from one of the donkeys wafted out of the valley, but mainly all was quiet except for the echo of hooves on shale.

Suddenly, they heard the familiar wavering whistle that reminded Luis of the bottle rockets that the kids played with around the Fourth of July. They heard another, and then another. Down in the valley, the Al-Qaeda heard them, too. They scattered like ants. Some ran up the hillsides on either side of the stream-bed, while others started trying to turn some of the donkeys.

It was way too late for any of this.

A massive explosion struck the end of the line farthest from Luis and Buddy. A second hit slightly farther up, followed by two that fell almost simultaneously a bit up from the first two. Luis crouched down and covered his ears against the crash of the steel rain. He counted a total of eight explosions, followed by a pause. The M270 could launch a total of twelve M26 rockets in the time that it took to say it, and he waited for the next four. He looked up as the radio crackled again.

"Echo four, this is Echo one. Tell me, Buddy, did we get 'em?"

"Roger, Sarge," Buddy said excitedly. "There are two or three of them on the hillsides that got away, but you scored a direct hit on the pack train. It's like a friggin' video game, man."

"Except that these donkeys don't walk away and play again," Luis said soberly. Luis had seen death before. He saw his grandfather die, and three men in his village who died in a scaffold collapse, but this was his first time to see mass casualties on a battlefield. He knew that this carnage ultimately saved coalition lives—maybe even those of Colorado Guard guys—but it was still sobering.

Buddy was already sighting his M16A4 on one of the Al-Qaeda who was trying to escape up the hillside on their side of the canyon. Luis watched as he squeezed the trigger. The Al-Qaeda stumbled, got up, and started to run. Buddy squeezed again, and the man toppled over, sliding a short distance in the loose shale in the steep terrain.

Buddy looked at Luis as if to say, *Your turn.*

Luis pointed his own rifle at another running man. On the second shot, he, too, fell.

Between Buddy and Luis—and the high-power scopes on their rifles—nearly all of the Al-Qaeda who survived the steel rainstorm went down. They were exposed on the hillsides where the loose gravel made running impossible, and they had a hard time identifying the location of the two Americans because of the way gunshots echo in a steep canyon.

That evening, the two men turned their position over to

another pair of Colorado Guardsmen with night-vision gear and made their way back to the Echo Battery bivouac. The mood was upbeat. In its first engagement, the battery had successfully interdicted a major infiltration. Letting the bad guys know that this line of infiltration was closed was also important, although several of the guys wondered out loud whether the enemy would just start bringing their weapons in from Pakistan by another route.

After dinner, Luis found a quiet spot and scribbled a few more lines in a letter that he was composing to Roxanna.

"*Maté a diez hombres hoy,*" he began, telling her simply that he had just killed ten men. "*Sé que esto es increíble para usted. Esto es increíble para mí. Muy extraño ser el gringo que protege la frontera.*"

He told her that such a thing seemed just as incredible for him to comprehend as it no doubt was for her. He shared with her the thought that had been running through his mind all day: that he now found *himself* in the strange role of being a *gringo* guarding a border.

"*Muy extraño matar a los hombres que desean cruzarse. Pero toman los armas y desean matar a nosotros. Esto hace mi trabajo bueno. Ironía grande.*"

It was ironic that the man who waded across the Rio Grande was now killing men for crossing a border—and thinking of himself as a gringo. All he could say to make her understand was that these men had guns, and that they would kill Luis and his men if given a chance. By this justification, he was doing the right thing, even if it meant becoming a gringo. Especially if it meant becoming a gringo.

Ironía grande.

As he looked up at the stars, Luis thought about that corner of the American flag with all the stars, and about what he was doing—and what he still had left to do—to make the dream of that night in the Rio Grande finally become a reality.

Manas Air Base, Kyrgyzstan
March 15

★ ★ ★

"Everybody down," Lieutenant Cindy Hunt screamed. "Get your heads down. Below the windows. *Now!*"

The pounding sound of heavy machine guns was very near. Cindy and her team were in a cinder block building whose walls were impervious to most calibers of small arms fire, but the windows were not. Anyone who looked up or out was just asking to get hit.

Machine guns could be heard to the left. Machine guns could be heard to the right. Smoke and dust were everywhere. People were running. People were screaming. A blinding flash that painted the wall of the room like a strobe light was followed a split second later by the sound of an explosion that shook the room and shattered the windows. Shards of glass were everywhere.

"*Omigod!* I'm hit!"

Cindy looked up to see Amanda Morgan, the young Specialist from Des Moines, kneeling in the middle of the room with blood on her hands.

"Get down, Amanda," Cindy shouted.

Amanda was frozen, a look of panic on her face. Cindy jumped up, grabbed her, and pulled her close to a wall, away from a direct line of sight from the broken window.

"I'm bleeding!"

"I know, Amanda, but you were just nicked by a piece of glass, you'll be all right."

Cindy tried to move away, but the girl clung to her. Amanda reminded her of students that she'd had at JCHS. In fact, she was just two years out of high school herself, one of those young women for whom Cindy had wanted to serve as a role model.

Suddenly the red dot of a laser range finder appeared on Amanda's frightened face.

A sniper.

Cindy closed her eyes and gritted her teeth as the door crashed open. Two large men with white armbands glowered at Cindy and Amanda.

"You're dead, both of you," one man said angrily.

"You three, you all survived," he said, looking at the other troops in the room. "Go take a break."

The horror of the past moments had merely been a training exercise. The explosions were real, but the sniper was not. Amanda's injury was real, but as Cindy had diagnosed, it warranted treatment no more invasive than a compress for five minutes and a Band-Aid. The implications of the exercise, however, were deadly serious. Had it been real, both Cindy and Amanda would have been—as the referee in the white armbands pronounced—dead.

Cindy took a deep breath and rose to her feet. She examined Amanda's wound and told her to apply the compress.

"That was brave of you, Lieutenant, but it would've cost you," the referee told Cindy. "In the real world, you can't trade two lives for one."

"Yes, I understand," she replied. The man was just a sergeant, but he was regular army, and he had a lot more experience that she did. Technically, she outranked him, but one of the first things that lieutenants fresh into combat have to learn is to listen to the sergeants. On the company and platoon levels, they are the ones who know what they're doing.

Lieutenant Cindy Hunt had yet to see real combat, but things were about to change. The orders that she had received a month ago stated simply that the 3rd Battalion of the Iowa Guard's 185th Regiment was deploying to Afghanistan. The unit that Cindy commanded, the 3313th Communications Company, was simply listed among the battalion elements. When she reported for duty, however, she was told that the 3313th would, instead, be going to Manas, the big American staging base in Bishkek, the capital of Kyrgyzstan. A tiny country in the heart of Central Asia, Kyrgyzstan is squeezed in between neighboring Kazakhstan to the north and China in the east. Since back in 2002, Manas had been a major base for coalition air forces operating in Afghanistan. Kyrgyzstan was not a pretty place, but at least they weren't shooting real bullets at you there.

On the evening of that terrible day when she said good-bye to Peter on the front steps of their home, she phoned him with the good news. She and the sixty men and women under her command would be processing paperwork well behind the lines. Both of them had been greatly relieved.

In the military, however, they tell you that good news has a very short half-life. The 3313th had barely gotten itself situated in Kyrgyzstan when the reassignment came down—to Afghanistan, after all.

The 3313th would be going down to Kandahar to set up a nonsecure communications network for information to be uplinked to Kabul so the Defense Department's American Forces Press

Service journalists could write press releases and news items. Cindy and her people were given twenty-four hours to repack their gear and go through a crash course in processing paperwork—under fire.

The flight from Kyrgyzstan to Kandahar, with the stopover in Kabul, was like a trip that Cindy had made last year from Cedar Rapids to Philadelphia, with a change of planes in Chicago.

However, as soon as their convoy of Humvees left the airport perimeter at Kandahar, it had become graphically clear to Cindy and the young Guardsmen in her communications company that they were no longer in a familiar world. Kandahar was a step back in time to a world of medieval misery punctuated by a few modern buildings that were shockingly out of place.

Cindy noticed Amanda staring, with a stunned expression on her face, at a group of women shuffling down the street in blue burkas.

"I didn't think that they still…" Amanda started to say. She paused as though unable to find the words.

"Yes, they still dress like that," Cindy replied.

"I just can't imagine it," Amanda said. "How can they even walk? How can they see where they're going?"

"I think they have a slit with mesh over it so they can look out," Cindy said.

"I thought they stopped making women do that."

"The government did, but out here in the sticks, a lot of women are still afraid," Cindy explained. "They're afraid that if the Taliban comes back, any woman who hasn't been wearing those things will get her throat cut. A lot of the warlords are the same way."

"And we thought we had gender discrimination back home!"

"It's a real eye-opener, that's for sure," Cindy agreed. "Those are the guys who we're fighting over here."

At last, the convoy reached a compound across Kandahar City from the airport. American, NATO, and Canadian flags were flying, and none of the women here had their faces covered by anything more intrusive than sunglasses.

"Welcome to the beautiful Arghandab Valley," a captain with a Tennessee drawl said as Cindy approached the command post. Cindy saluted the senior officer; he returned the salute and reached out to shake her hand.

"The 3313th Communications Company is here to report for duty, sir," she said.

"We're happy to have you," he replied. "We had a communications outfit from the New York Guard here until two days ago, when they rotated out. The sergeant will see that your people get some tent space, and tomorrow, y'all be helping our people get the Jitters."

As Cindy knew, "Jitters" was the way everyone in the army pronounced JTRS, which was the acronym for the Joint Tactical Radio System, which was supposed to be the next-generation radio for use by the military to transmit voice and data in field operations. She also knew that the first phase of the program had to be restructured in 2005 due to significant cost and schedule overruns, and that air force and army helicopters were removed from this phase, reducing the scope of Jitters to ground vehicles and fixed locations only.

"How much of the Jitters gear has been installed?" Cindy asked.

"Out at the field locations, pretty much next to nothing," the captain said, gesturing out into the hills beyond the sandbagged perimeter. I think that there are some UHF or VHF land mobile radio sites and such, but don't ask me nothin' about bandwidth and all that. I'm not a techie, and I've got a helluva lot else on my plate to worry about."

"How am I going to find out where things stand?"

"Well, it's too bad you didn't get here a couple of days ago when the New Yorkers were still around. You coulda just asked 'em."

"We didn't even get our orders to come down here until a couple of days ago."

"Doesn't surprise me." The captain grinned, shaking his head.

"So we're kinda playing catch-up," Cindy said tentatively. "What would you do if you were me? I mean how can I figure out what's been done and what we need to do at the field locations?"

"Well, ma'am," the captain said, again gesturing to the distant hills beyond the fortified edge of the camp. "I guess you're gonna just have to get out into the field and see for yourself."

Bagram Air Base, Near Kabul, Afghanistan
April 2

★ ★ ★

Jimmy Ray Flood squinted as he stumbled down the gangway leading out of the massive, gray C-17 Globemaster that had lugged the 33rd Infantry Battalion (Provisional) all the way from America. The weather was cold, but the sky was clear and, at nearly five thousand feet of elevation, the midday sun was bright.

The sunlight was especially glaring for the Georgia boys—and a few women—who had been cooped up in the nearly windowless transport plane for hours—many, many hours. Jimmy didn't have any idea how long it had been. He didn't have his watch. He had given it to Cathy at the mall in Atlanta when they said their tearful good-byes. Well, for Cathy it was tearful. Jimmy didn't start bawling until after he dropped her off at her mother's place and headed downtown to the Greyhound bus depot. The tears started just as he got on MARTA, and he was still crying when he got down to Forsyth Street and bought his ticket to Charleston.

Little did he realize that the U.S. Army was going to take him and the rest of battalion *back* to Georgia for nearly a month of training at Fort Benning. Then they put them on buses in the middle of the night and took them back up to Charleston again, where they had to sit around for a day waiting to board the planes. Everybody hoped that the month at Benning would count against the six months of their deployment—*if* it was only six months.

Now, here he was, halfway around the world. Bagram looked a whole lot like the base that he had flown out of in South Carolina. There was a row of the same whalelike C-17 transports, with a few American warplanes and a lot of big, white civilian transport planes as well. The big difference was the range of rugged, snowcapped mountains that seemed to be looming up just beyond the flight line. You don't see a lot of those in Georgia and the Carolinas.

"Whaddya suppose time it is?" one of the guys asked Jimmy as they stood waiting for the pallet with their gear to be lowered from the back of the C-17.

"I dunno," Jimmy said. "I left my watch in Georgia."

"Whatja do that for?"

"Like I told my kid when I was leaving, I said I figured that the army would know when things needed doing and that they wouldn't be tellin' me it was time till it was time."

"I guess you're right about that," the other guy said, satisfied with Jimmy's assessment of the situation.

"I figure it has to be Wednesday or maybe Thursday," another guy interjected. "I seen at least a couple of sunrises or sunsets while we were comin' over. Couldn't tell which."

The Georgians gathered up their duffel bags and rifles and boarded a line of vehicles that took them to a sprawling tent camp. Somebody said something about welcoming them to Kabul, but the place they were at sure looked a lot more like an army camp than a city.

The troops were given billets in a line of B-huts, and each

one claimed a cot. Jimmy crashed onto his and fell asleep almost immediately. So did most of the guys around him. He had dozed off during the flight, but lying prone on a cot was a lot better that trying to sleep sitting up in a bouncing, vibrating airplane. The sound of forty or so snoring soldiers was a lullaby compared to the incessant bellowing of four Pratt & Whitney F117 turbofan engines.

Jimmy slept and dreamed. Big D was in the yard, at his shack, not at his mother's house. As Jimmy drove away, the big dog started to run after him. If Big D was chained up, it was a long chain, because he kept coming. He ran and ran. The faster Jimmy moved away, the faster the dog ran. The dog was running as fast as he could, but he never reached Jimmy. Finally Jimmy reached out to his dog. Jimmy's hand was almost touching the big panting, slobbering face when there was suddenly a loud noise, and Big D disappeared.

"Up and at 'em, you clowns! Chow line in five minutes. We move out in thirty!"

The sergeant who served as the alarm clock for Jimmy's B-hut was not being gentle with the slumbering Georgians. Just as Jimmy had deduced, nothing happened until the guys with the brass on their shoulders said it did, and when they said it, they passed it down to the sergeants to make it happen. Jimmy wondered what time it was, but as he had told Cathy, he was in the army now, and it didn't matter.

It was still dark outside, but to Jimmy, it felt like the afternoon. Maybe this was what they call jet lag? Until now, he had never traveled far enough on a jet to know what jet lag was all about.

The hot breakfast wasn't bad. At least the army fed the men well—so far. After the men had eaten, they were ordered to get their gear and report as companies to an assembly point. As

Jimmy arrived, Captain Randolph was explaining what Lima Company was going to be doing next. There had been some talk on the plane that they would be pulling guard duty at the United States Embassy in Kabul. If that had once been the plan, the army had changed its mind.

The company commander told his troops that they were being assigned to support operations in Helmand Province. Jimmy had never heard of the place, but a guy standing near him had. By the tone of his voice when he said, "Oh shit," Jimmy figured that this mysterious place was not a good place to be going.

Helmand Province, Afghanistan
April 2

★ ★ ★

"Die, you motherfucker!" Raymond "Spider" Rhead screamed in frustration as he squeezed the trigger of the M240 machine gun, splattering the window across the street with 7.62 mm rounds. Another face and another weapon appeared at another window, and Spider hurled his deadly fire at this one. "These fuckers are like fucking bugs, you can't kill 'em all."

The wall behind where Spider and Justin were crouching erupted in a hail of broken plaster and ricocheting metal as yet another Taliban gunner tried to splash the Americans with AK-47 fire.

Both of the Californians ducked down, breathing heavily and waiting for the bad guy to stop shooting. As they pressed their heads as low as possible, they were within inches of either side of the M240's smoldering barrel. The heat stung their cheeks. It was so hot they could *smell* the heat through the stench of burned powder. The piles of steaming-hot, expended brass stung their hands as they rooted around, trying to find a safe place out of the withering fire being hurled at them now by several Taliban gunners.

Three days had passed since Alpha Company's 3rd Platoon had rolled into Sherishk to see and be seen. Everybody in the outfit had taken to pronouncing the name of the town as Sure-Stinks, but whenever Justin heard this, all he could think about was the melodic way that the NGO girl had pronounced the word. From her lips, it was almost like poetry. But thinking about this only got Justin thinking about the way those lips had quivered in shock as she clung to him and died in his arms.

He couldn't get the sound of her voice nor the image of her eyes out of his mind. Nor could he get her blood out of his shirt. He had tried to wash it out, but that had failed. He had washed it again, but it was still stained with her blood. He had another shirt in his gear back at Alpha Company headquarters, but he'd have to get there first. They were supposed to have been back there yesterday, but plans had changed.

Three days had passed since Alpha Company's 3rd Platoon had rolled into Sherishk on a patrol that was to have been a forty-eight-hour roll-through. They were there to see and be seen, to let the Afghans in this part of the province know that the coalition was still around.

It was the "hearts and minds" game. The way it worked was that the people were afraid to cooperate with the coalition, because if the Taliban caught them doing that, heads would roll—literally. If they felt that the coalition was paying attention to them, they were less likely to suck up to the Taliban.

If the bad guys saw the coalition coming around, they'd lay low or go bother somebody else—most of the time.

If the Taliban did come around, it was usually something sneaky, like a car bomb or a hit-and-run. The Taliban didn't like to stand and fight. Their advantage was surprise. When the surprise was over, they were gone—most of the time.

The coalition had the firepower and the ability to put a large force pretty much anywhere they wanted to—most of the time.

In Helmand, however, the coalition was stretched thin. The Brits were feeling it, and the small force of California National Guard that the regional IASF commander sent in to back them up were feeling stretched just as thin.

It turned out that Alpha Company's 3rd Platoon was right on the thinnest part of the stretch. The Taliban had seen the Cal Guard roll in with just thirty-one guys in five Humvees and licked their chops. For once, the Western devils were outnumbered. That was three days ago. Now, it was twenty-seven guys and three Humvees. Taliban mortars took out one of the vehicles with a direct hit and damaged the other one to the point that it would need some heavy maintenance to drive out of Sherishk under its own power.

Four guys had been wounded in the constant sniping by the Taliban: two of them really bad, the others bad enough. They were taken out on medevac choppers, but Lieutenant Sloan's repeated requests for attack choppers to back up the platoon were still unanswered. Battalion headquarters said they'd do what they could. So far, that was nothing.

When the Taliban figured out what was going on—or not going on—they apparently decided to stick around for a while and make life difficult for this small gaggle of infidels.

"I think it's stopped," Justin said, rolling his body into a slightly more comfortable position on the bed of spent cartridges from the M240 and his own M16A4. "Do you suppose those assholes have moved on?"

"I dunno," Spider postulated. "There's still a lotta shooting over around the command post, but these guys here are quieter. Maybe they're just waitin' for us to stick our heads up?"

"Do you wanna take a look, or shall I?"

"I dunno," Spider said. "Who wants to be the first to die for this stinkhole?"

"Let's try this, like they do in the movies," Justin said, pulling his helmet off and putting it on the butt of his rifle. The cool breeze felt good on his sweaty scalp as he raised the helmet slightly above the parapet. If the Taliban gunners were still looking their way, this would draw their fire—that is, unless they had seen the same movie as Justin.

"Nothing," Spider said tentatively. "Maybe the motherfuckers moved on?"

"I dunno. Do ya think?"

"All right, let's have a look," Spider said, hoisting the barrel of the M240 above the parapet. As he peeked over, scanning the building through the gunsight, he let out a long, low whistle.

"What is it?" Justin said, strapping on his helmet and rolling into a position where he could see the other building.

"We got us one Talibanger," Spider said as they stared across the thirty yards that separated their position from the building where the Taliban had been. Through one of the windows, they could see an enormous blood spatter on the opposite wall. At the base of the spatter, a man with a black beard appeared to be sitting on the floor, his back against the wall. His head was tipped to one side, and they could see the whites of his unblinking eyes.

"The other ones must have run for it when this guy got wasted," Justin said, staring at the dead man. "Wonder why they left their buddy."

"Probably figured there was nothin' they could do for him." Spider shrugged. "Probably figured that he's off somewhere screwin' the one hundred and seventy-five virgins that they're supposed to get when they get killed."

"I suppose," Justin said, staring at the dead man with the blank look on his face. He realized that this could have been him.

"Whaddya think we ought to do?" Spider asked.

"The lieutenant told us to patrol this sector and report back."

"Well, I guess we better report back," Spider answered. "I sure as hell don't wanna try to chase after the ones that got away and get suckered into a trap."

The sounds of the firefight near the command post had died down by now, and making their way back sounded like a safe and prudent thing to do. Neither Justin nor Spider felt like being a dead hero today.

When they had left this morning to go on their little recon patrol into the southwest corner of Sherishk, the platoon command post had been an orderly place. Lieutenant Sloan had located it inside an enclosure surrounded with a low adobe fence. This would keep the Americans relatively safe from car bombers. He had turned the Humvees in such a way that their radiators were less likely to be hit if a sniper started shooting.

What Sloan hadn't expected was a full-out assault on the command post. Unfortunately, this is what had happened.

Spider and Justin had returned to find the place in chaos. One guy, nervous and trigger-happy, almost shot them as they rounded a corner opposite the ruins of the 3rd Platoon position.

Two of the Humvees had been totaled by mortar rounds, and one was still on fire. Smoke and dust and shouting swirled everywhere. Justin and Spider were surrounded by men covered with blood. Some were walking, some lying on the ground being attended to by other men covered with blood. Chuck Ellis and another man were carrying a large object wrapped in a canvas tarp. Justin felt the puke rising in his throat as he realized that it was a human body. Who? How?

The lieutenant was talking on the radio. Actually, he was shouting on the radio.

"All right, yes *sir*!" Sloan shouted, as he terminated his conversation.

"Listen up, people," he said, trying to get the attention of men swarming here and there, picking up debris and comforting the wounded. "I've just been on the line with regimental headquarters. They've already sent out medevac, and they're sending us reinforcements. As soon as the wounded are taken care of, we're gonna mount up and go after those bastards."

"Who's coming in?" Sergeant Alvarez asked. "Is it 2nd Platoon? How many men are coming?"

"No, the rest of Alpha Company is engaged," Sloan explained. "So is Bravo. ISAF Headquarters up in Lashkar is sending in two platoons of guys from the 122nd Regiment of the Georgia Guard. Poor bastards just touched down. They were supposed to be coming in to guard the fuel dumps, but their mission got preempted."

"When are they going to get here?" Justin asked.

"Today, I mean real soon," Sloan said. "The first bunch are coming in on the Chinooks that are gonna take out our wounded."

Sloan paused. He had meant to say "dead and wounded," but obviously, he just couldn't say "dead." He trembled slightly. Justin thought he had been doing a damned good job of keeping things together in a really bad situation, but he was a Guardsman, too. In real life, Sloan worked for an insurance company in Bakersfield. In real life, he wore a suit and worked in an air-conditioned office, where the only blood came from paper cuts. Now, he was here.

Helmand Province, Afghanistan
April 3

★ ★ ★

"Nothing but motherhumpin' desert down there," Billy Idelson said for about the eighth time since the big twin-rotor CH-47D Chinook helicopter had taken off from Bagram Air Base. Jimmy Ray Flood just nodded. Billy was right. Aside from desert, they could see literally nothing beneath them. Most of the streambeds were just dry gullies, and the one or two roads since they had passed over Kabul and headed southwest were deserted.

Seen just before sunrise from the air, Kabul looked like just about any city looks from the air in the darkness. There were headlights and taillights on the roads, and there were some newish-looking tall buildings downtown. After the sun crested the mountains to the east, things changed. Now that they could see details other than lights, they could make out residential areas that looked progressively poorer as they moved outward from the center of Kabul's urban sprawl. The shacks down there made Jimmy's "cottage" back in Waycross look like a palace. Then things just faded into grayish, brownish desert.

The Georgia Guard guys had boarded three of the big choppers, but these Chinooks could carry only part of Lima Company.
They had waited. There were supposed to be more helicopters
showing up to airlift the rest, but they didn't. Somebody higher
up the food chain must have told Captain Randolph that he had
better get his ass in gear, so he ordered the three choppers to go
ahead and move out.

Randolph left his executive officer in charge of the troops still
milling around on the tarmac at Bagram and boarded the lead
chopper, the one that Jimmy was on. He was a hands-on kind
of guy. In real life, Randolph ran a construction company down
around Valdosta, and he was used to being in charge and being
involved.

"Okay, listen up, everybody," Randolph shouted over the
whacking sound of the big rotors and the thunder of the Lycom-
ing T55s after they had been airborne for an hour or so. "We've
been ordered to drop in and back up a platoon of guys from the
California Guard who are suppressing Taliban in a place called
Sherishk. These guys have been taking Taliban fire *today* so this
place is a *hot zone*. We're gonna be going in about ten minutes
from now. Make sure your vests are strapped on right and that
y'all are ready for anything. We're gonna have to hit the ground
running."

"That doesn't sound too good," Idelson said. Jimmy had figured that Billy talked more than any other five guys in the platoon. Some said he talked too much. "Do you suppose they're
gonna be shooting at the chopper?"

"Why don't you just shut up, Billy," another guy said. "A lot of
us just don't want to think about this thing getting shot at or shot
down."

"Yeah," Jimmy added. "Let's just take it as it comes. There
ain't nothin' we can do about it. Besides, from what I hear, most

of these assholes over here can't shoot straight. That's why they have to do chicken-shit stuff like blowin' up car bombs."

"Hope you're right," Idelson said. He always liked to have the last word.

The ten minutes seemed to drag on for thirty, but suddenly, they felt the chopper falling hard and fast. Several of the men gasped instinctively. Somewhere behind him, Jimmy heard the sickening sound of somebody loosing his breakfast.

Just as suddenly, the helicopter jerked to a stop. The falling sensation was the steep descent that the choppers use in combat zones to minimize potential exposure to ground fire. It's rough on the men, but less rough than risking being shot at during a slow, smooth landing. Outside, the men could see nothing but swirling clouds of rust-colored dust. They strained to hear the sound of gunshots, but that was impossible over the sound of the engines.

"Out, out, get the hell out of here *now!*"

The loadmaster was screaming as loud as he could as he opened the trapdoor at the end of the chopper, and the pilot settled down the last few feet onto the ground.

Jimmy rose out of his seat and grabbed his gear in a single motion. Every man was running as fast as his heavy load allowed him, each heading for the daylight at the end of the helicopter. Everybody had one thing in mind, and that was that the cumbersome aircraft was the biggest, noisiest thing on the battlefield, and hence the biggest and easiest-to-hit target for the bad guys. Everybody wanted to be far away from it as fast as possible.

Jimmy nearly tripped as he ran off the ramp but caught himself. He heard another guy behind him who was not so lucky, but he didn't bother to look back. Ahead of him, he could see only the ghostlike images of the guys as they ran into the dust cloud. He didn't know where he was going, he was just running *away* from the chopper and following the crowd.

As he at last broke out of the swirling dust storm, Jimmy could still taste it on his tongue. He coughed and spat a couple of times. That felt better, but not a whole lot better. The dust clung to everything, and even outside the cloud, the smaller pieces seemed suspended in a floating haze.

The men were forming up along a low stone fence, crouching down and looking around. The captain had said there might be shooters, and nobody wanted to be the first casualty.

Jimmy stooped down and looked back. He saw the captain running toward a place where there were several tents and some Humvees. Two of the three choppers were already airborne again, and some guys were loading something into the third. Jimmy didn't realize that the "something" was actually California National Guard casualties that were being evacuated.

"Do you hear anything?" Idelson asked rhetorically. "I don't hear any snipers. I think we made it."

"Oh yeah, man," grinned an Irish corporal from Atlanta named Mel Cooley. "We really got it *made*, now. Our troubles are all over. We just got dropped off at the gates of the Garden of Eden."

A couple of people laughed, but most of the guys were looking around and taking in the view of this place. This was no Garden of Eden. Around them was a town that consisted of single-story shacks that spread out across the flats for as far as they could see. Jimmy saw a few curious civilians watching them. There were some guys in turbans and a couple of women in burkas. He had heard that they liked to keep their women in sacks over here, but it was weird to see it. He imagined the hell that any guy would have to go through if he tried to put Kadeefa into one of those.

As Jimmy looked into the distance and saw that the Chinooks were already just specks in the eastern sky, the realization hit him that he was truly cut off from the real world—and he had no idea what to expect in this world.

Captain Randolph was walking toward the men with another officer, and the guys formed up to hear what he had to say.

"This is Lieutenant Sloan of Alpha Company of the one hundred and eighty-fourth," the captain said, nodding to the other man. The contrast was obvious. Randolph's uniform was so fresh that it could have just come from the cleaners. Sloan's was dirty and scuffed. His knees were the same dark color as the ground. "His men have been engaging the enemy here for the past two days. We are here to help him make sure that the coalition does not lose Sherishk."

"When's the rest of Lima Company going to get here?" Idelson asked. The sixty or so men who had squeezed into the three choppers were less than half of the men in the company. They had brought very little of their heavy equipment and supplies. They had no vehicles and little ammunition beyond what each man carried on his back, and what the two M240 machine crews had lugged.

"It's not going to be today," Randolph said. "Transport in this country is a little bit squirly, and it only gets more squirly the farther out in the boonies you get. So we're going to make do and go to work. Lieutenant Sloan will tell you what the situation is."

"So this is it, pretty much," Sloan explained. "The Taliban are somewhere in the hills south of town. They rushed us this morning, but we beat 'em off. Their MO is that they like to hit towns like this when we're not around. When we show up, they sort of pick at us and wait for us to move on. What ISAF wants is for us to take the fight to these bastards and *hold* this place. We know that they're nearby, so I want to find out where and hit them before they hit us again."

"What we have in mind is to get a patrol out there who can get on top of the bad guys where they don't expect it," Randolph added. "If we send choppers, they'd hear us coming. We'll do it after dark, so they can't see what we're doing. Sergeant Alvarez of Alpha Company is going to take the lead, and I want five of our guys to go with him. When you've located their nest, we'll call in an air strike. We'll send a small patrol...big enough to take care of itself...but not so big that they'd kick up a lot of dirt and get themselves detected. Just a recon patrol. Get in and get out...and let the air force plaster the bad guys with JDAMs."

The captain glanced around, saw Cooley standing nearby, and said, "Corporal, why don't you take Baio and Sheldon with their M240, and two other guys, and go introduce yourself to Alvarez."

In turn, Cooley nodded to Idelson and to Jimmy, who were standing to his right, and said, "you guys didn't have any other big plans for tonight, did you?"

Helmand Province, Afghanistan
April 3

★ ★ ★

Sergeant Ricky Alvarez sized up the crew that he would be leading on patrol. He picked Dude and Spider and SpongeBob Ellis. Even though he looked to be in his early twenties and had no combat experience, the wisecracking Irish corporal named Cooley from Atlanta would be his second-in-command. This was simply because he outranked everybody in the patrol except Alvarez, and the sergeant figured that he hadn't made corporal for sitting around with his thumb up his ass.

The Georgia Guard guys had been in country so short a time that they didn't even have nicknames yet. There was an M240 gunner named Baio and his ammo donkey, a guy named Sheldon. The two other Georgians were a study in contrasts: a white guy named Idelson who talked constantly and a black guy named Jimmy Ray Flood who said very little.

Alvarez gave the men a quick pep talk and then dismissed them with the advice that they had better get themselves fed and try to find someplace dark to get some sleep. He didn't want anybody dozing off on the nocturnal patrol.

"My name's Justin Anderson, but they call me Dude," Justin said, introducing himself to Jimmy as they gathered up their gear and headed toward the tattered scrap of canvas and aluminum tubing that passed as the mess tent. Alvarez had decided to pair off his Alpha Company guys with the Georgians. He figured that Spider would be a good match for the talkative Idelson, and he matched Ellis with the machine gun team. He had more experience with M240s than most of his guys. That left Justin and Jimmy.

"I'm Jimmy Ray, but they call me Jimmy. Where's the Dude come from, Dude?"

"They think I look like a surfer dude." Justin laughed.

"Are you?" Jimmy asked. He wanted to kid the kid and say that all white people looked alike, but he figured he'd better get to know him a little better. All the same, he had sized up the guy as the easygoing kind who could probably take a joke.

"Yup." Justin grinned.

"Never tried it myself," Jimmy said, wondering for a minute what it might be like to actually ride waves. Frankly, he had never thought about it much. In fact, he had never thought about doing it himself *at all*.

"If you ever get to LA, look me up." Justin grinned. "I'll show you how it's done."

"Okay."

Ordered to make a night patrol so that the Taliban would have a harder time seeing them, the nine men had sacked out and tried to catch some sleep before the sun went down. Jimmy had a hard time falling asleep, as he lay in the half-light of a tent wondering what it would be like to get shot at by somebody who you didn't even know. When he was growing up in Chicago, he knew several guys who had been hit in gang shootings, and one had died. He guessed that Afghanistan was just a big gang war. It all seemed to be about one gang wanting another gang's turf. Just like Chicago. With that disconcerting thought, he finally dozed off.

Alvarez rousted his men just after sundown. They'd have an hour to check their night-vision gear and get ready. They packed as though they were going away for a long weekend. They figured that it could be at least forty-eight hours before they spotted the Taliban. They loaded their packs with MREs, plenty of extra ammo, and water bottles—lots of water bottles.

Unlike most of the regular army guys, not all National Guard troops had been issued night-vision equipment, but Alvarez scrounged a set of the delicate and finicky goggles for everyone.

When it came time to paint their faces, Jimmy got a good laugh. "Sure is a hoot to see all you white guys tryin' to make yourselves look like us black folks," he chuckled.

Everyone else laughed. It was a good way to cut the tension that everyone was feeling.

The Taliban were presumed to be camping in the hills to the south toward the Pakistan border, so Alvarez deliberately took the men due north along the road toward Lashkar Gah. They'd go east, then circle back under cover of darkness, but in the meantime, anyone watching from the hills would think that the Americans were following the road north. The Taliban stereotype of Americans was that they were in love with roads where they could use their vehicles, and Alvarez wanted to play into the stereotype. He also knew that the Taliban had snoops inside Sherishk, and he wanted them to report an American patrol headed north, not south.

"Sure is dark out here," Billy Idelson said as they hiked along the road. Nobody else had much to say. "It sure gets dark out here when the moon's just a sliver. You can sure see the stars."

Alvarez and Cooley let him talk. It wouldn't hurt the tactical plan to have him rattling on and on while they were still distracting the attention of unwanted observers in Sherishk. However, when the lights of the town disappeared over a rise behind them, and Alvarez turned and pointed east, Cooley told Idelson to zip it.

They hiked in silence for about forty-five minutes until they reached the base of a line of hills that ran parallel to the road. Here, they turned south, keeping themselves hidden in the uneven terrain where the flats met the slopes. A half hour later, they had reached a point opposite Sherishk, and they continued south into the dangerous world that they supposed was Taliban country.

It was like a creepy movie, deathly quiet and cast in the weird green light of their night-vision goggles.

Alvarez had the men spread out; there was no sense making the entire patrol a good target if they happened to run into the Taliban. There had been a time when the Americans "owned the night" with their high-tech night-vision gear, but times were changing. The bad guys were gradually getting the gear, either by stealing it or buying it on the black market from armies and militias supposedly friendly to the United States who had been given the equipment by the Americans themselves. Then, too, the Iranians could buy it easily from arms dealers in Europe, and they were only too happy to see that it got shipped across the border to the enemies of the infidels.

The National Guardsmen moved quietly as they worked their way through the desert. The sergeant would hold up his hand every few minutes, and everybody would stop and listen. The only thing they had heard so far had been a couple of small animals running through the brush and the cold wind blowing out of the mountains along the border. Fortunately, the wind was blowing *toward* them. Justin remembered reading somewhere that the wind carried sound waves. That meant that if there were any bad guys up ahead, the Americans would hear them before being heard.

Alvarez had let Ellis take the point because he knew that this assistant manager of a copier place in Glendale was careful and meticulous. His job at the copy shop also made him a good listener. He knew when something sounded right—or wrong.

A couple of uneventful hours took them several miles south of Sherishk to a place where two canyons came together before spreading out into the broad, flat plain where the town was located. Suddenly, Ellis began waving his hands in the air, and everyone stopped in his tracks. The point man crouched down and pointed to his ear. Everyone made himself as still as possible and listened. Through the sound of the wind, they could hear voices. Somebody was having a conversation. It sounded like two or three people talking about fifty yards away over a low rise ahead and to the left.

Alvarez gestured for the troops to stay put as he crept quietly up to where Ellis was.

Jimmy and Justin looked at one another. With their goggles in place, neither could read the other's expression, but all the same, they knew what the other was thinking.

Ellis and the sergeant put their heads together for a moment, and Ellis nodded. He moved forward, creeping up the low rise. Alvarez had obviously told him to go take a look. They watched as he disappeared out of sight and counted the minutes until he reappeared. Again, he huddled with the sergeant, and finally Alvarez moved back down the slope to where most of the others were clustered.

Gesturing for the men to gather around, Alvarez explained the situation.

"There's a bunch of Toons down there about half a football field from the ridgeline," he whispered. "There's about a dozen. Maybe less. Can't tell if they're Taliban or just Toons. There's another town about a mile up that canyon. Bob says he thinks it's a lot smaller than Sherishk, but he can't tell, 'cause there's only a few lights on."

"Is it on the map?" Idelson asked. "I don't remember seeing a town on the map at the briefing."

"That's 'cause the friggin' map we got ends just outside of Sherishk, 'cause that's where the main road ends," Cooley explained.

"No shit?" Idelson asked. He always liked getting in the last word, however pointless.

Cooley traced his finger across his lips in a zipping motion, and Idelson nodded.

"What we're gonna do is this," Alvarez continued. "I figure those clowns are either stupid or they're not Taliban. If they were Taliban, they'd be here on this ridge, guarding the high ground and looking back down toward Sherishk. They wouldn't be camped over on the other side. That means we're lucky for a minute. What we're gonna do is climb up higher on this ridge. We gotta get ourselves some high ground and make sure that the Taliban ain't got the high ground up here. We're gonna climb up on this side of the ridge till we got a good view of that other town and all the ground between."

Justin looked around and up the slope. The sergeant was right. If the Taliban were serious, they'd have somebody on one of the hills overlooking this place where these two canyons came together. Maybe it was this hill, or maybe it was on another one. In any case, it was a good idea that the Americans also get up there on one of the hills.

The climb took the better part of an hour, because they were moving as quietly as possible, but at least they found a perfectly defensible spot among some boulders. They could see the lights of the town now, and a little speck of light that was the embers of the campfire belonging to the guys whose voices they had heard.

"Dude," Alvarez said, looking at Justin after everyone had shed his backpack. "I want you and Georgia here to recon up this hill to the top. Leave your gear here so you can move quick and get on up there. I wanna make sure there ain't no Taliban on this hill."

"Got it, Sarge," Justin said with a nod and a lump in his throat. Jimmy just nodded. Neither man really wanted to go off looking for Taliban, but at least they could move more nimbly without their packs, and logic told them that it was better to be hunting bad guys now than to get surprised by them later.

The climb was uneventful, and dropping the heavy packs was a rejuvenating experience. After the hours of hiking, being fifty pounds lighter made the men feel one hundred pounds lighter.

They made the top of the ridge in only about twenty minutes and sat down to rest. Justin pulled off his goggles and helmet and wiped his head with his sleeve. The cool breeze felt good on his sweaty scalp. Jimmy took a slug from his water bottle and studied the slopes of the hill with his PVS-23 night-vision binoculars.

"Guess nobody's up here 'cept us," he said at last.

"That's the good news I'm hoping to hear." Justin smiled, sipping a little from his own water bottle.

"Can't tell much about that town over there," Jimmy said, studying the town with the binoculars. "Pretty much like that town we were just at... 'cept a lot smaller."

"Anything else crawlin' around out there that you can see?" Justin asked.

"Not that I can see," Jimmy replied.

"Probably asleep like we oughta be," Justin observed.

"I gotta question," Jimmy said as he lowered the binoculars and removed his own helmet. "What in the hell's a Toon?"

"A Toon?" Justin laughed. "That's what Sarge calls the civilians. A lot of them are Pashtuns, and Toon is sorta short for Pashtun."

"I got another question," Jimmy said as he sprinkled a little water on his shaven scalp. "What in the hell's a Pashtun?"

"That's the people who live around here, y'know, they live all across this part of the 'Ghan and across the mountains into Pakistan and all around," Justin explained, using the soldiers' abbreviated nickname for Afghanistan. "It's kind of a tribe or an ethnic group or something."

"What do the Toons here in the 'Ghan call us?" Jimmy asked.

"I dunno, really," Justin admitted. "Infidels, I guess. Pretty much everybody in this part of the world calls us infidels...or foreign devils...or worse."

"And infidels are people that don't believe in their religion, right?"

"Some people just can't stand people that aren't like them."

"Yeah," Jimmy nodded. "I've seen shit like that back home."

Justin looked at him. In the darkness, only the whites of his eyes were visible. Justin watched as they flicked slightly, directing Jimmy's pupils toward him.

"I guess that bein' a white guy living in LA...I'm pretty much insulated from all that shit back home," Justin said, anticipating what he thought Jimmy must be thinking. "Y'know, like UCLA's been integrated forever, but y'know that shit doesn't really get noticed by white guys, anyway. I guess we're lucky that way."

"Not as bad in Georgia now as it was when my mama was growin' up," Jimmy said, taking another sip of water. "Least that's what I hear. I grew up in Chicago. It's worse up there. It's not as bad in Georgia, but there's one son of a bitch I wish I could..."

"Well, over here, I guess in the eyes of the Toons, we're all sons of bitches," Justin said.

"I sure wish the world wasn't such a fucked-up place," Jimmy said sadly. "I wish I could just take my kid fishin' and not have to go halfway around the world to get mixed up in somebody's gang war. This shit's just like Chicago. Up there you got the Mickey Cobras and the Disciples...back in the day you had the Latin Kings and the Insane Deuces and shit. Over here it's the Toons and the Al-Qaedas. Same shit."

Justin just nodded and looked out over the deceptively peaceful landscape where Californians and Georgians, like Pashtuns and Al-Qaeda, rested quietly beneath the brilliant dome of stars that spread across the cold night sky. He thought about that night under the same stars on the beach with Laurie at Malibu and wished that the gang wars—all the gang wars—would end.

CHAPTER THREE

A Day in Their Lives

Helmand Province, Afghanistan
April 4

★ ★ ★

"They're on the move," Sergeant Ricky Alvarez hissed.

Justin Anderson awoke with a start, completely disoriented and wondering what time it was. The sky was purplish pink, but the sun was not yet up. Justin realized that he must have dozed off after he and Jimmy had come down from the top of the hill.

He looked down into the place where the two narrow canyons came together to form the valley where Sherishk was located. The sergeant was right. About two dozen or more heavily armed men were making their way north toward Sherishk, watching the sky, looking for American helicopters, which they knew were their biggest nemeses. Like the Americans the night before, they stayed close to the base of the hills. Here, there were plenty of rocks and boulders behind which they could hide if they detected the familiar *chop-chop* sound of a helicopter. They apparently had not imagined that the Americans could possibly be on the ground this far from a road.

The one thing that elicits a numbing, constant fear in every

American soldier in a combat zone anywhere in the world is the threat of being ambushed. Roadside bombs. Improvised explosive devices. Rocket-propelled grenades. They are the many heads of the same monster, the monster whose menace is constant. Today, a handful of Americans were in a position to turn the tables. With the M240 and a few grenades, they could probably do a lot of damage, but they were just a recon patrol. Their orders were to look, not to touch.

When the enemy fighters had disappeared into the tumble of boulders and were safely out of earshot, Alvarez contacted Lieutenant Sloan on the radio and apprised him of the situation. He gave the coordinates of the canyon and estimated how fast the Taliban were traveling. Sloan was pleased. He told Alvarez that the air controller at Bagram Air Base had promised an air strike as soon as Sloan could give him a time and place.

"And another thing," Alvarez added. "There's another town up here. It's off the map that we have, but it's pretty obvious from the air. That's where the bad guys came from. You should have the Air Force hit the hive along with the bugs."

"Probably can't do that," Sloan said. "They don't like to hit towns. It's against rules of engagement. Collateral damage and all. They don't like to have civilian casualties."

"It's the friggin' Al-Qaeda and Taliban," Alvarez pleaded. "They didn't much care about civilian casualties on 911. That's why we're friggin' *here*, isn't it?"

In the regular army, a sergeant usually wouldn't speak to an officer quite so forcefully, but this was the National Guard.

"I know," Sloan replied. "You're preaching to the choir here. I'll tell them about it, but I know what they're gonna say. There isn't much we can do. We don't know who's in that village... unless you can get close and check it out."

"We *could* do that," Alvarez said. "But we're just a recon patrol.

We aren't big enough to take down a whole town, even if that big batch of fighters are out fighting, and it's less well defended now than it would've been an hour ago."

"Watch your backs," Sloan said. "Don't take any unnecessary chances. Just take a look and get out. If you get into trouble, let us know."

"Let's move out," Alvarez said, looking out over the landscape as the fiery orange ball of the sun began peeking over the eastern horizon. "Let's get this over with."

The night before, the men of the Alvarez patrol had moved under the cover of darkness. That advantage was slipping away, but they still had the advantage of being undetected in a place where the enemy was not expecting them to be.

As on the night before, the going was slow. To keep from being seen, they deliberately avoided the well-traveled path through the bottom of the canyon, and it took about an hour to cover most of the distance to the village.

"Not that I'm complainin'," Jimmy said as he picked his way through the loose rock along the hillside, "but it seems like we're getting a little bit far from Sher…whatever the hell that place is where we started."

"Sherishk," Justin said with a smile. "It's called Sherishk, but everybody just calls it Sure-Stinks, because it sure does."

Alvarez had the two men bringing up the rear, where they were tasked with keeping their eyes peeled for an ambush from behind. Given this fact, Jimmy was getting a little edgy as he looked for bad guys behind every rock.

"Never know what I'm lookin' for," he admitted to Justin.

"You'll know it when you see it," Justin said soberly. "Better to see it, though. Better to see 'em before you hear 'em. Better to see anything than to have the shots be the first thing you hear."

"What's it like? I mean gettin' shot at."

"Lot like a training exercise. 'Cept with live ammo. You just take cover and shoot back."

"Shi-it!"

"That's pretty much the way it is." Justin shrugged. "I've been in a couple of firefights. The best thing to remember is one thing I was told once by a guy who'd been over here a long time."

"What's that?"

"He said that the best thing to remember is that more than ninety-nine percent of the shots fired in a firefight never hit anything but dirt."

"Oh yeah?"

"Yeah. People get in a firefight and start spraying bullets. Nobody much aims. Most of the shots are just wild. But you do have to watch out for the other one percent."

"That long-timer, that guy who told you that, did he get to go home, or did he have his fuckin' tour extended?"

"He's dead. Went home in a bag."

Jimmy didn't say anything. What could he say? The two men continued in silence until Alvarez halted the patrol on a bluff overlooking the Afghan village.

As Alvarez studied the place with his binoculars, they could hear the sound of jets in the distance, and the sounds of explosions as the air strike plastered the enemy fighters—or at least the place where Alvarez had told Sloan he *guessed* they would be.

"It looks deserted," Cooley said, squinting at the squalid collection of hovels. There were about two dozen structures, each about half the size of a single-wide mobile home, strung out along both sides of a dirt main street. There were no vehicles visible, but there were a couple of rudimentary corrals where livestock might be kept. There were no goats or donkeys visible, however. The only sign of life was a pair of dogs the color of the dirt that they were lying on. One was asleep, but the other was vigorously chewing at fleas on his hind leg.

"Yep," Alvarez agreed. "Maybe the Toons checked out of Toontown."

"At least for the day," Billy Idelson added. "Y'all know, I was just thinkin' that maybe this isn't no town at all, but maybe it's one of those terrorist camps where the motherhumpin' Al-Qaeda are. Maybe them who live there are them who we saw leaving the place this morning. You said it weren't on the map, so, well, what if it's not a town at all, but it's the base where those motherhumpin' punks we saw this morning live and operate out from?"

"Possible," Alvarez said, deliberately using as few words as possible as a reaction to Idelson's chatter.

"Long as we're here, should we go in and take a look?" Spider Rhead asked almost rhetorically. "That way, we can confirm to the lieutenant that there's no civilians, and if we do find it's like Idelson says, full of weapons and shit, then the air force jocks can come back and flatten the motherfucker."

"It does look deserted…" Alvarez said thoughtfully. "It looked a lot more active last night with all those lights."

"I don't see any electrical lines coming in from anywhere," SpongeBob Ellis said. "Must have been lanterns and campfires or something."

"Well, are we gonna just sit around talkin' about the damned place, or what?" Baio, the M240 gunner, asked. "Let's get in there and get the hell out before those bastards get back."

"You don't think the air force got 'em?" Idelson interjected. "Sure sounded to me like they were droppin' a whole lotta shit over yonder."

"At least part of 'em had to have got away," Spider said. "The

Talibangers are like bugs, scamperin' all over the place. Can't hit 'em all from the air, even if you try."

"If all that's right, I figure we got about an hour before they could get back here," Alvarez said. "I wanna have us in and out in twenty minutes tops. They'll probably be coming back the way we saw 'em go out, so we'll get our asses up on this ridge and follow the ridge all the way back to Sher-Shit so we don't cross their path."

Alvarez proceeded to lay out his plan. With Baio and Sheldon providing backup with the firepower of the M240, the others would check each of the buildings along the dirt road that functioned as the main street of "Toontown." They would take turns, with a two-man team kicking in the door and the others covering them as they entered. They'd rotate to the next team to hit the next building, and so on.

Spider and Idelson went first, pushing open the door, crouching and entering the mud-brick shack with their M16A4s at the ready.

"Clear," Spider shouted from inside after a moment.

"There's nobody here," Idelson added. "And I don't see no weapons or shit. There's a lot of gear and dishes and stuff, though…"

"Just leave it," Alvarez interrupted. "Don't mess with anything. If possible, I don't want them to know we was here and come after us. Let's keep going and get this done quick."

One by one, the Guardsmen examined each of the shanties. By the time they had done a dozen, they had found four with sizable caches of rocket-propelled grenades and RPG launchers, as well as AK-47s and assorted boxes, clips, and belts of ammunition.

Things were going smoothly. When they worked out their system and established the rhythm of kicking and covering, they worked their way through nearly the whole hamlet in about fifteen minutes.

"Looks like we're gonna make it in twenty minutes easy; no way we ain't," Idelson said, observing that there were only six more houses left.

"Don't say that shit," Jimmy said angrily. "It's bad fuckin' luck."

As Idelson looked at Jimmy, and then around at the others who had been within earshot, he could tell that everyone agreed. The process had become repetitive, but it *was*, in fact, "bad fuckin' luck" to say that they were going to make it easy. It was Murphy's Law.

For once, Idelson had nothing else to say.

Jimmy and Justin were up next. Justin hit the door hard with a piece of fence post they were using for bashing doors. Nobody wanted his hand or foot on a door that might be booby-trapped if he could help it. None of the doors had been so far, but to assume that this meant there were none was foolhardy.

The door swung open, and Jimmy entered the building crouching, while Justin dropped the post and entered behind him with his weapon at the ready.

"Holy shit," Justin said.

"What is it, Dude?" Alvarez shouted. Part of the routine had been for one of the men entering to shout, "Clear." When Justin didn't, Alvarez was alarmed.

SpongeBob was the first to follow the two men through the door, ready to provide backup.

"People," Justin shouted. "We got two women in here. At least, I think they're women. Otherwise it looks clear."

"Whaddya mean, you *think* they're women?" Alvarez said as he stooped to enter the hut. "That sounds like a line out of a Bangkok whorehouse."

Alvarez soon saw what Justin had meant. In the corner were two small, slender people wrapped entirely in pale blue burkas.

Both of them were trembling as though expecting to be raped or shot.

"*Moaf-me-ka*," SpongeBob said, crouching down and looking at the two people. "*Assalam-o-alekum*."

"What are you saying to them?" Alvarez asked. "I didn't know that you spoke Toon."

"I don't," he said. "I read up on a few phrases when I knew I was coming over here. I don't know that I remember much.

"What was that you just said?"

"I said, 'Excuse me,' and 'Peace be with you,' that's about all the Pashto I know, except *sora*, which means 'how much?'."

Ellis pointed to his lips, said "Pashto," the Pashtun word for their language, and shook his head to indicate that he didn't know much of their language. He added "*Assalam-o-alekum*" again as Alvarez ordered Justin and Jimmy to lower their rifles.

"Do we pull off the hoods and confirm that they're women?" Justin asked.

"Might as well look at their privates," Alvarez said. "It's the same. A lot of women over here don't like to be looked at. Cultural sensitivity and all that."

"Cultural sensa-bullshit," Spider observed. "A lot of women over here are suicide bombers. We know that the Talibangers came from here, so we gotta figure these gals, if they're gals at all, are in with the bad guys. I say we search 'em both."

"Okay," Alvarez said, heading for the door. "Ellis, they seem to think you're a peace-be-with-you kind of guy, so you stay here and keep an eye on these two Toons while we finish searching those last shacks. We gotta get finished and get the hell outa Dodge here."

The remainder of the search turned up another cache of ammunition but no more people.

"Sarge, I think we need to do something with those women,"

Idelson said as he walked back toward their hut with Alvarez. "If we leave 'em, they'll be sure to tell the bad guys we was here."

"What do you suggest?" Alvarez asked.

"I guess we have to either shoot 'em or take 'em with us. Of course, if we shoot 'em that's the same as leaving 'em. The Taliban will know that we was here or somebody was here. No matter who they think was here, they're gonna come after us for killing their girls, but if we take 'em with us, they might think the gals just went off somewhere or something, y'know."

"He's right," Corporal Cooley said. "We don't have much of a choice."

"Okay," Alvarez started to say. When he was thinking on his feet, he usually began his sentences that way. "Okay, here's what we'll do. Ellis, you're the peaceful Toon-talker in the group. You gotta figure out some kind of culturally sensitive way to confirm that they're women and not walking, talking booby traps. Then we'll take them and get the fuck outa Dodge."

Suddenly cast as the man of peace with the wealth of Afghan cultural knowledge, Ellis told Justin and Jimmy to leave the building. He laid his M16A4 aside and sat down. He elaborately removed his helmet, looking at it and at them, trying to make eye contact through the crocheted grillwork that covered their eyes. As his own eyes became accustomed to the darkness of the room, he thought he could see the flickering of their eyes inside. He pointed to the helmet as he set it on his head and pointed to the head covering part of the nearest woman's burka.

The two women, huddled next to one another in the corner, looked at one another and began whispering in Pashtun. It seemed to him that they were arguing. Finally, one of them leaned toward Ellis, reached up, and pulled the hood from her head. She was, indeed, a woman, although Ellis guessed her to be barely older than eighteen. Her hair, mussed from being inside the tight-fitting hood, was light in color, as was that of a lot of the Afghan people he had seen. The other woman followed the lead of the first, shaking her hair and smoothing it with her hand. She was about the same age as the other one: late teems or early twenties. Both of them seemed glad to have the hoods off their heads.

The first girl began speaking rapidly to Ellis in Pashtun, probably thinking that he understood. At one point he asked her if she spoke any English. She just shrugged and continued speaking in Pashtun. Finally, she reached across to a low table and picked up a framed picture of a man. Ellis didn't know who the guy was. He had a dark beard, a turban, and that angry expression that one always sees on the faces of Afghan warlords or Taliban leaders. It was obvious that she cared little for the guy, and finally she confirmed her feelings by spitting several times on the picture and flinging it across the room.

The other woman laughed and began speaking rapidly to Ellis as well. Fighting to get words in edgewise, the two women battled for his attention in a way that Ellis found almost comic. Finally, one of them leaned over and hugged him.

"What the hell's going on in there?" Alvarez shouted.

"I think I've figured it out," Ellis said in reply. "I think these gals are comfort women. "They're prisoners that whore for the Taliban. They're glad to see us."

"I'm glad to see them, too," Alvarez said. "Now, let's get on the road."

Kandahar Province, Afghanistan
April 4

★ ★ ★

"That was the first field location with a UHF SATCOM interface," Amanda Morgan said, shaking her head. The young Specialist from Des Moines was getting over her initial culture shock and doing what she was trained to do. She still couldn't grasp the concept of women wrapped in cornflower blue sacks who lived in mud huts in the twenty-first century, but she understood more about radios than most people in her unit. "At least it was the first one that was Mil-Standard 182 or higher."

"And at least they had their TADIL tactical data links up to 960 to 1215 megahertz," Lieutenant Cindy Hunt added, looking into the Humvee's rearview mirror at the small U.S. Army outpost receding into the distance. The job of the Iowa National Guard's 3313th Communications Company was to make sure that the American Forces Press Service could get their information out of Kandahar, and the only way to access the communications hardware at remote locations was to go out and look at it.

In the early months of the war, there had been a problem with getting the proper body armor to the troops. Now that problem had been largely taken care of, but communications gear was emerging as the new signature shortfall out here in the boondocks. Tactical communications were one thing, but nonsecure communications so that AFPS could write press releases was high on nobody's list. For Cindy and Amanda, it was a thankless, almost pointless job—but it was *their* job.

Having discovered that Amanda had an exceptional technical aptitude for radios—she was an electronics major at Iowa State—Cindy brought her along on the survey excursions.

When Cindy made the decision to go out and survey the field locations, she looked at a map and decided that she and Amanda could get out and see them all in a series of day trips, but that plan only looked good on paper. They hadn't been back to their base in Kandahar City for several days. With the Taliban insurgency boiling beneath the surface everywhere, the only safe way to travel was as part of a convoy, so the 3313th's Humvee had to wait for one slow-moving line of trucks or another in order to move from place to place. At the same time, the convoys were magnets for car bombs and Taliban with RPGs. Not only was this a thankless, almost pointless job, it was turning out to be a very dangerous job.

"What now?" Cindy said in disgust as the big supply truck ahead of them shuddered to a stop.

"Looks like the lead truck must've broke down," shouted the burly young Guardsmen with the M16A4 who was riding shotgun in the Humvee's top position. Andy had better visibility than those riding in the cab. The armor around the Humvee's windows protected the occupants but limited their field of vision.

Cindy shoved the gearshift into neutral and stepped out to look ahead. Sure enough, there was a crowd of people standing around, staring at the first of the five tractor-trailer rigs in the convoy.

"I think he must've broke an axle," Andy said, squinting up the line.

"That's all we need," Cindy said in disgust. "To be stuck out here at night."

"Especially if it starts to rain," Amanda said, looking at some ominous black clouds building in the distance. "They were saying that when it rains out here in this desert, you get flash floods. Having to deal with a washed-out bridge wouldn't be too cool."

"Looks like the major's comin' back this way," Andy observed. One of the Humvees that was ahead of the line of trucks had made a U-turn and was driving toward them, stopping at each of the trucks as it came. Finally, the Humvee pulled to a stop adjacent to where Cindy was standing outside her vehicle.

"Lieutenant, we've had a breakdown up ahead, but we have to get these supplies to Hirwaiz before nightfall," the major in charge shouted, leaning across his driver. "I'm gonna leave one Humvee here to guard that one truck until battalion can get a repair crew out here. The rest of us gotta press on."

"Yes, sir," Cindy said, saluting casually. Things were less formal out here in the desert than they were in the armory back home.

"This isn't a good sign," Amanda said as they drove past the broken-down big rig. The worried looks on the faces of the men left behind were unnerving. "I would sure hate to be those guys. It could've been us."

"Don't worry, Amanda." Cindy smiled. "It's going to be fine."

Cindy could tell that Amanda was more than just a little worried. She was just a kid. A young college girl just two years away from being the queen of her high school prom, and here she was driving around in a Third World war zone. Cindy was worried, too. She smiled reassuringly at Amanda, but behind the grin, she, too, felt that the breakdown was a bad sign.

The jarring, jerking motion of the Humvee on the bad road made everyone irritable. An hour passed. Hirwaiz was still more than sixty miles away, but at the rate they were going, it would be at least another two hours. The Humvees could probably get there faster, but a convoy moves at the speed of the slowest vehicle, and the truck drivers were taking no chances. One broken axle was enough for one day.

Suddenly, there was an enormous crashing sound.

"What was that!" Amanda shouted as the truck ahead braked suddenly and started to swerve.

"I think that something happened with that truck," Cindy said, turning to the side and braking hard to avoid hitting the trailer.

"I see smoke," the young soldier up above shouted. "There's fire! The truck ahead of the one ahead of us is burning. Must have been a mortar or an RPG!"

Cindy could smell it now. She had smelled that smell a time or two during training exercises, and it took a moment to realize that for the first time, it was *for real*.

Her training told her that the best reaction was to press on. When a convoy is attacked, the thing to do was to just floor it and keep moving. A moving target is always harder to hit. Contradicting this, however, the truck ahead of her had stopped, and she couldn't see what was going on up ahead.

"What can you see up there?" Cindy shouted to Andy, who had the better field of view. "Are they moving?"

"I can't tell," he said, squinting through the smoke. "Yeah. I can see them now.

"Yeah, the two trucks are stopped, but everybody else is way up ahead."

Cindy had a sinking feeling. They were last in the convoy and stopped. Everybody else had followed the rules and kept moving.

"Hang on, we're getting the hell outa here," she said, jamming the accelerator with her boot and turning hard to the left. She caught herself flicking the turn signal and realized in a split second how absurd that was.

"Ohmigod!" Amanda screamed as they lurched into the left lane and the burning truck came into view. The whole truck, both the cab and the trailer, were engulfed in dark orange flames that fingered upward into a surging cloud of dirty black smoke. The truck ahead of them had been so close that it had rear-ended the burning truck, and that was why the driver had stopped.

As they passed the first truck, the driver jumped out, waving to flag them down. Cindy slammed on the brakes, and Amanda opened the passenger side door.

Just as the truck driver clambered in on Amanda's lap, they heard a noise that at first sounded like hail hitting a tin roof. As Cindy looked forward again, she saw two men running in the road ahead. For a split second, she couldn't tell what they were doing; then her mind caught up to processing the fact that they were shooting at her.

At first, she couldn't make out the guns—because they were pointed directly at her! Then she saw the muzzle flashes. The racket that sounded like hail was bullets hitting the Humvee. Its armor—as well as the heavy glass in the windshield—was enough to stop the 7.62 mm rounds of the AK-47s, but if these men would have had anything heavier, such as a .50-caliber weapon, the rounds would have punched into the vehicle like a kitchen knife into a cardboard box.

A month ago, Cindy had been carpooling with other day care moms, and now the kids in her car were being shot at by people who would go to any lengths to kill them.

There was only one thing to do: drive and drive fast. The two Taliban were standing directly ahead of her in the middle of the left lane next to the burning truck. She decided not to swerve. It was like seeing something in the middle of an icy road. It's best to steer *into* it rather than swerving to miss it and risking loss of control.

The two men grew larger and larger. Cindy could see their faces. One man recognized that she was not going to turn and ran to get out of the way. The other man just kept shooting. She stared at his face. It was directly ahead of hers. She saw the angry sneer as he expended the last of his ammunition. A split second later, she felt the impact as six thousand pounds of Indiana-built American steel slammed into the man.

The body bounced up onto the hood and hurtled straight at Cindy. For a moment, time seemed to stand still. For a moment, as time stood still, the bearded face stared through the thick glass of the windshield at Cindy's face from a distance of just a few inches.

There was a terrible ripping sound as the body tumbled off the hood, and the view through the blood-smeared windshield was that of the open road. Cindy could see nothing but the road ahead. Where were the other vehicles? How fast was she going?

She glanced down at the speedometer. She was going nearly fifty, and the Humvee was shaking madly as it smacked the potholes.

She freaked.

What if she blew a tire?

She'd run on the rim.

What if she broke an axle?

They'd all die.

Cindy touched the brake and glanced at the side mirror. Nobody was following them.

She looked at Amanda, who was still white as a sheet. The young truck driver, who in civilian life would have yearned to be this close to someone as attractive as the civilian version of Amanda, was not in a good mood. He had vomited all over himself and Amanda, and he was squirming to get away from her.

"Get in the back," Cindy shouted at him. "Crawl between the seats. Andy, help drag him back there. Andy, give us a hand."

As the truck driver struggled to get between the two front seats, he brushed Cindy's cheek. The stench was horrific, but somehow it didn't seem too bad, compared to what they had just been through.

Cindy screamed again, demanding that Andy pitch in and help. She looked in the rearview mirror, but her view was blocked by the truck driver.

"Amanda, what's wrong with Andy?" Cindy demanded of the younger woman, who still seemed to be in a state of shock. "What's he doing back there? Andy, what are you doing? Help out here!"

Amanda shook her head as though waking up from a trance, glanced at Cindy, and turned her head toward the rear of the jostling Humvee. Amanda's blood-curdling shriek made the hairs on the back of Cindy's neck stiffen, and she steered to the edge of the road and stopped the vehicle.

What Cindy saw when she looked into the back was enough to make *her* vomit and scream. The young truck driver, his clothes drenched in the fetid contents of his stomach, was slouching next to Andy, who was covered with blood.

"Do something," Cindy shouted, turning to crawl toward the young soldier. Stop the bleeding. Apply pressure. Where's he hit?"

"I dunno, there's so much blood," the truck driver said, turning toward Andy and feeling his arm and torso for wounds beneath the blood spatter. Andy was slumped backward, his head tipped to one side. There was blood everywhere, on Andy and splattered all over the interior of the rear compartment of the

Humvee. Cindy wormed her way back, disentangled his finger from the trigger guard of his rifle, and started looking for the wound that had caused all the bleeding.

"We gotta do something," Cindy said, reverting to her take-charge track coach persona. "Get his helmet off, stop the bleeding."

She had seen young people in her charge injured a number of times. That's what this was: an injured kid. It was many orders of magnitude worse, but it was the same. She felt his torso. No bullet had penetrated his body armor. A bullet had grazed his helmet, but it hadn't punctured it. Maybe the impact had knocked him out?

She reached up and gently patted his face. The cheek that was turned away from her was sticky with blood. She carefully turned his head and saw what she had neither expected nor wanted to see. A bullet had struck his cheek, just at the base of the eye socket, crushing his skull and carrying a hailstorm of bone fragments ripping into his brain. Death had probably been instantaneous.

When Cindy was driving headlong toward the Taliban, Andy was at his position atop the Humvee, probably returning fire. His face was almost the only unprotected part of him that was exposed, and he had been hit with a lucky shot as the bad guy sprayed the vehicle.

"Cover him with something," she told the truck driver. "We'll call for him to be evacuated when we get to Hirwaiz."

Clambering back to the front of the Humvee, Cindy looked at the road ahead and glanced in the side mirror. The road ahead was absolutely deserted. The remainder of the convoy was long gone. Behind, she saw only a smudge of black smoke on the horizon that marked the distant, burning truck. They were absolutely alone in the middle of nowhere, with a dead man aboard, only a quarter tank of gas, and just a vague idea how to find Hirwaiz.

Cindy took a deep breath and put the vehicle into gear. She

prayed that if they came to a road junction, the way to Hirwaiz would be obvious.

Suddenly, they heard a popping sound of something impacting the Humvee. Amanda, her eyes as big as dinner plates, made a gasping sound. All that either she or Cindy could think of was the sound of the AK-47 rounds hitting them.

Cindy looked away from Amanda and out toward the road ahead. She relaxed—a little bit. The objects hitting the Humvee were merely raindrops, big dollops of wetness falling from the big black clouds that were moving across the sky.

Soon, the road would be a morass of mud, but at least the rain would wash the Taliban blood off the bullet-pocked glass of the windshield.

Helmand Province, Afghanistan
April 4

★ ★ ★

The shriek of bare brake pads against metal came without warning. It was followed by a wave of simultaneous scrapes, creaks, and thuds. In turn, there was the hiss and tinkle of breaking glass.

The screams that came next were from anger, not pain, and Zalmai Nawsadi cautiously opened eyes that he had clamped shut at the first moment of the shrieking brakes.

Taking cover had been instinctive. It was not a function of fear but a function of experience. Zalmai had grown up with this. He was in his teens when the Russians came. He had them, and he had endured the Taliban. He had even spent time in a Taliban jail. Next, he watched as the new coalition of outsiders came to try to push them out of power. He had lived with this all his life.

With hardly a glance at the car wreck, he continued walking east on Garmsir's main street. It had only been a three-car pileup, not a bomb or a rocket-propelled grenade or any number of other things far more serious than an old Japanese sedan with bad brakes and a truck driver who was paying no attention to where he was driving.

Zalmai was angry, not at the drivers now hurling insults, who had interrupted his walk, but at the bombs and rocket-propelled grenades and any number of other things far more serious. He was angry at these things, and he was angry at the Taliban, who continued to hurl them not only at the coalition of outsiders but at Zalmai and his family and his friends.

He had made an important decision yesterday, and now he was going to make good on it. He was going to join the Afghan National Police.

What an irony, he thought to himself. What an irony it would have been if the sound really *had* been a car bomb. What an irony it would have been if he would have been blown up—after all these years—on his way to join the Afghan National Police. If they had blown him up, nobody would ever have known that yet another recruit was dead.

He hadn't even told his wife. He had thought about telling her, but he hadn't. A lot of Afghan men didn't discuss things like that with their wives, because in most Afghan homes, especially out here in this district capital in south Helmand Province, wives were people you told things *to*, not people with whom to discuss things.

This was true with many Afghan wives—probably most—but not Shahla. It was partly because of her that he was doing this. When the coalition came, and the Taliban left, she had become a nurse. A year before, women could have their hands—or even their heads—chopped off for getting educated, but Shahla learned to be a nurse. Even now, she was risking her life, walking into poor neighborhoods all over the district giving children the free polio shots that the international agencies made available. The coalition celebrated her for this, but the Taliban would kill her if they caught her running around with vaccine and syringes under her burka. They believed that the Qur'an said that women shouldn't work. Was preventing misery for children in the Qur'an? The Taliban thought so—if a *woman* did it. This was especially true if the vaccine came from the coalition. The Taliban had spoken, and many people lived in fear.

If Shahla was going to risk her life to do something to help make life in Afghanistan better, then Zalmai decided that he must do so as well. He was no longer content to sell lettuce in the marketplace and watch the country continue to tip back toward the nightmare it had been under the Taliban. His own sister had been killed by the Taliban, and he worried about his children. Most of all, he worried about Shahla. If she died, that would be terrible. If she died while he was selling vegetables, he wouldn't be able to live with himself.

Zalmai had thought about joining the Afghan National Army. That would be safer, because they had bases and better equipment, and they operated in larger numbers. On the other hand, he would have to go up to Kabul for training, and that would take him away from his family. In any event, the army was a younger man's life.

The police station near the Helmand River was a forbidding place, its masonry facade pocked by the impacts of bullets of various caliber fired over the years by gunmen from factions of various allegiances. It was surrounded by barbed wire and barricades. The Afghan flag fluttered in the cold wind, its shadow passing over the bearded men in gray uniforms who stood guard.

"I'm here to join," Zalmai said in Pashto, approaching one of the guards.

The guard looked at him suspiciously and nodded for him to pass through the first barbed wire barrier.

Inside, he was asked to remove his coat, and two men meticulously patted him down. All too often, people who showed up at police stations claiming to want to join were actually suicide bombers. These guards did not want to take a chance.

The Afghan National Police personnel inside the building were a lot friendlier. One of them even offered Zalmai some tea. A man with no beard took his name and told him to wait.

Finally, he was shown into a room where a man with a closely cropped gray beard was seated behind a desk. He had red tabs on the collars of his gray jacket denoting his rank.

"I'm Hamid Sediq," he said pleasantly without smiling. "I'm the chief of police here in Garmsir District. You must be Zalmai Nawsadi. They tell me that you wish to join the Afghan National Police?"

"Yes, that's right."

"Why?" Sediq asked. "Most men are afraid to join us…afraid of what the Taliban will do."

"I used to be afraid of the Taliban…I still am…but I'm more afraid of what they will do if they come back. I've heard what happens in places where they have returned. I don't want these things to happen to my wife."

"I see," the man said.

"Don't you agree?" Zalmai asked.

"That's why I'm here."

"What do I have to do?" Zalmai asked. "How do I sign up?"

"There will be papers to fill out," the chief said guardedly. "Are you willing to do this?"

"That's why I'm here," Zalmai said, repeating Sediq's words.

The chief smiled at this, and sent Zalmai down the hall to another room. Here, another man asked him casually which warlord he had fought for during the war against the Russians. He said that Zalmai looked to be about that age. The man looked at him suspiciously when he explained that he hadn't been in a militia. He told the man that he had small children, and he could better feed them by selling vegetables in the market.

He didn't tell them that he had spent most of a year in a cell in Khadwal-i-Barakzayi because the Taliban later accused him of having sold vegetables to the Russians. He didn't tell them about Khadwal-i-Barakzayi because he didn't want to remember what had happened there.

In another room, a man in mismatched hospital scrubs with a stethoscope around his neck asked Zalmai how he felt. He asked Zalmai if he had any wounds from fighting in a militia while the Russians were in the country, and Zalmai repeated what he had said to the other man. When this man in the scrubs looked at him skeptically, Zalmai repeated his earlier story.

"Why now?" asked the man. "Why did you not fight then...and now you want to join the police?"

"Do you have a wife?" Zalmai asked.

The man nodded.

"Do you want your wife to have to suffer under the Taliban? If they aren't kept at bay by those of us who will actively work to keep them at bay, who will protect my wife if they come back? I have daughters. Who will protect them?"

Again the man nodded. He gave Zalmai a couple of inoculations and sent him down the hall to another room. As Zalmai left, the man looked at him and said, "May Allah protect you and your family."

Khost Province, Afghanistan
April 4

★ ★ ★

"How can you tell?" Sergeant Charlie Schlatter asked as the two men climbed among the boulders high above the rugged Afghanistan-Pakistan border. "How can you tell anything after that flash flood washed away their tracks?"

"There, look under that outcropping," Private Luis Carillo told him confidently. "You'll see."

Schlatter peered carefully into the half darkness beneath a nondescript boulder. Suddenly, he saw it: a parcel wrapped in what seemed to be a crude form of burlap.

"Do you think it's booby-trapped?"

"No, but jab it with a stick...a long stick...just in case."

The sergeant did so, and nothing happened. He then dragged the thing out into the open with his stick and unwrapped it. There were several packets of jerky, some dates—the kind you eat—four banana clips—the kind you do *not* want to eat—for AK-47s, and two American-issue water bottles.

"Wrap it up and shove it back up in there," Luis counseled. "Make it look like it wasn't disturbed."

"How'd you do that?" Schlatter asked. "How did you figure that the trail came through here?"

"You gotta think like them. Where would you go if you were coming through here? Part of it is looking for places to cache ammo and rations."

Luis Carillo had developed a reputation within the 3rd Battalion of the Colorado National Guard's 157th Field Artillery for being the man who could find these mountain trails that no other American could see. Thanks to his skill, the gun bunnies of Echo Battery racked up an impressive record since they went into action. To the other guys, Luis was now a kind of celebrity, a superstar of artillery spotters.

As often happens among troops in combat, Luis earned a nickname. At first, they started calling him Eagle Eyes, but then someone pointed out that in Spanish, that was *Ojo del Aguila*. Gradually, the Spanish variation was shortened to *Ojo*, which everyone pronounced with an English *J*, and Luis became Ojo with an English *J*. He didn't mind. He preferred English. He had enlisted in the National Guard to prove himself worthy of being an American.

Gradually, thanks to Ojo, Echo Battery was becoming the most respected MLRS outfit in Khost Province. When the Colorado Guard had come down here to stop the infiltration, it had seemed like an impossible job. The Americans had the firepower, but the Taliban—and to a lesser degree, the Al-Qaeda punks—knew the lay of the land. They could slip through the eye of a needle to evade the big guns. Then, Ojo Carillo came in to pinpoint the needles in the haystacks of mountains and valleys, and the steel rain of MLRS projectiles put withering firepower through the eyes of those needles.

The lieutenant kept the battery's six M270 MLRS launchers

on the move so that the bad guys couldn't keep track of where they would be next. With a range of more than twenty miles, the Taliban rarely got close enough to hear the M26 rocket's big turbine engines.

That range, however, meant that Luis Carillo rarely got within earshot of the rest of the guys in the battery, either. With Luis acting as their scout, Sergeant Schlatter led small five- or six-man patrols out from the launcher locations to look for potential infiltration routes and keep an eye out for the enemy. They stayed roughly within a twenty-mile radius of the launchers and radioed coordinates when they spotted targets.

So far, Echo Battery had done a great deal of damage.

"Here they come," Luis said, looking across the valley from the position where they had found the cache of supplies under the outcropping. "This place probably connects to that place through the place down in the gully where there's those big boulders that look like Tina Hornschau's ass."

The half-dozen guys in the patrol all chuckled. Tina Hornschau was a soft-core porn model who they had discovered in a pile of naughty German magazines that they took from the body of an Al-Qaeda who they had killed. She had become both a star pinup at the battery bivouac and the punch line of a never-ending series of jokes, both off-color and plain stupid.

"So they're coming our way?" Schlatter asked.

"I guess so," Luis said, looking through the binoculars. "Unless there's a fork in the road down there somewhere."

"Echo one, this is Echo nine," the sergeant said into the PRC-148 radio as he studied his map. "Do you copy?"

"Roger, Echo nine. What do you have for us today?"

Schlatter checked in with the command post at prearranged times, so when he contacted Echo 1 at an odd time, they knew it was to call in a strike.

"Assholes at Alpha-Bravo-twenty-two through twenty-three, now."

"Roger that, we have targets at Alpha-Bravo-twenty-two and Alpha-Bravo-twenty-three. Stand by."

The familiar hiss of the M26 rockets could be heard in the distance but coming closer fast. Luis could see through his binoculars that the Taliban heard it, too. As they tried to disperse, the first of several projectiles arrived, unleashing its steel rain of hundreds of submunitions.

It was all over in less than a minute.

"Okay, gang, let's go," the sergeant said, shouldering his pack.

Echo Battery's usual drill now involved having the spotting patrol go into the MLRS kill box after a barrage to poke around for any useful information that might be obtained from documents that could be retrieved. The Arabic writing was just scribbles to most of the guys, but somewhere back behind the lines, there was an analyst who could decipher all those squiggly lines.

It was a bloody mess. It always was. The results of hundreds of grenades raining out of the sky on a column of infiltrators was never pretty, but neither were the results of the car bombs and IUDs that these Taliban would have planted across Afghanistan.

"Here's something, Sarge," the man known as Deuce said, pulling a wad of papers from a blue nylon day pack.

"Looks like maps and stuff," Deuce's friend Ace observed. The pair had earned their nicknames from their incessant card-playing.

"Whoa, this really is a big deal," Schlatter said as he made his way over to where Deuce and Ace were leafing through their find. "These are maps of towns and streets. This looks like Kabul; I recognize that place there where all the streets cross that square. I remember that from one of the maps they gave us when we deployed."

"What the hell's with all the red and pink dots?" Deuce asked as he leaned over the sergeant's shoulder.

"I dunno," Schlatter said. "Could be safe houses or places where they want to plant bombs or where they make bombs?"

"Could just be good places to get laid," Ace suggested.

"Yeah, I think I see Tina Hornshau's house." Deuce laughed.

There was no doubt that they had stumbled across something important, and everyone crowded around for a peek. Everyone, that is, except Luis Carillo. He stood about thirty yards from the others, staring quietly up into one of the canyons that led back up into Pakistan.

"Sarge," he said at last, still staring at the hills with his binoculars. "I think I see something funny."

"What is it, Ojo?"

Everybody looked toward Luis. When Eagle Eyes saw something, everyone paid attention.

"See the birds. See that big flock of birds over there."

"Yeah. the black ones? Yeah," the sergeant said. "So what?"

"That whole bunch there, they all flew up all at once and moved away."

"Yeah…" Schlatter said, wondering why, in the scheme of things, these birds were important.

"Somebody's up there," Luis said. "Somebody's moving around up there, and they just spooked that bunch of birds."

That got everyone's attention.

Every man in the patrol knew that anyone who was between them and Pakistan was a bad guy, and that bad guys on the Afghanistan-Pakistan border did one of only two things: they tried to kill you or they succeeded in killing you.

"Eyes down," the sergeant ordered. "Don't look in that direction. Don't let them know that we know they're there."

Every man in the Echo 9 patrol suddenly felt as naked as he

had been on the day he was born. The patrol was out in the open, hopelessly exposed, just as the Taliban infiltrators had been on this same patch of ground a half hour before.

"Everybody start heading back," Schlatter said. "Let's head up there for the rocks where we were so we'll have some cover. Spread out and don't walk so fast that it looks like we're running. Move out."

The sergeant waved toward their former position and shouted, making it look to anyone watching that he was signaling to unseen American troops hiding in the rocks and covering the patrol. He wished that he really had left a couple of guys up there to cover the patrol as it went Dumpster diving amid the splattered Taliban. Next time—and he said a silent prayer asking that there *be* a next time—he would remember to have a couple of guys cover the patrol.

"Ojo," he said as Luis Carillo came abreast of where he was walking.

"Yeah, Sarge?"

"I really do hope that just this one time, you were seeing something that wasn't there."

"You and me both, Sarge."

Both men wanted to turn their heads and look back, but neither did. It was best that the people who spooked the birds not see them doing that.

The six men of Echo 9 had almost made it to the safety of the boulders on the opposite side of the canyon when they heard the unmistakable cackle of an AK-47 on full auto.

Schlatter did not need to issue the order to run for it.

The good thing about being shot at by someone shooting on full auto was that their fire was inaccurate in the extreme. The sound of a banana clip being emptied at ten rounds per second was terrifying, but at this range, only a lucky shot connected.

Another bad guy began shooting, and then another. The sound of a banana clip being emptied at ten rounds per second was terrifying, but the sound of a bunch of banana clips being emptied at ten rounds per second was *extremely* terrifying.

"*Aieee!*" Buddy Sorrell gasped.

Luis turned to see his friend tumble to the ground and grasp his thigh. Only lucky shots connected, but there often were lucky shots, especially when there were as many shots being fired as there were today.

Ace, who had been running next to Buddy, paused, extending his hand to the fallen man. Just as they touched, a bullet hit Ace, spinning him around and tossing him to the ground.

"Take cover!" Schlatter screamed as another man paused and looked back toward Buddy and Ace. He was making one of the toughest decisions that a sergeant ever had to make. He had two men down, and he couldn't risk the lives of the rest of the patrol.

As Luis dove behind a boulder, some of the other guys were already returning fire. He lifted his M16A4 and sighted back across the killing field. He could see several Taliban scurrying around, and he squeezed off a couple of rounds. He had his rifle on single shot, knowing that he was much more likely to score with a carefully aimed round than by just spraying the opposite hillside.

"Buddy, stay down," Luis shouted. He could see his friend moving, starting to crawl, but he cautioned him to remain where he was. Buddy had fallen into a shallow indentation, so as long as he kept low, he was out of the line of fire. Ace was not moving.

Helmand Province, Afghanistan
April 4

★ ★ ★

Shahla Nawsadi smiled as she passed the back door of a little shop on a side street near the center of Garmsir. The men inside were playing cards, and she could hear music. Under the Taliban, that would never have happened. Those men would have been beaten or stoned. They probably would not have been killed, however. She knew for a fact that some of the Taliban had secret card games going. Of course, hypocrisy was not the worst fault that she could attribute to the Taliban.

Shahla looked forward to the day when a woman in Afghanistan could sit down in the back room of a shop in Garmsir and be dealt in to a hand of cards. Someday, but not yet. Under the Taliban, such a woman *would* have faced the death penalty, and women were still skittish about the Taliban. Shahla was skittish about the Taliban. When she was in Kabul training to be a nurse, she had worn jeans and had gone bareheaded. Here in Garmsir, to go into the poor neighborhoods where people needed her help, she wore a burka. It was best not to take a chance. Even if

Garmsir was secure—fairly secure—there were still Taliban and many sympathizers lurking about. It was a lot easier for these fearless soldiers of Allah to abuse a lone woman in a back alley than to break in on a group of men playing cards.

It was best to just wear the burka and not to take a chance. Shahla wore the burka, and so did her daughter Zahra. Her other daughter, Zalima, had moved away five years ago, first to Kabul and then to London as soon as the first passports were issued. She did not wear a burka in London. Shahla had just heard that Zalima was working with an NGO and that she might soon be coming home. Both Shahla and her husband, Zalmai, were excited that they would see their daughter again.

As soon as she was through the gate in the wall that separated their home from the street, Shahla peeled off the pale blue bag and took her long, dark hair out of the knot into which she had tied it at the back of her head.

Inside the house, she could smell lamb cooking. Zalmai must be home. Most Afghan men still found it demeaning to cook for their wives. For some reason, Zalmai had never cared. It was one of many things that she liked about him.

He shouted a greeting, and she replied, telling him that she was hungry.

As she walked through the house toward the small kitchen, she saw something out of the corner of her eye that caused her heart to skip a beat.

"Zalmai!" she shouted.

"Yes, Shahla."

"What's this?"

Zalmai was in the doorway, and his wife was pointing at the table. There was a stack of folded, gray garments topped with a gray cap.

"Is there someone else in our home?" Shahla asked nervously.

"No."

"That's an Afghan National Police cap," she said. He could tell that the wheels in her head were turning to the unthinkable.

"It's mine," he said. "I joined the police."

"What?" Shahla gasped. "Why?"

"Because I'm tired of all this. I'm tired of the Taliban. I'm tired of thinking that we were lucky that our daughters escaped genital mutilation under the Taliban. If that's what we have to be thankful for, then this is a sorry place."

"We count blessings the outsiders take for granted." Shahla shrugged.

"I want to count the blessings that the rest of the world counts as blessings," Zalmai insisted. "That's something that we cannot do when everyone fears the Taliban."

"But if you put on that uniform and wear it in the street, it will be like wearing a big sign that says, 'Shoot me, here I am, shoot me.'"

"If I don't, and if nobody else does, then what does the big sign say?" Zalmai asked. "It says that Helmand Province contains only two types of Afghans: Taliban and cowards."

"But it doesn't have to be *you*," she said, tears pooling in her eyes. "You would be risking your life."

"You go out and risk your life every day," he countered.

"I hide behind a burka. There are ways to do things without announcing it to the world."

"I'm doing this so you do not have to hide behind the burka," Zalmai explained.

"But I'm careful."

"Doing what you are doing is never careful," he told her. "Even under the burka, you are a woman doing man's work. It would be easy for them to kill you…as easy as it would be for them to kill me. We have to stop living like bugs in a hole. The more of us who stand up, the harder it will be for the Taliban."

Shahla embraced her husband and sobbed quietly.

Helmand Province, Afghanistan
April 4

★ ★ ★

"Up this ridge and around to the back of that cliff, and then we head straight northwest back to Sure-Stinks," Sergeant Ricky Alvarez said, pointing up the hillside away from the village that had turned out to be a Taliban or Al-Qaeda arms dump.

For the two women that SpongeBob Ellis had befriended, it was probably their first time outside in fresh air without being bagged in burkas, and they were obviously pleased. They were also glad to be getting away from the Taliban and a life of being enslaved to the carnal hunger of these gangsters.

When they had first learned that the women were coming out with them, the Guardsmen expressed concern that the two small women—barely more than teenagers—would have trouble keeping up with the big soldiers who were in peak physical condition. The two girls quickly proved them wrong. Wearing thin leather sandals, they glided up the hill like a pair of pale blue garbage bags being blown by the wind. At one point, Justin noticed them giggling as they paused to wait for the heavily laden Americans to catch up.

The girl with the lighter hair reminded Justin a little bit of Laurie. It was her easy smile and the way she laughed. What a difference it was, entering adulthood on the UCLA campus, compared to a dead-end existence in the mountains of the 'Ghan.

Justin found himself thinking a lot about Laurie. Maybe he was in love. Without thinking, he had used the word to sign his last e-mail to her, so maybe it was true. He didn't know what she had said in reply. He hadn't been anywhere near a place with e-mail access for days. On the other hand, maybe he just wanted a second date to end up in his bed as the first one had. If it wasn't love, he was sure thinking a lot about how he *liked* her.

Maybe he was thinking about her too much as he trudged up the slope. He was awakened from his daydream by a startling buzzing sound followed by a snap in the air near his head. Next, he heard the pop of gunfire off to his right. Somebody was shooting at him.

"Go!" Sergeant Alvarez was shouting. "Get over the top. Your ass is exposed out here. Go!"

Justin looked up. They were almost to the summit of the ridge. The shots were coming from the right and slightly below. On the face of the hillside, they were wide open for the bad guys. If they could get over the crest, which lay just ahead, they had some cover. Alvarez wanted everybody to run for it. Some of the guys were across the crest already. He saw the pale blue of one of the Afghan girls running. She made it. He didn't see the other one. She must have made it already.

Justin had been daydreaming, just slogging up the hill and daydreaming. He should have been paying attention. Those few seconds that it took him to get his bearings might have cost him his life. He was in control now—sort of. He was running as fast as he could for the gear he was lugging, but the bullets were sizzling through the air all around him.

Running next to him, Jimmy gave him a look. He could tell that Jimmy was thinking about what Justin had said earlier in the day about ninety-nine percent of bullets fired in battle being misses. They both had the one percent on their minds.

It seemed like forty-five minutes, but it was a lot closer to forty-five seconds when Jimmy and Justin vaulted the crest of the ridge. Just as Jimmy dove for the dirt, he felt something hit him in the side. It was like a fist. Had it not been for the fact that he was hitting the dirt anyway, the impact would have knocked him down.

"What is it, man?" Justin asked.

"What...?" Jimmy realized that he must have screamed or groaned or something when he was hit. He felt disoriented. He just lay on his back looking up at the sky and wondering what to do.

What happened?

What should he do?

A split second later, he pulled himself under control and rolled onto his belly.

"Are you hit?" Justin asked. Jimmy just looked into the blue eyes scarcely a foot away. Imagine that. A white boy genuinely concerned that he might have been hit.

"Yeah, I think so," Jimmy acknowledged.

"Where?"

"In my right side...below my armpit. Doesn't hurt bad or nothin.'"

"Yeah, I see it,....You're damned lucky, man. The slug is embedded in your body armor. It didn't penetrate."

"Ain't this my lucky day?"

"Ain't it though!"

Elsewhere, it was not a lucky day.

Baio had also been hit. Ellis was wrapping a strip of gauze

around his left hand. It didn't look life-threatening, but there was a lot of blood. Jimmy looked to where the two Afghan girls were crouching. Their expression of wide-eyed horror made them look younger than late teens or early twenties. It reminded him a little bit of the look on his daughter's face when he and Kadeefa screamed, yelled, and threw things. These girls had a lot more at stake. The bad guys were throwing things a lot more deadly than dinner plates, and they knew that a bullet was a happy alternative to what they could expect if the Taliban won this shoot-out.

The air was filled with the pop and crackle of small-arms fire, but for the moment, the Guardsmen and the girls were safe—and much luckier than they felt. If the enemy had opened fire five minutes sooner, the Americans and the Afghan girls would have been totally at their mercy. As it was, the Taliban had committed two serious tactical errors. They had waited to open fire until their quarry was almost to the top of the hill, and they had opened fire from below. The Americans and their young charges were now on the relative safety of the high ground. They also had the good fortune of finding themselves in a shallow, crater-like indentation at the top of the hill. It was too shallow to safely stand, but they could easily sit or crouch and be sheltered behind a rim of rocks and loose dirt around the edge of the depression.

Alvarez had realized all of this when he screamed at everyone to dash for the crest, but now he realized that their good fortune was thin and fleeting. His small patrol could certainly defend themselves from this position, but there was no way of knowing whether they were outnumbered and no way of knowing if—more like when—the bad guys would try to surround them and overwhelm them. He also knew that they had lost their biggest advantage. Ever since they had begun the patrol, they had moved undetected. Now, that part was over.

Spider Rhead peeked up from behind the rock where he was

hiding and poured a stream of obscenities and 7.62 mm rounds down the hill toward the direction of the firing, but the sergeant stopped him.

"Conserve your ammo," Alvarez shouted. "Don't shoot unless you got a clear target. We need to preserve our ammo as much as possible. Get the M240 set up and ready to open fire if they start coming up the hill. Dude, you and Georgia, move down and cover the opposite side in case they circle around."

The thought of being surrounded popped into everyone's head, but nobody wanted to think too hard about that. Being pinned down like this was a frightening experience for the Guardsmen, but as long as they still held the high ground, they were reasonably secure.

It helped make them feel not quite as alone when they heard the sergeant talking to the command post back at Sherishk on the radio. They listened as he explained that the cluster of huts previously thought to be a village was devoid of civilians and clearly a target for an air strike. They listened to his side of the conversation as he outlined their current situation and asked for backup.

"How long?" Alvarez shouted.

"I'm not sure…" he continued. "I suppose…Six hours is a long time to wait for a chopper to get in here to take us out. What about an air strike?"

All eyes should have been scanning the surrounding hillsides for Taliban, but they were on Alvarez as he rolled his own eyes and listened to the chattering sound of the officer on the other end of the call.

"We'll hang on…No, there are no casualties…not really… One guy was nicked…but we're petty much okay for the moment…under the circumstances."

"Are they sending in an air strike?" Billy Idelson asked when Alvarez had signed off.

"Not for the time being," Alvarez said. "The jets that made the attack up at Sherishk are long gone, and there's some kind of big shit goin' on over by Kabul that's got all the airpower preoccupied."

"Are they gonna send a chopper to get us out?"

"Six hours. They might be able to get one out here in about six hours. In the meantime, we could hope that this bunch will break it off and we can just walk out of here."

They all knew that the Taliban often favored hit-and-run tactics, breaking off their attacks after they figured that they had done enough damage. The bad guys liked to stay on the move and to avoid getting into long sieges, because it increased the odds of an air strike. The gunfire had lessened somewhat, and the men hoped that this was a good sign.

It was also good news that the enemy fire was still coming from below. The bad news was that it was coming from higher up the hillside below than before. The Taliban were inching their way up the slope. The other bad news was that in order to get away from the Taliban, they'd have to climb another fairly steep hillside behind them. They were relatively safe where they were, but to get away completely, they would have to expose themselves again.

"Whaddya see?" Idelson asked as Alvarez peered through his binoculars at the enemy position.

"They're still out there. Looks like they're working their way up this way."

Turning to Spider, who he knew to be the best shot in his California contingent, he said: "Spider, you're so anxious to shoot…why don't you put it on single shot and see if you can hit those bastards right there that are coming up the slope."

Without speaking, Spider grinned and did as Alvarez ordered. His first shot kicked up a puff of dirt and broken rock, but the second found its target. One of the Taliban crumpled, fell, and rolled a short distance down the hill. Spider managed to get off six shots before a hail of return fire began peppering the American position. Two of the shots had hit bad guys.

"How's your hand?" Alvarez asked Baio. "Can you shoot the 240 okay?"

"Yeah, Sarge," Baio said bravely. His hand obviously still hurt, but he didn't want it to get in his way of doing his part. "It's only my left. My trigger finger is fine."

"Great," Alvarez said. "I want you to put short bursts right in there where Spider shot those two. That's where they're tryin' to come through. That's an open space that they have to cross if they're gonna make it all the way up to the same elevation as us."

Baio looked and nodded.

"You want a short burst against anybody that tries to get through there, right?"

"You got it."

Almost immediately, three Taliban sneaked across, and Baio simply mowed them down.

The quick simplicity of the way they just fell startled Jimmy. He had never actually seen someone get shot before. Twice he had seen people lying on the street after a gangsta execution. He fancied himself streetwise in this regard, but he had never actually seen someone get hit by a bullet and fall in that clumsy, unnatural way that bodies fall when they are suddenly no longer animate objects. It neither frightened nor sickened him, but it startled him.

"Way to go!" Idelson said happily. "You smoked their mother-humpin' asses."

For Idelson, it was neither unnatural nor startling. It was a video game. His elation was short-lived as the response to the dead Taliban was another fusillade of enemy gunfire. Just as Baio had been able to target a choke point that the enemy had to cross, the Taliban gunners knew exactly where the Americans were, and it was easy to zero in on them. The infidels were hard to hit in their little defensive position, but it was easy for the Taliban gunners to keep them reminded that they were pinned down.

A half hour went by, then another and yet another. The shootout appeared to be devolving into a stalemate. This pleased the Americans, because they still held the high ground, and every minute that ticked by brought the situation closer to the point when either a helicopter would arrive to extract them, or the Taliban would figure that it wasn't worth waiting around for an air strike.

Each of the Guardsmen got off a few shots at the enemy, continually admonished by Alvarez to make their shots count. He was obsessed with preserving their ammo. He couldn't get the six-hour ETA for an extraction chopper out of his mind.

"It's getting a little close up here," Idelson observed, having taken a break from his video game to take a sip of water. He was right. The nine Guardsmen and two women had been squeezed into a small depression about half the size of a typical American coffee shop for about two hours, and the moment had come and gone for the first bathroom break, an awkward moment made more touchy by the presence of representatives of both genders and the fact that nobody dared leave their perimeter.

After Cooley broke the ice by being the first to take a leak, everyone accepted the embarrassing situation in stride, but the fact that it was too dangerous to go far in the answering of nature's call meant that the growing stench was starting to become, in Idelson's word, "close."

Because of the latter, nobody really felt like eating their remaining MREs, but everyone was craving a drink. The long climb, the final dash to safety, and the lack of shade was a prescription for dehydration, and now the water was starting to run short. It wasn't a hot day, but there was no shade and no clouds anywhere near where the sun hung in the deep blue sky.

Everyone just stared at Idelson after he articulated the obvi-ous; he *always* had a knack for articulating the obvious. Nothing more needed to be said. Finally, Cooley just broke into a laugh.

"It's a fuckin' Garden of Eden," he muttered, reprising his comments from the day before when he first stepped off the CH-47 in Sherishk. Everyone laughed hysterically in that way that people laugh when someone says something that is so far beyond ridiculous that it is actually hysterical. Even the two girls smiled, though they had no idea what he had just said. They, like everyone, just laughed at the frightening absurdity of their predicament.

Was it really just a day? Jimmy Ray Flood thought it felt like weeks.

"What's it like, Dude?" Jimmy asked, turning to a startled Justin. "What's it like to be a surfer? Really, man, I ain't never even been in the ocean. What's it like?"

"Sure seems a helluva long way from this shit," Justin said, responding to an honest question that was, in its way, as absurd as their laughing about the open sewer where they huddled for fear of their lives. Jimmy was obviously wanting to change the subject, and that was a *good* idea. "Well, you paddle out in the ocean far-ther than us to them. You paddle out until the swells are higher than you can stand, and you wait for the right waves. You sit there and you feel the power of the waves under your board."

Justin looked around. Except for Spider and Baio, who were staring at the Taliban position, everyone was looking at him with rapt attention. "You learn to feel them. Each one has a personality…like a big monster or an animal of some kind. You wait for the right one, and you just half catch it…and half let it catch you. You get up on your board, and you got sometimes half a minute or more of the most total freedom you can imagine. Wish to hell I was there now."

Everyone nodded.

"I want to try me that shit," Jimmy said emphatically.

"Me, too," Idelson said hungrily. "Sounds fantastic."

"When this shit is all over, you all come to LA, and I'll show you."

"Count me in," Idelson said. "Put me down."

"Add my name to the list," Sheldon grinned. Justin smiled at him. The fresh-faced kid was barely eighteen, if that. In every group of Guardsmen, there was always one kid who hadn't really even started to shave yet. In this group, it was little Sheldon. He was probably younger even than the Afghan girls. "Surfing safari, man. Let's go."

Everyone nodded, even the girls, who had no idea what they were agreeing to. It obviously just seemed like a good idea. Justin wondered whether they even knew what an ocean was, much less a surfboard.

"Alpha Command, this is Alpha Patrol," Alvarez said, deciding to take this moment to contact Lieutenant Sloan back at the Alpha Company command post.

"This is Alpha Command, Sergeant," Sloan said. "How are you guys holding up?"

"How are things coming with that chopper?" Alvarez asked, ignoring Sloan's query. "And the air strike. We're still pinned down here and could use a hand."

"No can do on the air strike," Sloan replied. "You mentioned civilians."

"What does that have to do with it? The civilians are with *us*."

"This is an ISAF area, pretty much all of Helmand is under ISAF," Sloan said impatiently. "ISAF is real hypersensitive when you start using 'civilians' and 'air strike' in the same sentence."

"What does that have to do with it?" Alvarez repeated. "I said the civilians are with *us*."

"Rules of engagement," Sloan said. "That's the rules of engagement. Civilians? No air strike. End of story."

"But we're surrounded," Alvarez pleaded. "There's no civilians out there with the Taliban. We could use some help here."

"I told you, Sergeant. They say their hands are tied."

"What about the chopper? Are we going to get pulled out of here?"

"They promised me one," Sloan said, sounding like someone who was trying too hard to sound upbeat. "They said they'd try to send a Black Hawk down from Lashkar Gah."

"When?"

"I don't know," Sloan admitted "What's the flying time from Lashkar Gah? Couple of hours? I don't know. Everybody's short-handed. There's a war on. I'll get back to you."

"What'd he say?" Idelson asked impatiently.

"He said there's a war on," Alvarez snarled.

"No shit," Cooley replied. "I'm glad he reminded us."

Almost on cue, a Taliban gunner who thought he'd get lucky unleashed a burst of automatic weapons fire that kicked up a small storm cloud of dry, reddish dirt along the rim of their crater.

"Fuckin' Garden of Eden," Cooley repeated.

Nobody laughed.

SpongeBob Ellis took out his water bottle and politely offered it to the girls. The one with the light hair reached for it eagerly and thankfully but noticed that there was just two inches left, and she declined. She understood that water was a precious commodity and only getting more so.

Suddenly there was another popping of automatic weapons fire. The Guardsmen had grown so accustomed to it that they hardly noticed when some Taliban cut loose with a few rounds, but this was different. All afternoon, they had been taking fire from below and to the southeast of their position. Now the sound of the shots was coming from the northwest.

"They're up there," Justin shouted, pointing to a place on the ridge in the opposite direction from the other Taliban.

"While we were waiting for the goddam chopper, they fuckin' surrounded us," Alvarez said angrily. "Get the 240 on that spot."

As Baio and Sheldon scrambled to get the M240 and their ammo moved and repositioned, a hail of bullets ripped into the crater in whose bosom the Guardsmen had felt somewhat secure.

"Oh my God, I'm hit," groaned Idelson.

Everyone turned and looked. He was clutching his shoulder, and his uniform was soaked in brilliant red. Nobody wanted to think artery, but to have soaked his shoulder so fast with so much blood, the injury had to be a bad one. Ellis was on him in an instant, pushing him flat on his back, partly to get him as far as possible from incoming gunfire and partly to get his head below the wound to help prevent shock.

Alvarez watched as Ellis shoved his hand into the wound to try to stop the bleeding, then turned to see if everyone else was okay. They weren't. One of the women was wiping blood from her head. Sheldon and Baio were both down in a single tangled clump— although there was movement and no immediate sign of blood. His first reaction was that this was a good sign, then he realized what had happened. Sheldon was not moving. All the movement was Baio struggling to get out from beneath an immobile Sheldon.

Justin and Jimmy leaped into the morass, grabbing Sheldon and pulling him up. His head, top-heavy with his helmet, flopped backward lifelessly. His eyes were wide in an unblinking stare. There was a single, neat hole about the size of a nickel about an inch or so above his left eyebrow.

Surfing safari. He'd never have the chance. He'd never have a chance for a lot of things.

Jimmy felt his hands trembling. He fancied himself street-wise. He had seen the bodies of dead people, dead people who died violently. Today, he had watched men shot, probably shot to death. But he had never held a man freshly dead, a man with whom he had just shared a laugh. He had never looked into the open, unseeing eyes of a man who had been alive a split second ago, a man wearing the same uniform, with the same Georgia National Guard shoulder patch. Like Jimmy, he had a mother across the world in the rolling, red dirt hills of Georgia praying for him. Her prayers would not be answered.

The Taliban at the new position to the west gave the Guards-men no moment of respite in which to ponder their new situation. The once secure confines of their defensive redout erupted again in a ripping, coughing nightmare of impacting and ricocheting AK-47 rounds.

Helmand Province, Afghanistan
April 4

★ ★ ★

It was Baio—Justin didn't even know his first name—who saved their day. At least he allowed everyone to wake up from a very real and very deadly nightmare. Having seen his buddy die so abruptly, he paused not a second. Coolly and methodically, he positioned the M240's bipod on the rim of the American position and pointed it at the Taliban who had done this terrible thing to Sheldon.

The hellstorm of gunfire was exactly that. For what seemed like an hour but that may have been as little as two minutes, the American defensive position was filled with the shrieking, snapping sounds of incoming rounds and the ear-numbing thunder of the M240. The air was filled with dirt and chipped rock, with ricocheting bullets and steaming-hot brass ejected from the M240. The stench of human excrement mixed with the stinging smell of burned powder.

The M240 fired the last shot in the exchange.

Justin had watched Baio kill at least four of the Taliban, and when two ran, Justin shouldered his own M16A4 and fired. One of the runners went down, but the other kept going. Justin fired again and again, but his rounds would not connect.

All memory of the UCLA campus, of the Pacific Coast Highway, of the waves off Malibu, or of anything beyond the borders of the 'Ghan, was gone. Justin did not even think of weird ironies. He thought only of killing so as not to be killed. He forgot about Laurie. He thought only of Sheldon and the bullet hole in his head and the need to kill the men who had killed him.

Justin Anderson had barely known Sergeant Ricky Alvarez before they came to this place at the end of the earth. He knew him from summer camp, but he didn't really know him. He knew that he was from somewhere over in Riverside County, but he didn't know where. He figured, because of his name and his complexion, that his family was from somewhere south of the border, but he didn't know where. He figured that he was born, or at least raised for most of his whole life, in the States, but he didn't know which. Before today, about all he knew was that he was an NCO and a bit of a wiseass.

In the past six grueling hours, Justin had watched Ricky Alvarez demonstrate himself as a true leader. Alvarez shouted and demanded, cajoled and encouraged, but he never lost his cool. He organized a defensive position, he demanded that the men conserve water and ammo, and he reorganized the defense when the tactical situation changed. He looked after the wounded, and he respected the dead. Justin had never thought much about medals, but he thought Alvarez deserved one. He didn't know much about medals—all those crosses and stars that people talked about—but he figured that there ought to be one of them for what Alvarez was doing today.

Ricky Alvarez didn't see himself as a hero. He saw himself as a failure. He had allowed his command to get ambushed. He had lost one man, the boyish ammo donkey, Sheldon, and he feared that another man, Idelson, was not far behind. Most of the others—including one of the Afghan girls—had been nicked pretty badly by shrapnel or debris kicked up by the enemy gunfire.

The catalog of his mistakes clanged in his head. His list of personal fuckups began with the decision to recon the Afghan village and led up to allowing their defensive position to get squeezed in a crossfire. Now they were sitting in what amounted to a giant open latrine taking fire and waiting for a helicopter that may never arrive.

Why had he not seen it coming?

In retrospect, it was obvious that the Taliban would try to get somebody behind the American position.

Why had he not seen that coming? What if they had just *not* gone into the Afghan village? What if he had been proactive instead of so fucking lazy? What if he had ordered his men to outflank the Taliban instead of letting the bastards outflank *them*? Why had he put all his eggs in the one basket of waiting for Sloan to get a chopper out to pick them up? Why the hell did the army put a furniture store delivery manager from Redlands in charge of the lives of young men in the godforsaken middle of godforsaken *nowhere*?

The shooting was more sporadic now, but the Taliban were still out there, and the shots were coming from all directions. Like a coyote circling a wounded deer, the enemy sensed that they had easy prey. The enemy sensed that it was only a matter of time before the Americans ran out of ammunition.

Another burst of gunfire splattered the gravel just outside the American perimeter, and everyone flinched instinctively—but this was not just any burst of gunfire, it was the first from an elevation *above* them. Their high ground advantage was over.

"That Talibanger sure as hell's a bad shot," Spider Rhead said, commenting on the fact that the burst had missed the American position by a wide margin.

"We can't count on him to miss forever," Alvarez said, hoping his desperation would not be evident in his voice. "We gotta take him out."

Baio was already looking up at the ridge from which the gunner had fired, hoping to see him and frame him as a target for his M240.

"We let the bastards outflank us once." Alvarez said. That fact gnawed at him—and hard. "Can't let it go. This time, we gotta take the initiative. We gotta take him out. Dude, you and Georgia get your asses up there. See that notch over there? Run like hell and get through there, and you can get up in there behind the bastard."

As the sergeant pointed, Justin and Jimmy both nodded. If they ran hard, they could cover the ground in maybe twenty seconds. It would be longest twenty seconds of their lives. Taliban gunners from all over the hillside would have a clear shot, although they would not be expecting to have two of the infidels suddenly bolt up the slope.

Without saying another word, they dropped all of their gear except their M16A4s and some extra clips. A few extra pounds shed could mean a few extra seconds off the time that they would be exposed.

When they were ready, Justin suggested that they do rock-paper-scissors to see who went first. They knew that they'd better make the dash a few seconds apart, because by making themselves two targets, it would be twice as hard to hit them both. Justin's rock was trumped by Jimmy's paper. The Georgia Guardsman would go first.

"Baio, on my signal, throw a wall of lead down there where most of the Taliban are," Alvarez told the M240 gunner when

Justin and Jimmy nodded that they were ready. "Spider, keep an eye on those rocks above where the shots came from. If you see anybody, you know what to do. We gotta cover these boys."

Jimmy took off at a dash the moment that Baio opened fire. Justin counted to four, clenched his teeth, and ran like hell. The sound of gunfire seemed to be everywhere, and Justin prepared to feel himself get hit at any moment.

It had been the longest twenty seconds of their lives, and both men felt truly surprised that they had made it without getting hit.

After they caught their breath, they moved out, picking their way as carefully as possible in the rocky terrain. The object was to circle around and get behind the place from which the shots had come. They circled wide, because if the bad guys had seen them running, they would pull back, hoping to turn the tables on the American attempt at an ambush.

Moments later, as they crept up a small rise, they heard voices on the other side. Justin and Jimmy froze. They held their breath and listened. The words were meaningless, but the tone of voices told them that these guys were unaware of Americans trying to outflank them. The Guardsmen breathed again and crept slowly to the top of the rise to take a look.

About twenty yards away, there were four bearded men in turbans standing around a long, narrow object in a duffel bag. To the eyes of men who were essentially average American civilians, the thing in the bag looked at first like some sort of tool or a piece of sporting equipment. It took a moment for the mechanic from Georgia and the college kid from California to realize that it was a rocket-propelled grenade launcher.

Justin and Jimmy looked at one another. An RPG round launched at the American position would be devastating, and they both knew it. Two rounds launched would almost certainly kill everyone who had escaped a violent, painful death with the first. It was incredibly fortuitous that they had arrived in this place now.

Jimmy pointed to Justin and to the Taliban standing on the right and indicated through hand signals that they start shooting left and right and converge on the two guys in the middle who were crouched over the RPG tube.

Justin put his target into his sights and squeezed the trigger. It was nice to see the bad guys on the receiving end of a hail of inescapable lead for a change. Justin knew that he had hit the guy on the right, but he couldn't tell about the guys in the middle. There was a lot of dust swirling and bullets flying.

Suddenly, one of the crouching Taliban leaped up and started running away, carrying the launch tube. Justin could see that there was an RPG attached.

Both Americans had their M16A4s on full auto, but they could not seem to hit the running man. It was the ninety-nine percent rule again, this time applied to the bad guy.

"We gotta catch that motherfucker," Jimmy screamed as he stood and started to run in pursuit. Luckily, he had chosen to run in the opposite direction from the American position, but there was no question that he had to be stopped.

As the two Americans ran past the place where the Taliban had been standing, Justin slowed to look at the three who had gone down. Two were obviously dead, but the third was squirming in pain, his torso drenched in blood.

For a moment, their eyes met.

Justin tried to read the expression of this man he had tried to kill, this guy who would have as happily killed Justin as to have looked at him. Did the expression say, *Please put me out of my misery*, or *Fuck you, you godless infidel*?

Impulsively, Justin raised his rifle and put a short burst in the man's head.

No more face. No more expression.

Jimmy was quite far ahead, so Justin ran as fast as he could to catch up.

As he ran, Justin began hearing a roaring, growling sound in the distance.

What the hell was that?

He had almost caught up to Jimmy when he saw it. Off to his left, over the canyon through which they had hiked early that morning, was a dark green helicopter. It was the Black Hawk that had been promised! They were saved!

"*No!*" Jimmy screamed.

Justin turned his head away from the chopper and saw what Jimmy was looking at.

The Taliban was about thirty yards away on the edge of the cliff that dropped into the canyon, aiming the RPG at the Black Hawk.

Jimmy was firing.

Jimmy's anger had welled up inside him. The anger that he had felt all his life for assholes like Lennie Cahner and all the others just overflowed. That single Taliban was a Lennie Cahner who had done to Jimmy and his band of comrades with bullets what the real Lennie Cahner did with words. He was an arrogant, self-righteous bastard. He was a holier-than-thou asshole who regarded Jimmy as an inferior infidel the way that Lennie Cahner regarded Jimmy as an inferior nigra.

Justin did not stop to shoot but ran to get closer and within range.

The Black Hawk was slowing. He must have seen the American position ahead of him. He was flying low over the canyon almost at the same level as the cliff where Jimmy and Justin were. Justin could see the pilot's green plastic helmet in the fading light of the setting sun, and the sunburned pink of his cheeks beneath his dark visor.

A plume of dirty gray smoke swirled out of the RPG launcher just as one of Jimmy's slugs finally—and amazingly for the range—found the target. The Taliban fell, but the RPG was on its way.

The two Guardsmen watched helplessly as the rocket-propelled projectile impacted the helicopter's left engine. The explosion was deceptively small.

Justin saw the head of the pink-faced pilot jerk around to look back.

Almost immediately, the helicopter began to fall. The explosion had destroyed the engine, but it had also severed the drive shaft to the main rotor, without which a helicopter had no lift. It suddenly became ten tons of debris hanging in the sky.

The helicopter driven by the pink-cheeked man had become now a ten-ton block of debris.

As Jimmy and Justin watched, the Black Hawk fell like a stone, then exploded in a fireball as it slammed into the boulders on the canyon floor at about a hundred miles per hour.

Khost Province, Afghanistan
April 4

★　★　★

Luis "Ojo" Carillo pondered the situation. It was a classic stand-off. The Taliban were reluctant to advance across the open ground toward the American position, and they were not ready to pull out and leave when they had their enemy outnumbered three to one. If this had been the United States border—as it once had been for Luis—they could have waited until the Border Patrol got hungry and went home. What a strange upside-down world it had become. Here he was, wearing a uniform that represented the same government as the Border Patrol agents with whom he once had played mouse to their cat. He was still the mouse. There was just a different cat.

"Echo one, this is Echo nine," Sergeant Charlie Schlatter said into the PRC-148 radio. "We have two men down, and we're taking hostile fire."

"Give me the coordinates, and we'll blast 'em," came the reply from the Echo Battery MLRS command post.

"Negative. No can do. They're too close to us."

The M26 rockets were pretty accurate, but Schlatter's patrol was very close to the enemy position, and he did not want those hand grenade–size submunitions raining down on top of his men.

"Can we get a gunship over here?"

An AH-64D Apache helicopter gunship could rip into the bad guys with the kind of surgical precision that an M26 rocket could not. When the distance between good guys and bad guys was measured in yards, surgical precision was preferable to the Cold War–era sledgehammer method of the steel rain.

The four uninjured men could easily escape at this point, but there was no question of the four abandoning the wounded two.

The Taliban had seen six infidels and that two of them had gone down. The fact that the four who remained were continuing to return fire meant that at least one of those who had fallen was still alive. If the four infidels weren't covering for a wounded comrade, they could have and would have gotten away. That was one of the many weaknesses that the infidels had: they never left their wounded behind.

Neither side was willing to pull out, and neither side was able to efficiently attack the other. The Americans needed something to tip the balance. In the huge inventory of extraordinary weapons possessed by the American armed forces, there were myriad balance tippers. It was just a matter—a very crucial matter—of getting them to the places where they could tip balances for specific American soldiers caught in specific classic standoffs.

An hour passed before Echo 1 called back with a reply to Sergeant Schlatter's request.

"Echo nine, there are no attack choppers in the area, but a Hog has been vectored out of Bagram to your position. Where are the bad guys exactly?"

"They are at Alpha-Bravo-twenty-one," the sergeant replied.

"That's on the side of the canyon toward Pakistan. Tell him to stay away from Alpha-Charlie-twenty-three... that's our position."

"Roger that, Alpha-Bravo-twenty-one, and *not* Alpha-Charlie-twenty-three."

Everybody in Echo 9 looked at one another. Nobody said anything, but everyone knew what everyone else was hoping that the pilot of the A-10 Warthog attack aircraft would not get the numbers mixed up.

"Hold on, Buddy," one of the guys shouted to Sorrell. "There's a Hog on the way. We'll get you out. How's Ace doing?"

"He's not moving, but I think he's still alive," Buddy shouted hopefully. "How in the hell is a Hog gonna get us out of this shit?"

"He'll kill 'em... or at least distract them long enough for us to get you out!"

"I can't walk, and Ace is not moving," Buddy replied, sounding increasingly nervous. "We need medevac. I'm hit in the leg. I think it's broken. You can't carry us all the way back. We need medevac."

"Don't worry," Sergeant Schlatter shouted back. "We'll take care of you."

By the look on the sergeant's face, Luis could tell that he was making it up as he went along, and that he really wasn't sure how they were going to take care of the two wounded men under fire.

"What's that?" Deuce said, pointing across the no-man's-land toward where the enemy was. "Looks like smoke. They started to cook dinner or something?"

Luis immediately glued his binoculars on the faint traces of smoke.

"They're smoking something," Luis reported.

"Weed? Shit, man. Wish we had some of that shit," Deuce laughed.

"That's all we need here," Luis observed. "Get ourselves loco from some marijuana."

"Are they blowin' some weed out there?" Deuce giggled. "For real?"

"They got a pipe," Schlatter said, watching the Taliban, who no longer seemed interested in keeping themselves concealed.

"Hey, man. I got it figured out," Deuce said, a lightbulb going on in his brain. "It's opium. They got tons of this shit here."

"Thought that their religion didn't let 'em get high," Luis wondered.

"I think that only applies to booze," Schlatter said. "Afghanistan's the friggin' opium capital of the world. These clowns are stoned all the time."

"If they're stoned all the time, how come they managed to hit two of our guys?" Luis countered.

"Maybe they weren't high yet," Deuce observed. "But they're sure as shit gettin' high now."

For dozens of centuries, the black and pungent putty known long ago as *hul gil* had enslaved countless millions across the globe. Nearly two centuries before Deuce and Luis came to the mother lode of the terrible curse, Thomas de Quincey sat in his English drawing room, musing that "Thou hast the keys of Paradise, O just, subtle, and mighty opium!"

Across the killing fields from where Deuce and Luis watched, a dozen Al Qaeda smoked not for paradise, but to calm the chemical change in their bodies, implanted long ago, that demanded the opium in order to maintain equilibrium.

"If they're getting loaded, maybe they'll be so spaced out that we could sneak over there and whack 'em," Deuce postulated.

"Why would they be getting stoned in the middle of a firefight?" Schlatter speculated rhetorically.

"I hear that they're just plain loco," Luis replied.

Suddenly, four of the Al-Qaeda burst from their positions, zigzagging madly across the no-man's-land toward Buddy and Ace.

"Loco!" Luis screamed, leveling his M16A4 and hurling a three-round burst at the closest bunch of opiated bad guys.

The two who survived Ojo's fusillade were oblivious to the two others who did not. They ran forward, firing wildly in the direction of Buddy and Ace, and were cut down in a hail of American fire.

"Shi-it!" Deuce said. "Guess those assholes get doped up to get brave. Too bad it don't make 'em bulletproof."

"Loco," Luis repeated.

"They don't mind dyin'," Schlatter observed. "They get all those sixty-nine virgins or whatever when they go to heaven."

"In the meantime, all they got's Tina Hornschau magazines," Deuce added.

"I guess that's for practice," Luis added.

The Warthog arrived without warning. The U.S. Air Force always had its attack aircraft airborne to support major ground operations, but this wasn't a major operation. Luckily, Echo 1 was able to get through to the regional command center, who got in touch with the tactical control center at Bagram, who happened to have a Hog who had just taken off for a routine patrol.

The scream of the Hog's twin General Electric TF34 turbofan engines did not reach the canyon until its shadow had streaked silently across the landscape. When the explosion erupted on the Taliban side, the Colorado men breathed a sigh of relief. At least he got the coordinates right.

They watched as the A-10 banked in the distance to return for another pass against the Taliban. With its straight wings and clumsy-looking fuselage, the Hog had a decidedly old-fashioned appearance. Indeed, it got the nickname Warthog because it was considered to be downright ugly. To ground troops in situations such as Echo 9 found itself, however, the A-10 was the most beautiful thing in the world—except, perhaps, for Tina Hornschau.

The A-10 came in again, low and fast, opening up with its GAU-8/A Gatling gun. The troops heard the ripping sound and saw just a hint of muzzle flash. By now, they could tell that the pilot could see the Taliban because the puffs of crud kicked up by the impacts of the 30 mm rounds ripped right through their position.

The Echo 9 guys cheered when they saw an Mk 82 dumb bomb tumble from the airplane's starboard wing, and kept cheering as it hit the Taliban position. By the time the dust began to clear, the Hog was already half a mile away and turning for a third pass.

Luis could see the Taliban moving again. This time, they were on the run and heading back toward the pass that led to Pakistan. A number of them were hit, and a couple were being carried, just as they would soon have to be doing with Buddy and Ace. As he watched, Luis saw one guy with a gray turban running into the open. What was that he was carrying?

As the A-10 came in low again, the thing the guy was carrying sprouted a plume of blue-gray smoke. It was a dreaded rocket-propelled grenade. The pilot jinked the plane hard to the right, rolling nearly ten degrees as he took evasive action to avoid the RPG. The plane was so low that Luis could look up and see the frightened expression on the pilot's face as he rolled.

Luis saw the RPG miss the Hog's engine by a matter of inches, but he did not see the other Mk 82 come off the wing.

Helmand Province, Afghanistan
April 4
★ ★ ★

Justin Anderson fought the urge to fall asleep. After twenty-four hours awake, and the exhaustion of the longest day of his life, his body demanded sleep, but Justin fought it. Something inside insisted that he stay alert. Everything inside insisted that he stay alert. Everything that he had experienced during the longest day of his life insisted that he stay alert.

He forced his eyes open but wished he could close his nostrils. A mass of humanity swarmed in the darkness, illuminated only by a couple of dim red lights that made it look like an abstract scene from somewhere in the depths of hell. There were more than a dozen people crammed into the Black Hawk's payload bay, but it was impossible to count them. Justin didn't even try.

When Lieutenant Sloan's request for a helicopter finally worked its way back up the chain of command to ISAF HQ, they—whoever "they" were at that level—had sent two. The first Black Hawk, armed with a pair of M60 machine guns, was supposed to have provided cover for the second, which had medics aboard. Alvarez hadn't mentioned casualties, but "they" knew. "They" had experience extracting soldiers from spots like this. "They" knew that medics would be needed.

However, like the first Black Hawk, this two-chopper plan had spun out of control, and a new plan had to be formed—instantly. The pilot of the second UH-60L had to improvise. As he watched his fellow flight crew—men with whom he had flown for the past four or five years—incinerated in a ball of burning aviation fuel on a nameless hillside half a world from their loved ones, he improvised. The men he knew were gone, but other people's loved ones still had a chance, and they depended on him.

The second Black Hawk spotted Jimmy and Justin, and the chopper had easily taken them aboard.

"Where are the others?" screamed the loadmaster.

"Over the hammering sound of the two General Electric T700 engines, Justin shouted directions and pointed to the Guardsmen's defensive crater. But the chopper couldn't land there—not enough room for the Black Hawk's fifty-four-foot rotor diameter.

The pilot set his ship down as near as possible, and Jimmy and Justin found themselves running *back* across the same ground as when they started out. Once again, they stepped into the cauldron of chaos and small-arms fire. Fortunately, in the gathering darkness, they now made poorer targets for the Taliban. The darkness also made for confusion. The Americans and the Afghan women needed no urging to understand that making a mad dash to the chopper was the first forty yards on the road to safety, but Justin and Jimmy knew they needed to go back to help carry the lifeless Sheldon and the dying Idelson back up the hill to the waiting helicopter.

Justin and SpongeBob Ellis took Idelson, while Jimmy and Spider Rhead scooped up Sheldon and struggled up the hill with his dead weight. The sound of rounds plinking against the thin metal skin of the Black Hawk were one of the most sickening sounds in the world. It turned Justin's stomach. He knew that it would take just one very lucky, well-placed bullet to screw up the Black Hawk's engine, drive shaft, or any number of other delicate and vulnerable private parts.

"Yeeow!" Ellis screamed just as they handed Idelson to the medics in the chopper.

"What is it, man?" Justin asked, looking into the face of the man who had pounded on his door in Venice that morning to give him the bad news that brought both of them to this unimaginable place.

"It's my leg," he said. "It's okay, just surprised the shit outa me."

"You're hit?"

"It's okay, man, let's get into the chopper."

Justin heaved himself easily into the crowded Black Hawk and reached out to give Ellis a hand. He lifted himself, preparing to swing his leg up when his face contorted in a grimace of terrible pain. He tried again. This time, Justin gave him both hands and dragged him in.

The pilot wasted no time. He, too, had heard the sickening sound of rounds hitting his bird. He, too, imagined—though it took no imagination—that his helicopter was only a split second away from the irretrievable end suffered by its sister ship. The moment the last Guardsman was aboard—it was Alvarez, who insisted on being the last—the pilot took off as fast as he possibly could, banked violently to get as much mountain as possible between his bird and the Taliban as fast as possible, and slammed the throttles to max power.

Justin watched as the medics, who had been working on Idelson, took one look at SpongeBob's pant leg, sopping with blood, and rushed to his aid.

"I'm all right," Ellis insisted. "Really, man, it looks worse than it is. It doesn't hurt too much."

At first, it hadn't seemed too bad, but Ellis felt dizzy and light-headed as the helicopter jerked airborne and felt himself just collapse. Meanwhile, the injury would not stop bleeding, and the medics discovered that the slug had nicked his femoral artery. Not good.

Justin stared at Billy Idelson, lying near the door next to Sheldon's lifeless body, and wondered whether he, too, had left the land of the living. The medics had given him a once-over, their form of triage, and had turned all their attention to Ellis.

He missed the talkative Georgian who wouldn't shut up. If Idelson was here, Justin thought, he'd be carrying on right now. Then he reminded himself that Idelson *was* still here—wasn't he?

Surfing safari. Justin could not forget those words, two of no more than a dozen that he had heard spoken by the kid Sheldon. Only two words, spoken by the kid who would never surf, never safari, the kid who lay growing cold on the floor.

Justin was exhausted, but the adrenaline and his own anxiety would not let him relax. He realized only after the chopper had taken off that he still had his finger inside the trigger guard of his M16A4.

This was not good, but of course, as Justin's eyes wandered about the half-light inside the chopper, he realized that not much—aside from being *out of there*—was good. It seemed that everyone had been hit, at least by shrapnel. Baio had been hit early on. Cooley had blood on his hand that he continued to wipe on his sleeve. One of the Afghan women had a terrible gash on her face. Justin noticed that as they were making their way to the chopper. One of the medics had given her a compress to push into it, and she sat in stunned silence, consoled by her friend, the one who Justin had thought looked a little bit like Laurie.

Oh God, what a world away! His thoughts about Laurie were like trying to remember a dream, the rapidly disintegrating fragments of memory growing dimmer as one moves from sleep to "reality." How was it possible, Justin asked himself, for Laurie and Nobu and Malibu Canyon to exist on the same planet with this girl, with Sherishk, and the nightmare mountaintop that he had just left?

How could I be the same person?

How can the guy racing to get to Haines Hall be the same guy who was racing across a mountain to kill a man with an RPG launcher, the man who paused to look into the face of a living man and casually blow him away?

Jimmy Ray Flood sat in the gyrating dark box trying to relax, but each time the low-flying aircraft hit a bump of uneven air, he felt his eyes pop open in a reflex action. Like Justin, he felt a void in the absence of Idelson's chatter and longed for it as indicative of normalcy.

Eyes closed, Jimmy replayed the events of the long and unbelievably intense day. They replayed not in a neat, consecutive time line, but as a random stew of vignettes: bodies falling, people screaming, and that awful stench.

He thought about Cathy, and about how he had felt her emotional disconnect in that last day before he shipped out. When he saw her again—that was *when*, not *if*, he reminded himself—how could he tell her about all this?

What *would* he tell her? What *could* he tell her?

Suddenly, the Black Hawk bucked violently.

Eyes open.

It was all there. It had not been a dream. Jimmy felt like crying, but he realized that he was way beyond tears.

In the darkness, Sergeant Ricky Alvarez reflected on the agony and misery of this long and terrible day and of the stinking, screaming abyss from which this stinking, screaming machine had just snatched him and the men whose lives had been entrusted to him.

Like Justin, Jimmy, and the others still conscious, he looked around at those who crowded together here, each breathing the deep breath of exhaustion—or not breathing at all. It was all his fault, he thought. One, probably two, men were dead because of his failed mission. An enemy arms cache that they had reconned would not be attacked, and the enemy who had ambushed them had not been defeated. As every soldier knows, the victor is he who holds the battlefield when the shooting stops. Alvarez knew that it was their enemy who still held the battlefield. As disgusting and awful as that place was, an unvanquished foe still held the ground.

How many furniture store delivery managers from Redlands would the United States have to send to these dreadful mountaintops before this war would be won?

Alvarez let himself relax a little bit. His body ached, especially his back. He must have wrenched it getting into the chopper just as the pilot pulled that bat-out-of-hell maneuver taking off.

His back ached, his lower back. It *really* hurt.

Mother of God, a hot bath would feel good right now. But he knew there would be no hot bath back in Sherishk. There wouldn't even be a cold bath. Hopefully, he could hose off the dirt with some clean water and sleep for a while.

Mother of God, a night's sleep in a bed would feel good. There wouldn't even be a cot back at Sherishk, just a sleeping bag on the ground, but at least he had leveled out his sleeping area back there. *Sleep itself would be a reward too great for a fuckup like me*, Alvarez said to himself, thinking of the men he'd lost to death or injury.

His back ached, his lower back. It *really* hurt.

Alvarez reached down to massage it, to put some pressure against it, but it only hurt worse. His pants were wet. He felt his pants, and they were *wet*. Had he fucking wet his pants?

What a fuckup! A failure in battle brings home his decimated command with his pants wet. He looked at his hand. It was dark. What was that? In the murk, he could tell only that the wetness on his hand was dark, like a shadow.

Could it be blood?

CHAPTER FOUR

Days into Months

Helmand Province, Afghanistan
June 22

★ ★ ★

"What would Idelson say?" Spider Rhead asked rhetorically.

"A whole motherhumpin' lot," Jimmy Ray Flood answered, knowing that Billy Idelson, the man who, in life, talked all the time, would be saying nothing. Ever. The phrase had become a shorthand comment, a sort of inside joke for the men who had survived the shoot-out atop Hill 989, and a way to remember those who had not.

They missed Idelson. Even the guys from Georgia, like Jimmy, who had been on that hill and had hardly known him before that terrible day. Now they couldn't forget him, and the ridiculous comments he made and the way that he always used *motherhumpin'* as an adjective for the oddest things.

They had hardly known each other before that day. None of them. Now they were almost like brothers—just like in the war movies. A random selection of guys from Alpha Company of the Cal Guard's 184th Infantry had been thrown together with a random selection of guys from Lima Company of the Georgia

National Guard's 122nd Infantry. They were people who never would have crossed paths in a million years, and now they were almost like brothers.

They hadn't even known that the hill was called Hill 989 until days later. They just knew it as the hill, the high ground above the still-unidentified village—the Taliban nest—that Sergeant Ricky Alvarez had called Toontown.

They missed Alvarez, too. On the hill, he had been their big brother, shouting, cajoling, encouraging, and keeping everyone together. When they left the landing zone, they hadn't even known that he was hit. He was the last man aboard the Black Hawk at the LZ, deliberately not boarding until everyone else had reached its precarious safety.

They hadn't even known that he was hit until they landed in a swirl of dust in the precarious safety of Sherishk. They found him unconscious in a pool of his own blood and didn't know that he had died until later in the day. They never saw his body. He had just been airlifted out, along with the others.

Justin Anderson thought that Sergeant Alvarez deserved a medal for the way he kept everyone together and organized up on the hill. He didn't know what kind of medal—he didn't know a Distinguished Service Medal from a Bronze Star—but he deserved *something*. Justin mentioned it to Lieutenant Stone and suggested that he ought to pass it along to Captain Van Dyke.

The harried Sloan said, "Later, maybe later." Those were his exact words. He had just lost a sergeant from his command. Maybe recommending a dead sergeant for a medal was like admitting that he'd made a mistake by sending out the patrol in the first place.

They had lost four guys up there: two Californians and two Georgians. Eugene Sheldon, the M240 ammo donkey, was the only one who actually died on the hill. They saw him die and did not even know his first name. Two others were dead before the Black Hawk landed. SpongeBob Ellis insisted that he was okay right up to the moment that he passed out, but by morning, he, too, was dead.

SpongeBob's death hit Justin especially hard. It wasn't that they were close friends, although they had gotten to know each other pretty well while they were "weekend warrioring" back home. SpongeBob—back when he was still Chuck Ellis—had brought the news that Justin suddenly had just five hours of normal life before he left for the 'Ghan. Now he was dead. That struck Justin as very eerie. Ellis was the man with whom Justin had stepped across the line from a distant and vastly different former life into this one. Now he was dead.

Last year Justin had gone to Cal Guard summer camp with Chuck Ellis. They had driven back to LA together. They had gone to Afghanistan together, and Justin had not even considered the possibility that they would not be going back to LA together.

The copy shop assistant manager from Glendale was also missed by everyone because he was a genuine nice guy. Everyone recalled that he had learned a few words of Pashto and that he had used it to calm down the two Afghan women. One of them had bawled her head off when she saw that her "friend" had been injured. Maybe she didn't know that he was dead.

Nobody knew what happened to the girls after the Black Hawk landed.

Justin had lost a comrade. He understood now why soldiers didn't make friends. Losing a comrade was hard. Losing a friend would be way too personal.

Justin had lost a comrade on the hill, but he gained a new one. He and Jimmy Ray Flood had been paired off randomly, just as the Cal Guard's Alpha Company and the Georgia Guard's Lima Company had been thrown together randomly.

Both remained in Sherishk. The cost of the fighting around
Sherishk and on Hill 989 had convinced the International Security Assistance Force command in Lashkar that Sherishk must be
held. Sherishk had become a de facto ISAF fortress. Somebody
said that it was like a shithole in Vietnam called Khe Sanh that
the U.S. Marine Corps held on to for months just to prove to the
bad guys that they could. Eventually, they just gave it up. France
had a place like that, too, when they were in Vietnam. It was
called Dien Bien Phu. Eventually, they just gave that up and went
home. Justin, Jimmy, and a lot of the other weekend warriors in
Sherishk wondered when ISAF would finally decide to give Sherishk back to the Taliban and go home. They did their wondering
to themselves. Nobody talked too much about it.

"They got a friggin' satellite TV down there," Justin said as
he approached the place where Jimmy and Spider were sitting in
the shade of a dust-colored tarp. Jimmy was drinking a Pepsi, and
Spider was cleaning his M16A4.

"No shit?" Jimmy asked rhetorically.

"No shit," Justin confirmed. "I guess you know that they're
meaning to have us here for a long time when they bring in a
satellite TV dish."

"This is permanent," Spider said in an ominous, resolved tone.
"They ain't never giving up this place. We'll be here for fuckin'
ever."

"What they got on TV?" Jimmy asked, ignoring Spider's geo-
political prognostication.

"Somebody said baseball," Justin replied.

"Shit, man, I gotta go see me some baseball," Jimmy said excitedly. "Let's us go see who's playin.'"

"Sounds like a plan," Justin agreed. "You comin', Spider?"

"Nah, I gotta work tonight. Got a patrol. Gotta go hunt the
Talibangers. I wanna kill 'em all."

Though thrown together randomly, Justin and Jimmy had continued to hang out together. Someday, Justin promised, they'd be surfing at Huntington or Manhattan. Meanwhile, their experience on the hill gave them a shared experience that neither had in common with most of the men here at Fortress Sherishk. Spider was still around, but he was becoming harder to talk to. The experience on the hill had made him moody and bitter. He wanted to kill them all.

The bosses, the captains and lieutenants who decided things, had decided that the men who survived the hill should be tasked with softer duty for the time being, but Spider continued to volunteer for anything that came up. He wanted to kill them all.

The area where the satellite TV was set up was to Fortress Sherishk like a carnival midway or a campus quad. It was the place where people could just hang out and pretend that the real world was not so far away.

"Didn't know you were a baseball fan," Justin said as they walked. "Guess we really haven't had much time to talk about it."

"Yeah, I'm a big old baseball fan," Jimmy said. "Cubs."

"Cubs? I thought you were from Atlanta."

"Not Atlanta. Waycross. But I grew up in Chicago. Can't like the Braves. My ex lives in Atlanta. How 'bout you?"

"I don't have an ex, but my team's the Dodgers."

"Dodgers?" Jimmy said in mock disgust, disparaging the other National League team. "Sorry man, but you ain't gonna see no pennant this year."

"We'll see about that." Justin laughed. "At least you're not a Giants fan."

"Fuck *no!*" Jimmy declared, glad to have someone with whom to talk about his favorite sport, if not his favorite team.

The next two hours were magic. Three dozen men and a dozen women were suddenly transported halfway around the world to Wrigley Field. As it turned out, the Dodgers were play-ing in Chicago, and as Justin and Jimmy arrived, Carlos Zam-brano was pitching a no-hitter.

Finally, someone got a hit. The Dodgers got two men on base in the fourth and a run batted in. The game seesawed back and forth until the ninth inning, when the Dodgers won it by a single run. The Cubs fans didn't seem to mind. Every baseball fan in Sherishk was a winner, for during those nine innings, they were *not* in Sherishk at all.

Los Angeles, California
June 23

★　★　★

Laurie Hall closed her laptop and stared out the window of the Starbucks at the traffic passing on Wilshire Boulevard. Three weeks ago, Justin Anderson had sent her an e-mail that he signed with "Love, Justin."

Those two words seemed to vindicate all of the emotions that she had invested in her memory of that perfect night with him at Nobu, on the beach at Malibu, and back at his place. They had been ripped apart so suddenly, without time to talk and to share their emotions about what it meant to have wound up sleeping together on a first date.

Then he had signed his e-mail with "Love, Justin."

She had been in heaven for the next few days, but after two weeks with no reply, she wondered what had happened. Her emotions ran from anger that he was dissing her to worry that he had been hurt.

Last night, she opened her laptop, and there it was in her inbox, an e-mail from Justin, glowing brilliantly like a jewel in a jewel box. Then she opened it. What she read confused her even more. He told her everything was fine and that he missed her, but the message seemed so lifeless. Most guys have a hard time expressing their feelings, but Justin's message had seemed deliberately stripped of feeling, as though it had been written by a machine. At the very least, it did not seem to be the Justin whom she knew.

This morning, when she opened her laptop at Starbucks, she read his reply to her reply. She had asked him why he hadn't written, and he curtly told her that there was no Internet access in most of the 'Ghan. Laurie had long since figured out that *'Ghan* was short for the remote and incomprehensible place where Justin was. She had asked him what he was doing, and he had said simply, "Mostly we're not supposed to talk about it in e-mails, and the rest isn't something I want to talk about."

Laurie had asked him about Chuck Ellis, the man whom she had met under somewhat awkward circumstances that morning in Venice, a man whom Laurie knew had gone overseas with Justin. The cold and emotionless way that Justin described the man's death chilled Laurie to the bone.

Helmand Province, Afghanistan
June 23

★ ★ ★

"Is it my imagination, or do a lot of the Toons seem to be glad to have us around?" Jimmy Ray Flood asked as he and Justin Anderson made their way along a dusty street on the periphery of the town of Sherishk as the rear guard of an eight-man patrol. He, like many of the others who had known Ricky Alvarez, had adopted his shorthand term for the Pashtun people. It was not used as a derogatory term but merely a description and even somewhat affectionate expression. A lot of the Americans had come to have a certain fondness for the Toons, and vice versa.

"I guess they're glad that we've sorta brought them order out of chaos and chased away the Talibangers," Justin said. "I guess we became okay in their minds soon as they figured out that we weren't gonna extort money and rape their women."

"Those girls up on the hill were sure glad that we sorta rescued them," Jimmy observed. "And real freaked out when they got to thinkin' that the Talibangers were gonna get their hands on them again."

The term *Talibangers* was *not* used in an affectionate way. It had become clear to the Americans—especially Jimmy, who had grown up around the Mickey Cobras and Insane Deuces in Chicago—that the Pashtuns regarded the Taliban and the other bandits run by other warlords the same way people in inner cities regarded gangs. When the Americans first arrived in Sherishk, the local population had been extremely reticent to have contact with them. At first, they, too, were regarded as just another gang. Now people were actually returning smiles, and many of the women had stopped bagging themselves in burkas. They were happy to see the Americans patrolling their town like beat cops. To the Americans, Sherishk was just Sure-Stinks, but to the Afghans who lived here, it was their whole universe.

"What's up, man?" Jimmy asked, talking to someone whom Justin hadn't noticed.

Justin turned. An old man with a white beard had approached Jimmy and was jabbering to him in Pashtun.

"Hold on, man," Jimmy explained. "I don't speak your language. Let's get us some sign language goin' here."

Jimmy and Justin had already interpreted enough of the man's body language to know that something was disturbing him, it was urgent, and he figured the Americans could help.

"What's up?" the sergeant leading the patrol asked as he walked back to where Jimmy and Justin were.

"Old guy's bothered about something or other," Jimmy said. "Looks like he wants us to go with him and look at something."

The old man was pointing nervously at a somewhat isolated cluster of mud-brick structures about forty yards away.

"What do you suppose it is?" one of the men in the patrol asked.

"Sure wish they'd taught us some of the language," Justin said.

"What the hell does the army expect, sending a bunch of

appliance salesmen and bank tellers to the 'Ghan?" another American asked disgustedly. "Watch this guy that he doesn't get you blowed up."

"If he was a suicide bomber, you'd already be dead," Justin said, glowering at the guy.

"Okay, let's split up and go take a look," the sergeant said, trying to think on his feet and appear decisive. "You three come with me, and we'll check it out. The rest of you cover us. Let's move out and get this over with."

The old man was still clinging to Jimmy's sleeve as they entered the first building. He was obviously very frightened.

"Holy shit," the sergeant gasped, gaping at what he saw. The building was stacked floor to ceiling with RPG launchers, ammunition boxes, and other assorted weapons. "All this shit, right here on the edge of town. Those bastards were...I mean, think of what they coulda..."

"Somebody sure coulda caused a whole lotta trouble with this stuff right here in Sure-Stinks," Justin said, leaning down to take a closer look. "Musta been moving it into town to launch an attack on us at point-blank range."

"This old dude saved a shitload of American lives," Jimmy said, patting the old man on the back and giving him a big, exaggerated, but genuine grin.

"There's more in here," the sergeant said, stooping under a low doorway.

"Old dude wants me us to follow him over to this other building," Jimmy shouted. The man was pulling on Jimmy's sleeve and pointing.

"Go ahead and check it out," the sergeant shouted.

Justin followed Jimmy and the man by about five paces as they entered the smaller mud-brick shack.

Pop, pop poppa pop.

The sound rattled out of the building just as Jimmy and his friend went inside. Justin processed the hollow sound as gunfire in a small, confined space and ran to Jimmy's aid.

After just leaving the other building, Justin's eyes adapted to the darkness quickly. The first thing he saw was movement in a corner.

There was a head turning.

A face.

A defiant expression.

An AK-47 muzzle in motion.

It all rolled by in a split second.

Justin aimed and cut loose with his M16A4.

He didn't think. He let his training, his instincts, and his experience take over.

The defiant face disappeared, swallowed in a cloud of broken fragments of bloody bone and mud-brick wall.

"Motherfucker shot the old dude," Jimmy told Justin before the dust had settled.

Justin looked down. The Georgia Guardsman lay in a heap, tangled in the limbs and loose-fitting cloak of the Afghan man. He was clutching Jimmy's hand, his chin quivering in a way that Justin had learned the hard way to interpret as an involuntary reaction of a man in a lot of pain.

There was a lot of blood. It seemed to Justin that there was always a lot of blood. He had seen a lot of blood so often that it almost didn't register anymore. Justin tried to help the Afghan up, but he grimaced and clung to Jimmy as though the Georgian was his last best friend.

"Ahhhhrgh," Jimmy said as he tried to stand and help the man up. "I'm hurtin,' man. Musta got nicked in the leg…and the fuckin' arm. Shit, that hurts."

"Let's get everybody outa this shack," Justin said. "The sarge is callin' for backup. We'll get medevac out here a-sap."

Jimmy and Justin half-dragged, half-carried the old man into the daylight and laid him down where the sun wasn't directly in his eyes.

It wasn't until Jimmy flopped on the ground with a long, teeth-clenched groan that Justin realized how badly he had been hit. The guy with the AK-47 had cut loose with a short burst, but it was at close range, so most of the rounds found their mark. He had apparently just pointed his weapon at their midsections, where Jimmy's body armor absorbed most of the slugs, but where the old man was totally vulnerable. His wounds were almost certainly mortal. Jimmy's body armor saved his life, but a couple of rounds had hit his extremities in places where the wounds were serious.

Their being within the environs of Sherishk meant that the response time for the medics was a matter of only about ten minutes. The first thing Jimmy said when they pounced on him was to ask how the "old dude" was doing.

"The old dude was hangin' onto me, man. Y'know, these people fuckin' *depend* on us. You gotta fix him," Jimmy insisted. "I'm okay. Fix the old dude, man."

Just as he could see that the old dude was beyond fixing, Justin could see that Jimmy was *not* okay.

After surviving that terrible day on the hill, Jimmy had walked into a shack within a half-hour stroll of the place where they'd watched the Dodgers and the Cubs and had gotten gunned down. Just as war is hell, war is a breeding ground of ironies.

Justin had come to really like this guy from Georgia—even if he was a Cubbies fan—but in war, you don't make friends.

This was the reason why.

Helmand Province, Afghanistan
June 23

★ ★ ★

Zalmai Nawsadi stepped into the highway and waved his hand.

The truck slowed to a crawl, then ground to a halt amid the hiss of its air brakes.

The driver complained loudly, then pouted behind his steering wheel as Zalmai patiently explained that this was a security checkpoint, and every vehicle was subject to search.

As Zalmai watched the cab, three other members of the Afghan National Police climbed aboard the battered Mercedes truck to pick through the man's load, looking for weapons. Finally, they waved to Zalmai, who gestured toward the open road ahead of the truck. As he slammed the big vehicle into gear and navigated around the concrete barrier in the road, the driver cursed under his breath without making eye contact with Zalmai.

It was a boring task, standing on a highway near Garmsir looking in truckbeds and car trunks, but it was necessary. The Taliban couldn't be allowed to carry weapons and explosives in or around Garmsir and Helmand Province with impunity. They could probably still do it secretly, but it was the job of the Afghan National Police to serve notice that they couldn't do it openly. Even more important, the police presence had to make it clear to the people of Garmsir and Helmand Province that the Taliban was not in charge. The driver of the battered Mercedes truck notwithstanding, most people were very glad to see the Afghan National Police manning the checkpoints.

Zalmai looked at the people coming through his checkpoint with goods they had bought or goods they wanted to sell, and he saw himself—or at least his earlier self. He saw, too, how far he had come. Being in the police had changed his image of himself. He was proud of his decision. Though she was afraid for him, Shahla was proud of him, too. She recognized that the uniform put a Shoot Me sign on his back, but she also understood that the growing number of gray uniforms in Garmsir sent the message to the Taliban that they were no longer the lords of Helmand Province.

It hadn't been easy. A lot of the men who signed up quit during the training. Zalmai did not. It was more rigorous than he could have imagined, but the trainers were professional and businesslike in a way that he had never before experienced. They were mainly foreigners, the kind of people whom Zalmai had always been taught to regard as infidels. The Afghan National Army was trained mainly by the Americans, but the Afghan National Police got its training from the Germans. He had heard that they were very precise and rigid, and as far as the training was concerned, this was true. Off duty, though, they could laugh just like anyone.

Since he had been in the field, Zalmai had met other foreigners. There were a lot of British and Canadian soldiers in Helmand, and a few American units. He had been on patrol with them a number of times. They were also more precise than he had been used to, but they were less rigid than the Germans.

Today, there were a few Canadian soldiers with his patrol,

but they were hanging back so that the faces the Afghan people saw stopping them at the checkpoint were those of their National Police. Everybody knew that the foreigners would go away eventually, but they had to know the Afghan National Police would not abandon them.

Zalmai stepped into the highway and waved his hand, and a small blue Japanese pickup slowed to a crawl. As Zalmai stepped to the side of the road, preparing to make his usual speech to the driver, he heard the scraping sound of him downshifting. This was followed by the roaring, spitting sound of gravel being kicked up as the driver accelerated in first or second gear.

In a split second, the small truck collided with two Afghan National Police guys and a Canadian soldier, slammed into the concrete barricade, and exploded. The explosion, in turn, hurled bodies into the air.

Zalmai was in the process of getting out of the way as the pickup exploded, and the concussion slammed him sideways like he was a bale of dirty laundry.

He caught his breath, stood, and picked up his gray uniform cap. He decided that he was not badly hurt and looked around at the checkpoint. A sheet of dark orange flame had erupted from the pickup, topped with a billowing cloud of dirty black smoke. He could see the driver, still sitting in the vehicle. The flames had burned the skin from his head, leaving only a blackened skull, its teeth clenched in a manner that struck Zalmai as both grotesque and comical.

Not comical were the bodies strewn about on the ground. They included both Afghans and Canadians; the suicide bomber had not discriminated. He recognized his friend Muhammad. The way he was lying there, Zalmai was certain that he had not survived, but he felt his neck for a pulse anyway. No surprise.

He ran toward the place where most of the people had been

standing. The Canadian medic had survived, and he was kneeling over a wounded Afghan soldier. An Afghan civilian was helping a wounded Canadian to stand.

Zalmai was trying to decide where to go, to whose aid he should go first, when he heard the unmistakable cackling sound of an AK-47. He turned back to the road. A second pickup was stopped there. He saw three men standing in the bed and one in the open door of the cab. Each one was armed, and they were shooting at the police and soldiers. It was a good thing that this driver had stopped about fifty yards back from the checkpoint. At that range, an automatic weapon fired from a standing position was not very effective.

Zalmai still had his own AK-47 slung over his shoulder, so he unslung it, dropped to the pavement, and returned fire. The angry Canadians were also shooting back.

One of the Taliban toppled off the back of the pickup as Zalmai poured a stream of fire into the cab.

Two of the surviving Taliban leaped off the truck and started to run.

Almost without pausing to think what he was doing, Zalmai got to his feet and started running after them. He felt his cap fly off his head as he ran.

He heard someone running next to him to his left. He looked around. It was Keith Mackenzie, the Canadian sergeant.

Together, they chased the two Taliban off the road and into a cluster of small buildings.

As they started to gain on the insurgents, the Taliban separated and went in different directions. Without a word spoken between them, Mackenzie went left, and Zalmai continued chasing the other man.

Suddenly, he was out of sight. He ran around a corner and was lost to Zalmai's view.

Zalmai slowed to a walk and carefully peeked around the corner.

The Taliban, obviously winded by the unexpected run, had also slowed to a walk to catch his breath. Just as Zalmai rounded the corner, he glanced back to see if he was still being followed.

As their eyes met, both men froze.

Each man was carrying his assault rifle at his side, and as such, neither man was in a firing position.

Through each Afghan mind ran the scenario for what should happen next. It was very simple. Each man knew and understood in a split second that he must raise his weapon, fire it, and kill the other man. However, each man knew that the other was thinking exactly the same thing. As they stood there frozen in space and time, each man understood that it was a matter of who shot first and who shot straightest.

They drew up their AK-47s in nearly simultaneous motion.

They squeezed their triggers in nearly simultaneous motion.

As Zalmai had understood earlier, and as both men knew, firing from a standing position was a detriment to accuracy, but in this situation, both men were standing. It was an even match.

There were a couple of women and an old man who watched it all go down.

There were two men and two automatic weapons.

The weapons were each on full auto, and in a sense, so, too, were both men.

Nobody counted nor knew how many rounds were fired.

In the end, it did not really matter.

Zalmai fully expected to feel the sting of 7.62 mm projectiles piercing his body, but in this, he was disappointed.

The Taliban spun sideways as he was hit, and his rounds went wild.

As Zalmai approached him cautiously, he saw that his wounds

had been fatal. The first bullet had struck his abdomen; the second, his chest. The third had hit his face, just beneath his eye.

What occurred to Zalmai first, strangely more striking than seeing a body that he had rendered lifeless, was the precise, even spacing of the three bullet holes. As the barrel of his AK-47 had risen, pushed higher by the recoil, it had stitched a pattern of three evenly spaced hits. As Zalmai comprehended the man he had just killed, he found it surprising that this was the first thing that had come to his mind.

He looked around. A small crowd had gathered. They had seen a Taliban die at the hands of a member of the Afghan National Police, and this was good.

Zalmai heard his name being called, and he looked over his shoulder. It was Keith Mackenzie.

Kandahar Province, Afghanistan
June 24

★ ★ ★

"Mommy is fine, Isabelle," Cindy said, trying to comfort her littlest daughter in a reassuring tone. "How was your day? What did you do in school?"

Staring at the small, fuzzy image of Isabelle on the laptop screen, Cindy summoned the bravest smile that she could. She had gotten up at five-thirty in the morning in order to talk to her family before bedtime the night before. The time difference was bad enough. The weird half-hour time zone in Afghanistan was disorienting. So, too, was life in Afghanistan. The frightening thing was that Cindy felt herself starting to get used to it.

"Everything is very nice here," Cindy lied to the little girl in the Little Mermaid nightgown. "I'm having fun, but not *too* much fun...I'm really looking forward to seeing you soon...Mommy will be home soon. Go to bed when Daddy tells you...I love you. Let me talk to Jessie."

Things were not fun. They were far from fun, but Cindy had settled into a routine. The violent death of young Andy on the road to Hirwaiz had both horrified and hardened her. Since then, she had seen death again and again. She had watched Amanda, the twenty-year-old former prom queen, grow noticeably older and less sensitive. Since the road to Hirwaiz, they had been on other roads to other remote locations. They had experienced other RPGs and other roadside bombs. They had set up the elements of a communications network that helped the AFPS transmit the words and pictures of this strange and violent place so that people in America could have some tiny sliver of an idea of what it was like.

Today, Cindy and Amanda would be taking Sean and Cory, a pair of AFPS photojournalists, out to a place called Bayat. The object of the exercise was to acquaint them with a compact satellite uplink facility that was a prototype of a new Jitters interface that the 3313th Communications Company of the Iowa National Guard had installed for nonsecure data traffic. The two photographers had been surprised to learn that there were no Wi-Fi connections in rural Kandahar Province. Cindy had laughed at the way Amanda rolled her eyes.

"Was I *that* naive when we first came here?" Amanda asked Cindy as they marveled at the cocky antics of the two men. Civilian employees of the Defense Department, Sean and Cory were familiar with military operations but totally unfamiliar with the realities of a war zone like Afghanistan. They suffered from the usual affliction of the novice: thinking they were better prepared than they actually were.

"They're way too smug for their own good," Cindy admitted. "But they'll learn. We all seem to."

Amanda just nodded soberly as they stowed their gear and prepared to head out.

As the convoy rumbled westward toward Bayat, the two photographers tried a time or two to flirt with Amanda, but she merely shined them on. They had seen the shape of her body before she donned her flack jacket and her long, blonde hair before it was shoved into a helmet. They had seen a glimpse of the prom queen in the rapidly maturing soldier. In them, she had seen merely a state of mind that she had left behind.

As the convoy passed through progressively more primitive villages, Sean and Cory gradually sobered up. Everyone did when confronting the reality of village life in Afghanistan firsthand. Cindy had. Amanda had. Everyone did.

Most of the time, coalition convoys tried to circle around the perimeter of the towns, but once in a while they found themselves on main streets, dodging donkey carts, stray goats, and people on ancient, rickety bicycles.

Amanda was driving today, and she was glad that their Humvee was far enough back in the convoy that most of the mass of people and livestock had parted to let the lead vehicles pass. Nobody liked to hit pedestrians, and fender benders often turned into major incidents if coalition vehicles clipped a jaywalker.

Today, their Humvee was second to last in the convoy, followed by another group of Guardsmen from the 3313th who were their armed backup. After the incident on the road to Hirwaiz, the battalion commander had decreed that whenever the 3313th went out, the troops should travel in a pair of vehicles to provide mutual assistance in emergencies. It must have worked, because there had been no more emergencies—at least not so far.

Suddenly, without warning, an enormous explosion rattled their eardrums, and a concussion shook the Humvee.

"What the hell was that?" Cory shouted.

"Probably an IED," Cindy said, far more calmly than she would have just a couple of weeks before. "Could you tell where it came from?"

"Up ahead, I think," Amanda said through nervously clenched teeth. She would be damned if she was going to show any vulnerability in front of the two clowns in the back of the Humvee. The truck ahead started to gain speed, and she pushed down on the gas pedal. "There, I can see the smoke now."

Outside, the civilians were running away from the site of the explosion. IEDs, like RPGs and car bombs, didn't discriminate. They killed anyone who was nearby, regardless of age or ethnicity, regardless of whether a person was an infidel from the West or a member of the same Muslim sect as the bomber.

IEDs, like RPGs and car bombs, also did not usually come alone. There was frequently a follow-up attack or a second bomb, timed to inflict further casualties among those attending to the initial batch of injured. That's why the reaction of a convoy under attack was to speed up and clear the scene as soon as possible. Just as on the road to Hirwaiz, it was harder to hit a moving target, although it was not impossible.

Sean and Cory gawked as they passed the truck that had been hit by the IED or the RPG or whatever it had been. The cab was engulfed in flames as the gas tanks burned, but the trailer was incongruously intact. Its load, a dozen or so pallets of cardboard boxes, looked pristine. It looked just like it would have at the loading dock of the Wal-Mart in Tysons Corner. Cory nudged Sean and pointed to three boxes containing General Electric refrigerators. People were already swarming. Within an hour, the truck would be completely unloaded.

Out on the streets, pandemonium reigned. The truck ahead was braking and swerving, and Amanda followed, praying that she wouldn't hit a civilian amid the chaos. As the swerving grew more erratic, and as the trailer bounced and twisted, Amanda backed off slightly, just in case something happened.

That was a good thing, because something *did* happen.

The trailer was lurching, then bouncing back down, its wheels all rolling on the pavement for a moment before bouncing up again. Suddenly, though, the trailer lurched and did not bounce back down. Cindy and Amanda watched in horror as it twisted and continued to twist.

The massive trailer, weighing several tons, rolled nearly 180 degrees before crashing in a cloud of broken boxes and splintered pallets. The forward momentum of the truck sent the trailer skidding forward in a shower of sparks. The tractor pulling the trailer, meanwhile, flipped on its side and was crushed as the trailer skidded against it.

Amanda slammed on the brakes, sending the Humvee into a skid that came to a stop about three feet from the upended trailer.

"Quick," Cindy said, climbing out of the Humvee. "Let's pick up the survivors and get going again."

The second Humvee pulled abreast of Cindy's Humvee, and she repeated her previous order. Two soldiers from that vehicle scampered into the wreckage to check on the truck driver.

"What next, Lieutenant Hunt?" asked the sergeant from the second Humvee. "We can't keep going in this direction. There's a canal or stream of some kind right there, and the wrecked truck has got the bridge blocked."

Cindy surveyed the situation. He was absolutely right; the big rig had jackknifed against the approaches of the bridge. There was no way that they could drive the Humvees over or through the wreckage. She looked into the distance. The waterway marked the edge of town, and beyond the bridge was open country. If the wreck had occurred twenty seconds later than it had, they would have been across the bridge. They could have just driven off the road, around the wreck, and been on their way. As it was, they were twenty seconds on the bad side of being trapped.

"How long do you think it would take to use the cable winch

on your Humvee to pull that wreckage out of the way?" Cindy asked, sizing up the situation.

"I don't think we can do it," the sergeant said, examining the diameter of the cable on his winch. "If the trailer was upright on its tires, it'd be a cinch, but we can't pull a piece of dead weight that big without busting the cable. Even if I had bigger-gauge cable, we're talkin' hours."

"Can't we just go around it?" Sean asked hopefully. He was eavesdropping as Cory wandered away, snapping pictures of the scene.

"The sides of that channel are too steep for us to ford it here," the sergeant said, pointing at the waterway. "It also looks too deep. Without the right kind of amphibious snorkel gear for the engine, we can't drive through water that deep without the motor conking out halfway."

"Why don't we have the right kind of gear?" Sean asked.

"Because Uncle Sam sent us to fight in a desert," the sergeant replied. "And he didn't figure that we'd be driving through three to six feet of water in a desert."

"Oh."

"I have an idea," Amanda said. Cindy had seen her walking near some buildings off to the left of the main road. "There's a narrow street down over there that seems to run alongside of the canal. It goes a long way up. Maybe we can drive up there and find another bridge or something."

"What do you think, Sergeant?" Cindy asked, turning to the man with the stripes on his sleeve. Junior officers often didn't seek the counsel of the sergeants under their command, but *smart* junior officers alawys did.

"Lieutenant, I think that's the best damned idea I've heard all day."

Cindy noticed that Amanda blushed slightly. The prom queen was becoming a soldier.

By this time, the two Guardsmen sent into the wreck site had returned with the driver. He was bruised and shaken but otherwise okay. Cindy counted their blessings.

Once they had passed away from the buildings that clustered around the bridgehead, the narrow, partly paved road paralleled the canal for as far as they could see. There were more buildings up ahead. There had to be another bridge.

As they drove, Cindy contacted the lead vehicle in the convoy by radio and explained their situation, including the fact that they had picked up the injured truck driver.

"Do you want us to come back?" asked the captain in charge.

"No, we can't get across the canal up here anyway," she told him. "We'll find another way across and then cut back overland. I'll let you know when we're back on the main road."

"We're at a location about nine clicks from the bridge," the captain explained. "We've got plenty of visibility here, so we'll just pull off and wait for you here. If you need us to come back or to meet you somewhere, just give us a shout."

"Thanks, Captain," Cindy told him as she signed off. Everything seemed fine, but in a war zone, just as everything seemed fine, it started to get *not* fine.

"I see a bridge," Amanda said, pointing ahead. There was a noticeable sense of relief in her voice. "It's about a half mile ahead by that pinkish-colored building."

Everyone relaxed as though the presence of the bridge was the end of their problems. It wasn't.

As they neared the bridge, all eyes were on it and not on the pinkish-colored, two-story building across the road from it. Unbeknownst to the unwitting Americans, the building was an Al-Qaeda safe house. It was off the beaten track of where the coalition usually went but close enough for use as a base for hit-and-run raids.

When the Al-Qaeda looked out their window and saw two American Humvees coming toward them, they naturally assumed that they were under attack. Little could they know that if unmolested, the Americans would have just made a right turn at the bridge and driven off into the distance.

Having waited for the two dust-colored vehicles to close within clear AK-47 range, the Al-Qaeda fighters opened fire. Unfortunately for them, they had only a single rocket-propelled grenade launcher, although they had nine of the eight-pound grenades to launch with it. Though an RPG's fuse sets the maximum range at just over nine hundred meters, it is not accurate past three hundred meters. Today, however, the Al-Qaeda gunner squeezed the trigger when the Humvees were only eighty meters from a second-story window in the pinkish colored building.

The explosion erupted between the two Humvees as the barrage of automatic weapons fire sprayed the vehicles. An RPG round can easily destroy even an armored Humvee, but the shooter had missed. While the eighty-meter range is within the accuracy specs for the RPG, it is no guarantee of a hit for a bad shooter. Both Humvees survived.

"There, second floor, see that," the sergeant shouted to the gunner atop his Humvee. While rocket-propelled, the RPG is actually launched by a gunpowder booster charge whose blast comes with a cloud of bluish smoke. The sergeant saw the telltale puff, and so did his gunner. Unlike Cindy's vehicle, the other Humvee was armed with a grenade launcher of its own. The Mk 19 belt-fed automatic grenade launcher—favored by troops who have to engage bad guys hiding behind stone or masonry walls—fires 40 mm grenades at a sustained rate of about forty rounds per minute.

"I see the bastard," the gunner shouted. Crouching behind his panel of steel armor plate, he lined up the second-story window and cut loose. Unlike the RPG, which had to be manually reloaded for the second shot, the Mk 19 used the blowback, or chamber pressure, from each fired round to load and recock it. It also had an effective range five times that of an RPG, but today that didn't matter. The range was very short.

The gunner lobbed five grenades into the second-story window and then began pumping additional rounds into every window where he saw a muzzle flash.

Inside Cindy's Humvee, the two photojournalists had been handed the greatest photo op of their careers, but they cowered on the floor as the hailstorm of 7.62 mm rounds hammered the vehicle's armor. The velocity of the rounds was such that their impact actually shook the Humvee. One round pierced the safety glass, but most its velocity was expended, and it ricocheted harmlessly—albeit frighteningly—inside the vehicle.

The firing seemed to go on forever, but it actually lasted only about a minute. When it subsided, the sergeant drove his Humvee closer to the building and ordered two of his men to approach and secure it. The gunner lobbed a grenade through the front door, and the two men scrambled through.

Even from outside, the other troops heard the sounds of them clomping up the stairs. At last one of the men appeared at a gaping hole where the RPG gunner had been.

"It's all clear, except we have some civilian casualties up here," he shouted.

Cindy and the two photojournalists entered the building.

The ground floor was just a single large open room with a primitive wooden staircase leading upstairs. As Cindy surveyed the scene, Sean and Cory began taking pictures of the four bloody bodies tangled with their AK-47s were they fell, killed by the blast of the Mk 19's grenades. There was a little bit of furniture and a few rugs. The rugs were covered with a fine white dust of pulverized masonry, and most of the furniture was broken. One piece, a very old and rustic sideboard, was amazingly untouched.

Having counted the bodies, Cindy started up the stairs to check on the civilian casualties. Up there, the scene was like the first floor, with broken masonry and splintered furniture scattered around. There were two rooms. In the first, there was a dead Al-Qaeda lying on his back, his AK-47 resting on his face. Elsewhere were pieces of the RPG gunner, dismembered when he took a direct hit. His launch tube lay bent and twisted near one of his arms. A month or so ago, this scene would have sent the high school teacher from Iowa City into convulsions. Today, Cindy felt a little sick to her stomach, but that was all.

As she passed into the second room, this would change.

A man and woman were lying in the corner, both staring blankly upward at nothing in particular. The woman's face was visible beneath the torn burka. They were obviously both dead. As Cindy approached, however, she nearly jumped out of her skin. There was a sound and a flicker of movement beneath the woman.

If, they were dead, how could this be?

She knelt down for a closer look and put her hand near where she saw the movement.

"There's something moving in here," she said without looking up. "There's a third person here...oh my God...it's a little kid....She's alive!"

"Get a first-aid kit up here *now*," the sergeant shouted.

Cindy reached beneath the woman's body, pushing it aside.

The little girl looked to be exactly Isabelle's age, with light brown curly hair that looked just like Isabelle's. She looked at Cindy with terror in her little black eyes, and her chin quivered from fright. As Cindy picked her up, she instinctively reached to grab Cindy's uniform. She seemed to weigh the same as Isabelle. Then she let out a low moan that Cindy thought sounded like Isabelle.

Cindy closed her eyes and hugged the little child. For a moment, everything else around her disappeared. The darkness behind her squinted eyes came alive with the little red and green table lamp that Isabelle got for Christmas last year. Cindy felt the cuddly warmth of the baby blanket that Isabelle slept with, and she heard the sounds of Jessie asking her dad for a drink of water.

Abruptly, the scene ended.

The child who was for a split second of a moment Isabelle, hiccuped loudly. Cindy opened her own eyes and looked into the little dark, terrified eyes. She saw the curly hair that could have been Isabelle's, and she saw the trickle of blood that had belched from the little mouth as the child had hiccuped.

"Oh man, the kid's got internal injuries," the soldier with the first-aid kit said as he reached to take Isabelle from Cindy's arms.

The girl shook with a sudden spasm, squinted her eyes, and let out a gasping sound. The little hands with the perfect fingers released their grip on Cindy's uniform. The little, squinting eyes relaxed and fell open. For a split second, they met Cindy's gaze, then rolled back as the small body fell limp.

"Oh no!" Cindy screamed.

"Okay, everybody out of here," the sergeant said, pushing the two photojournalists and the Iowa Guardsman with the first-aid kit out of the room. Having waited a few moments, he went back into the room. Cindy was still clutching the small body. Like him, she was a civilian soldier, but she was also a mother. However, she was an officer with responsibilities for others. He had given her a bit of private space, but it was time to move on.

"Shall we mount up the troops, move out, and get everyone

down to Bayat, Lieutenant?" he asked quietly, putting the emphasis on *Lieutenant*.

"Yes…yes. That's what we need to do," Cindy said. They *did* have to move out. They were in a hostile war zone, and she was the lieutenant, with the responsibility of five other Guardsmen, two photojournalists, and a wounded truck driver. There was a convoy exposed to potential attack waiting for them nine kilometers away, and they still hadn't gotten across the canal.

In the best of all possible worlds, she could have wrapped up the bodies and delivered them to local authorities personally, instead of reporting it to someone who would tell someone else to report it to the locals.

Of course, in the best of all possible worlds, she would not be gently placing a dead child Isabelle's age next to dead parents. In the best of all possible worlds, Al-Qaeda would not have taken over their home as a safe house. In the best of all possible worlds, there would be no Al-Qaeda, no Taliban, and no need for Cindy to be half a world away from Jessie and Isabelle.

As Cindy walked out into the sunlight, most of the people were loading themselves back into the Humvees. Amanda was standing a short distance away talking with the sergeant. When they noticed Cindy emerge from the building, the sergeant started toward the Humvees, but Amanda paused, looking back near the corner of the building. Something had caught her eye.

With an alarmed expression, Amanda pointed and shouted, "Look out!"

Cindy turned; a man with a turban and a black beard was running toward Amanda and the sergeant. She immediately saw that he was carrying a hand grenade. He had apparently been watching the Americans from the cover of a small shed at the side of the building.

Instinctively, Cindy ran toward the would-be suicide bomber.

It was all she could think of to do. She had no conscious plan of what she would do to stop him, she just had to try. The strong legs of the Jackson County High School girls' track coach allowed her to intercept the man before he could reach Amanda and the sergeant.

Cindy just body-slammed the man, knocking him to the ground. In a split second, he was facedown with her on his back, grabbing for his wrists to try to bring him under control.

She pinned his arm with her knee, seized the hand with the grenade, and struggled to pry it loose before the safetty lever was released. If she could only get it away from him, Cindy could keep the damned thing from going off.

She almost had it, but the grenade slipped out of his hand. It bounced twice and came to rest a few feet to her left.

CHAPTER FIVE

Not the Same Old World

★

Rochelle, Colorado
August 26

★ ★ ★

Roxanna Huerta stared out the window of the old Chevrolet van at the row upon row of three-bedroom, four-bathroom homes. The first time that she had seen this spectacle, it had taken her breath away. The first time that she had stepped inside of one of these homes, she could not contain her amazement at the fact that anyone could live like this. Nor could she comprehend the fact that for as far as the eye could see, all the gringos lived like this.

Roxanna came north from Chihuahua for two reasons: dollars and Luis Carillo. Luis had come north for two reasons as well. The first was the same as for Roxanna, and the same as that which brings millions of Mexicans into the United States every year. For Luis, the second was that he truly believed in what he called *"el sueño Americano,"* the American dream.

Roxanna was in love with Luis, and she easily accepted the notion that the streets in *los Estados Unidos* were paved with gold. Everyone in dirt-poor rural Chihuahua believed that, but it was not until the twenty-year-old woman actually reached Colorado that she saw how true it was. The first time that she came into a gringo home to clean its floors and take out its trash, she was astonished. Maybe there really was something to this *sueño Americano* that Luis kept crowing about.

Gradually, her perspective began to change. She came to realize that the barrier represented by the Rio Grande was inconsequential when compared to the barrier that existed between her world and the gringo world. Luis had worked long and hard to get his *targeta verde*, his green card, and to make himself eligible for the *sueño Americano* life that he wanted to live.

Roxanna was a long and potentially insurmountable distance from living *el sueño Americano*. Like so many others, she found herself trapped in the shadowy world of the *mojados*, the people whom the gringos called "illegal aliens"—except, of course, when they called them to clean the floors of their three-bedroom, four-bathroom homes.

When she arrived in Rochelle, Colorado, she took up residence with her cousins in Galeana Poco—Little Galeana—named after the *municipio*, or municipality, in Chihuahua from which most of the *mojados* in Rochelle lived. Galeana Poco was an old part of Rochelle that the gringos had gradually abandoned as they moved into the new subdivisions.

She found ready employment with a cleaning service run by longtime *mojados*, who hired newly arrived *mojados* and paid them less than the gringos were paid to do work that gringos didn't like to do. The first time that Roxanna found herself mopping a floor while a woman her own age sat on a sumptuous sofa watching an enormous television set, Roxanna was amazed. Now she was used to being regarded with disdain by the gringos or ignored as though she were an inanimate appliance.

When Roxanna came north, Luis was away in a distant place

called Afghanistan. He told her that he was helping the gringo army protect a *frontera* thousands of kilometers from Colorado or Chihuahua. He called it *"ironía grande."* Roxanna was inclined to call it "loco," but she loved Luis and respected his decisions.

Luis told her that when he returned to Rochelle that they would work hard, and that they would live *el sueño Americano*. She wrote to him about the three-bedroom, four-bathroom homes, and he wrote back that they would one day live in such a home and that it would be sooner rather than later.

A lot of people around Galeana Poco had called the people who joined the U.S. Army loco, but Roxanna loved Luis, and she respected his decisions. Gradually, news began coming back from this place called Afghanistan. It was news that made Roxanna proud to love Luis and proud of his decision to become a soldier. She heard that Luis was being called *Ojo del Aguila*, because he could see things that were invisible to the gringo soldiers. A great many people around Galeana Poco were proud of Luis, glad to see that one of their own was regarded as a hero.

There was even an article about Eagle Eye Carillo in the Rochelle newspaper. Eagle Eye Carillo was the hero of the 3rd Battalion of the 157th Field Artillery of the Colorado National Guard. Roxanna couldn't read all the words, but she recognized the picture of Luis—*her* Luis—resplendent in his uniform. She knew that this handsome man on the front page of the gringo newspaper was the man she loved, the man she would marry, and the man with whom she would live in a three-bedroom, four-bathroom home of their own.

Roxanna loved Luis, and she was proud of her hero.

At last, Roxanna heard the news that Luis was coming home. The news came unexpectedly, months before the date that Luis said he would be coming home. She got the news from her cousin one night as she came home after nine hours of mopping gringo floors and scrubbing gringo *tocadors*. Her cousin had heard it from his cousin who heard it from someone else. They said that Luis had been hurt, but he was coming home. Roxanna didn't worry, because Luis had told her not to. He was coming home, so she didn't imagine that he could be badly injured.

She didn't go to the airport to meet Luis Carillo when he came home. If you are a *mojado*, you know better than to go somewhere that is crawling with nervous gringo police. Instead, she put on her best dress and went with her cousins to Luis's cousin's home, where a welcome home fiesta was planned. Crepe paper banners were strung between the house and a lone shade tree in the front yard. There were flags—both Mexican and American—and tin wash pans filled with ice and Corona. Roxanna asked to help the women as they cooked the lunch, but they told her that was foolish. Her job today was to look beautiful for *Ojo del Aguila*, her hero and her future husband.

At last, she saw him. She saw his face in the passenger's seat of his cousin's big car. He was grinning from ear to ear. She would have known that grin anywhere!

Roxanna ran to the vehicle, reaching it before it stopped. "*Mi amor!*" Roxanna screamed.

The moment that she grabbed him, their lips met. They kissed deeply and passionately, oblivious to the fact that two dozen people were standing around, watching. Her head spun. She wanted to give herself to her hero, to surrender herself to him body and soul. She wanted to feel him inside her. She wanted to start the family of which they had often spoken, and she wanted to start it *now*.

Roxanna laughed when she realized that she hadn't even let him step out of the car yet. Laughing, she jerked open the door and pulled him toward her.

She laughed when he tumbled out and fell on the ground. She

thought it funny to see the great *Ojo del Aguila*, whom she had seen on the front page of the gringo newspaper, just lying awkwardly on the ground in his beautiful new uniform.

She noticed his ribbons and thought of the medals and the heroism that they represented. She was so proud of her hero and her future husband.

As Roxanna bent down to kiss Luis again, she stopped laughing. His ear-to-ear grin was gone, replaced by an expression of awkward embarrassment.

What was wrong?

She saw him struggling to sit up and leaned down to help him. His eyes were darting around nervously. Roxanna looked up and saw the expressions on the faces of the others. No one was laughing. No one was grinning.

Luis's cousin popped the trunk and pulled out something that looked like bicycle tires in a black canvas bag. A moment later, as he unfolded the object, she realized that it was a wheelchair.

Iowa City, Iowa
August 26

★ ★ ★

The banners reading "Welcome Home, Mrs. Hunt" hung in the cafeteria where the luncheon had taken place. School was out for the summer, so the celebration was much smaller than the big pep rally in the gym that had seen Cindy off to war. The luncheon had been mainly teachers, although the student body officers for the coming year were present, as were nearly all of the girls from the track team. As Cindy had predicted before she went overseas, there were several state champions among them, including the girl who set a new state record in the long jump.

Track season was over. Jackson County High School would not actually need a girls' track coach for many months, but they would need history teachers in a couple of weeks. Cindy Hunt had returned home to find that, as they had promised, they had kept her teaching job open for her.

A great many good words had been spoken at the luncheon. As usual, the principal went on much too long, but he had good things to say. Everyone had good things to say about Cindy.

Everyone had good things to say to Cindy, but she sensed that the things they weren't saying *to* her were a lot different. She sensed that by the way she caught them looking at her. They were friendly but uneasy. It was as though she were being hugged, but at arm's length. Cindy had changed, and they hadn't.

When she read the banners that read Welcome Home Mrs. Hunt, she had felt as though she had finally come full circle. She had come home to the job that she had missed a thousand times more than she had imagined. She had felt as though she had finally come home, but she realized now that she had not. So too, did the others. The banners read Welcome Home Mrs. Hunt, but it was no longer home. The Mrs. Hunt who had received the magnificent send-off so long ago had gone away, and someone else had returned in her place. It was someone they did not recognize.

Cindy had realized on the morning she awoke at the U.S. Army's Landstuhl Regional Medical Center in Germany that things would be different. She did not yet know how different. The skies were blue, and a light breeze was ruffling the chestnut tree outside the window. Inside the room, machines were beeping and whirring. Nobody was in the room when she woke up, and she didn't know where she was.

The first thing she noticed was that she ached all over.

The second thing she noticed was that she was mostly wrapped in bandages. She lifted her right arm. There were clips and monitors and cables attached to her fingers. She opened and closed her fist a couple of times, and some of the monitors fell off. She heard them hit the floor, but she couldn't move to look to see where. That was when someone came in, looked, and went away shouting to someone else.

"Your patient is awake...she just woke up!"

In a moment, there were several people in the room, fluttering about like birds, mainly ignoring Cindy and fussing with their beeping and whirring machines. Finally, they told her what happened. There had been a hand grenade. She had been nearby when it went off, but she had no memory of being near a grenade. They told her that she had saved the life of Amanda Morgan, a young Specialist from Des Moines, and a sergeant named Carter from Waterloo. Cindy remembered Amanda, mainly her face and her expressions. She couldn't remember a sergeant named Carter.

They asked her what was the last thing she could remember. Cindy told them that she thought she remembered being in a convoy, but she added that there were a lot of jumbled memories of convoys. She admitted that she could not place these recollections in any order.

Gradually, they got around to explaining what was beneath the bandages. The grenade had bounced away far enough that the explosion didn't kill her, but it had done a lot of damage. Her body armor had saved her torso, but her left leg was badly mangled. They told her in great detail about tendons and ligaments. As a runner, she understood tendons and ligaments. They used words that were strangely abstract, but which all meant ripped and shredded. Why couldn't the doctors just say "ripped and shredded"?

They had done their best to put the ripped and shredded tendons and ligaments back together, but as with Humpty Dumpty, there hadn't been much to work with. They told her it was fifty-fifty whether she would be able to use her leg, and she told them she would beat those odds.

She could see that her unbandaged right arm had sustained only a few scratches, but they told her she had nearly lost her left. She had come into the hospital with a thumb and one finger. They were able to reattach the thumb. There was no place to attach the finger.

Her helmet had protected her head but not her face. This news, they spun in as positive a light as they could. They explained that wonderful things were being done with prosthetic eyes and ears these days. They made it sound like an infomercial. They said they were doing skin grafts to reconstruct her cheek. They made it sound like she was getting a tooth filled. By the way, they added, she now had fewer teeth to fill.

Cindy looked at her right hand. She looked at it a lot as she lay there in the Landstuhl Regional Medical Center. Except for the television set, with its depressing English newscasts and German soap operas, there was not much else to look at. At least she still had a right hand and a right eye with which to see it.

Welcome Home Mrs. Hunt.

Cindy felt that she had come a long way from Landstuhl when she walked into JCHS. They had given her a standing ovation when she entered the cafeteria and limped across the room. They had heard about her leg and about the probability that she would never walk again. They remained standing as Cindy, aided by Peter, hobbled to the head table on her cane. Her hair had started to grow long again, and from the right, you would not have noticed her injuries. She still had her lips, and she still had her smile, but there was an ugly red scar that extended from the corner of her mouth. The rest of her face remained bandaged, as did what remained of her left wrist and hand.

The bandages were due to be removed, but she put it off until the next day at the VA Medical Center in Iowa City. She self-consciously did not want to have these injuries on display in front of people whom she knew. Not yet, anyway. People stare. She knew that it was only human nature. They don't want to be rude, but people stare.

"The principal was pretty upbeat about expecting you back in front of class in the fall," Peter said as they drove home from the luncheon.

"I'm not so sure that I'm ready for that," Cindy said, staring out the window at the familiar sights of Iowa City. The strip malls and fast-food drive-ins seemed so peaceful and so far removed from the horror of Afghanistan. The typical suburban Midwestern street where she lived, with an SUV in every driveway and brightly colored children's toys on every well-kept, deep green lawn, was unimaginably far from Afghanistan. A year ago, Cindy could not imagine what she would later see in Afghanistan. Now she thought she could never forget.

"The doctors say there's no reason why you can't go to work in the fall," Peter reminded her. "You've gained back about half the weight you lost, and you're getting your strength back. They said it was fifty-fifty that would wouldn't be able to use your leg, but look at you."

"I just don't know whether I'm ready to be stared at," Cindy admitted. "You saw them today; they were all looking when I wasn't looking. What's it gonna be like when the bandages come off?"

Peter was glad that they wheeled into the driveway at that moment. He had no answer.

Inside, the house was a mess. Cindy had been home for nearly a week, and the mess was starting to grate on her. At first, she was just happy to be back with her family under a familiar roof and surrounded by familiar things. Now, the fact that those familiar things were in such disarray was starting to get to her.

"We've got to get this house picked up," she said, putting down her purse and wriggling out of the jacket she had worn to the luncheon to hide as much of her withered left arm as possible.

"It's not so bad," he said, glancing through the mail and adding it to a big and growing pile on the kitchen table. He was a bit perturbed that the first thing she said when they got home was that the house needed to be picked up. "We can deal with it later."

"That's what I mean; you keep putting it off," Cindy said, pointing to the pile of papers on the table. "You have got that pile going. You got piles going everywhere. It needs to be picked up. All this crap all over the place needs to be picked up."

She kicked the overflowing plastic laundry basket a few feet across the room, then leaned down to try to pick it up, awkwardly trying to use her bandaged left hand.

"*You* have to start doing the laundry," she sobbed. "I can't even lift this damned thing anymore."

"Okay, okay," Peter said, lifting up the laundry basket and carrying it to the laundry room between the kitchen and the garage.

"Things have to change around here…" Cindy started to say as the front door burst opened and two little girls raced into the room shouting, "Mommy."

"My babies," Cindy said, leaning down to hug Jessie and Isabelle. She was so glad to see them—more glad every day. She had missed them so much when she was away. Cindy hadn't remembered the little Afghan girl until she saw a picture in a magazine. Taken by one of the two photojournalists who were there that terrible day, it showed Cindy holding the child. She had a sad and desperate expression in this last picture ever taken of her face. Circulated around the world, it had briefly made Cindy famous. The picture had been the subject of much talk and a great deal of blogging. Some saw it as a symbol of American compassion, others as a symbol of American violence against Third World civilians. A few even saw it as a mother reacting to a child.

Cindy hadn't remembered the little Afghan girl until she saw a picture in a magazine. Now Cindy could not forget her.

The memory of that event came back to Cindy when she had

seen the photo, and she wished that it didn't exist. She remembered looking into that girl's eyes and seeing Isabelle. Now she could not look at Isabelle without remembering the other girl and the helplessness of feeling her die in her arms.

"Look what Megan bought us, Mommy," Jessie squealed, holding up a colorful beach ball.

Cindy glanced up as Megan came into the room carrying one of the girls' backpacks.

"Thanks so much for picking the girls up at summer camp, Megan," Cindy said, standing up. "That thing at the school took longer than expected."

"No problem, Mrs. Hunt." She smiled. "I like the girls a lot. Oh, hi, Peter."

"They seem to like you, too, Megan," Cindy observed, feeling warily jealous of the enthusiastic way they hugged Megan whenever they saw her. Megan had graduated from JCHS a couple of years ago, making her about the same age as Amanda Morgan. They looked a little bit alike as well: tall, slender, blonde, and well tanned. Megan had been in Cindy's history class when she was a junior, but Peter had been her faculty adviser and had known her much better. While Cindy had been overseas, Peter had hired her to drive the kids around and babysit once in a while.

"I'm glad that Megan's been able to help out," Cindy said after the younger woman hugged Cindy's children good-bye and left in her Volkswagen Jetta.

"Yeah, it's been great," Peter agreed.

"But it sure worries me that she was carrying the kids around in that small car."

"Maybe we should let her drive the SUV," Peter replied.

"I don't think we'll need her to do that anymore," Cindy said. "I'm back now."

"Yeah, but you're going to be having to have your surgeries…all the reconstruction and all…and you'll be having your physical therapy and…"

"Peter, I'm their mother. I can certainly drive them to summer camp."

"Are you sure that you'll be okay driving?"

"Dammit, we have an automatic," Cindy said, exasperated. "I have two feet and two arms, and all you really need to drive is your right foot, and my right foot is fine."

"Okay," Peter said as he left the room. "I was just trying to think of you."

Cindy felt exhausted and decided to go try to take a nap. She longed for a shower, but that would not happen until the bandages came off. Hopefully, it would be tomorrow.

She waited until Peter was out of sight before she started up the stairs. She didn't want to follow a conversation about how independent she was by having him watch her as she went through the slow and difficult process of climbing the stairs. The pain in her left leg was less and less every day, but she had no strength. Most of the muscle had been blown away, and it was only through the amazing skill of the surgeons that she had the tendons to make it bend and flex in some semblance of normal.

Cindy was slowly taking off her clothes when she caught sight of the woman in the master bedroom mirror: a woman with a bandaged arm and withered leg streaked with red scar tissue and jagged seams. She remembered the woman at whom she had looked before she went away. Cindy put her left foot into the closet and looked at the woman now. With the reflection's right half obscured, she looked almost like the woman that Cindy used to see in this mirror. She was a little thinner, and the circles under her eyes were darker, but all that wouldn't be hard to change.

"You don't look so bad," Cindy lied to the woman in the mirror.

The image of Megan came to her mind, the image of pretty, perky Megan with her shorts and her perfectly shaped, unblemished legs, of Megan with the tank top that barely covered her perfectly shaped breasts. *It's sad*, she thought, *that a woman has to watch her youthful body slowly age.*

She started to say out loud that it's even sadder when a woman sees half her body suddenly torn away, but she stopped herself.

Waycross, Georgia
August 26

★ ★ ★

"When y'all goin' down to see Mr. Cahner?"

Jimmy Ray Flood had heard his mother come home from work. He had heard her slam through the screen door. He had ignored her when she said hello, and he ignored her when she asked, for the umpteenth time, when he was going down to Cahner's Quick Lube to ask for his job back. He had no answer to her question.

When Jimmy had come back from Afghanistan, his mother had hugged him for a full five minutes. There had been excitement all around. There was a lawn party at the house, and they even had a supper at the Baptist church. Jimmy had come home in one piece, and there was a lot to celebrate. Now, the celebrating was over. Days had turned to a couple of weeks.

Jimmy had sat down on the sofa in front of the television set, and he hadn't moved.

Jimmy had come home with scars that those around him could not see. The scars remained when his leg and arm had healed, but you couldn't see them unless Jimmy wore his wife-beater shirt. The scars inside were even harder to detect.

He hadn't realized that it would be like this.

Jimmy had nightmares about watching helplessly as the Talibanger with the RPG shot down the Black Hawk, but it was the old dude on the edge of Sherishk whom he could *really* not pry out of his brain. The old dude had probably lived in that stinking hole for a hundred years, watching the gangs come and go. It was like Jimmy's mom in the projects in Chicago, but a thousand times longer in time and a thousand times worse. Finally, somebody had come along who the old guy thought he could trust, and a half hour later, Jimmy was flat on his ass as the old guy twitched to death on top of him.

Every time Jimmy dozed off, the old dude's final expression, his death mask, drifted across the inside of Jimmy's brain.

Part of Jimmy's angst was how fast they shipped him home. He got himself medevaced out of the place so fast it made his head spin. That in itself made him feel guilty. He felt that he had just picked up and abandoned the old dude's people just as he started having an intense feeling of getting attached.

Jimmy also felt as though he had just picked up and abandoned the other soldiers with whom he had bonded. He thought about Surfer Dude, the easygoing white boy from California. He thought about Sheldon, the Georgia kid who said he wanted to go surfing and then got shot in the head two minutes later. Jimmy had nightmares about the way the kid's head just flopped around.

Jimmy had a lot of nightmares, and they weren't always at night.

Jimmy sent a couple of e-mails to Surfer Dude, and he understood why the replies were few and long in coming. There weren't a lot of Internet cafés in Sherishk. In his last e-mail, Justin had said that he wasn't in Sure-Stinks any longer. At church that Sunday, Jimmy actually *prayed* that this meant that ISAF hadn't just pulled out and hung all those people out to dry. He hoped that God would understand the metaphor.

"When y'all goin' down to see Mr. Cahner?"

"Dammit, Ma, I just ain't ready yet," Jimmy said.

Jimmy knew that he needed to get his ass in gear. Except for Big D, lying around on the front lawn or lying on the rug at Jimmy's feet, Jimmy was the only member of the household who wasn't pulling his own weight. His nephew Lamar had a job down at the bait and tackle, and Jimmy's mom, of course, virtually ran that pretty big insurance agency. Even the partners did as she told them.

"I'm barely from the 'Ghan, Ma. I haven't been around here on my ass all that long, and I was up to Atlanta for more'n a week."

"Don't be using that 'ass' language in this house, boy," she replied. "I raised you to use respectful language in the home."

"Sorry, Ma."

Jimmy's mom bit her tongue. She knew that Jimmy had been through hell, even if she couldn't comprehend the dimensions of that hell. On the other hand, her mother's instinct told her that the best thing for her son was to get him busy and get his mind on something besides that hell through which he had been. With that thought in mind, she was determined to hassle him until he went back to work.

"When are you going to get Cathy down from 'Lanta to visit her grandma?" Jimmy's mother asked. Jimmy spent nearly a week up there, but his mother had not seen her granddaughter in a year.

"Yeah, I will, Ma," Jimmy shouted from the bedroom he shared with Lamar.

"Are you stayin' home for dinner, boy?" she asked.

"Naw, I'm gonna go down and shoot some pool."

"Don't be out late again. Worries me to hear doors slammin' at all hours."

"No, Ma."

Off and on since he came back, Jimmy had been hanging out at the pool hall with some of the guys from around town. His mother didn't like to see Jimmy swimming with those sharks and spending time with the kinds of people who spent time at pool halls, but what could she do? She also suspected that he had started drinking again, and that troubled her greatly.

Jimmy *had* started drinking again. Not a lot, but a few beers at the pool hall. After Afghanistan, he had a lot to forget, and after his disastrous trip to Atlanta, he had a lot more to forget. Kadeefa had evolved from merely an intolerable ex-wife into a deliberately arbitrary bitch who used her right of sole custody like a hammer over his head. Meanwhile, Cathy—who he loved more than anything else since the day she was born—was becoming a teenager. Every time he saw her, she seemed to have drifted farther away and into the netherworld of being a teenager.

★   ★   ★

Jimmy's first glass of Sweetwater 420 Pale Ale tasted good and went down smooth. He craved another but decided to pace himself, so he drifted into the back of the tavern where the pool tables were.

He and a friend played two other guys for beers and won, so a couple of rounds were shared. Jimmy was feeling pretty good as the place started to fill up with the usual boisterous crowd.

The girl, hardly more than twenty-one, who serviced the pool room with her big tray was running herself ragged, taking orders, delivering drinks, and carting away the empties. Jimmy had wondered why they didn't set up a bar facing back this way but figured that it was none of his business.

"Hey bitch, where my muh'fuck shots?" roared a dude in a backward Marlins baseball cap as the girl passed him.

This struck Jimmy as awfully rude—the girl was obviously working as hard as she could—but he figured that it was none of his business.

It was Jimmy's turn to break, and he got the seven in the corner pocket. As he moved around the table, Marlins was at it again. The girl had delivered a tray of shot glasses to Marlins and his entourage in record time, but he couldn't let it go.

"Slowest bitch in Georgia," Marlins said, bopping slightly as though imitating a hip-hop video, while glancing around at the entourage he was obviously trying to impress. "Wouldn't mind gettin' a piece o' yo' slow ass."

The girl ignored Marlins and continued her rounds.

Jimmy continued to shoot pool.

"Hey there, slowest bitch in Georgia, we need us some mo' shots."

The dude in the Marlins cap was now making a point of harassing the girl every time she squeezed into the pool room with her tray. People were starting to notice, and an aura of tension was growing in the room.

She was just trying to ignore his taunts as she tried to do her job.

Jimmy saw him grab for her posterior as she went past.

She did not see his hand as it grabbed her, and she lost her balance. Jimmy instinctively grabbed for her tray as it toppled, and luckily, only one half-filled beer glass fell across the pool table. It was still a huge mess.

"Why don't you fuckin' leave her alone," Jimmy told the dude angrily as the girl regained her composure and took her tray.

The crash and spatter of the glass hitting the table had gotten the attention of nearly everyone in the pool room, and all eyes were on Jimmy and Marlins.

"Wha'd you say, muh'fuck?" Marlins asked.

"I said, 'Fuck off,' *muh'fuck*."

Marlins saw a challenge to his role as the alpha male wannabe within his entourage. Jimmy saw red. He looked into the face of the man with the backward Marlins cap and the gold neck chains, and he saw red.

Jimmy's mind exploded as the sneering face before him morphed into the sneering face of the Talibanger who had shot the old dude on his terrible last day in Sherishk.

"Why don' y'all go crawl back into your chicken coop, country boy," Marlins laughed, sneering at Jimmy with teeth that were plated in gold the way they do up in cities like Atlanta.

Jimmy exploded. All of the anger that he had felt in his life, all of the anger he had brought back from Afghanistan, just exploded.

His fist exploded into Marlins' sneering face, crashing into those teeth that were plated in gold the way they do up in cities like Atlanta.

Jimmy was seeing red.

Everyone in the room was seeing red: blood red.

The blood from Marlins' broken nose was splattering everywhere.

Jimmy was aware of men shouting and women screaming.

He found himself on the floor, kneeling over Marlins and pummeling his face. It no longer sneered but looked up at Jimmy with an expression of terror.

Jimmy felt hands on him. They were trying to stop him, trying to pull him away.

Jimmy saw red. He saw the Talibanger with the RPG shooting down the Black Hawk, and the sneering Talibanger who killed the old dude. He saw the old dude's death mask.

Why don't these assholes just leave people like the old dude and the girl with the tray alone?

Why do bullies have to keep doing this shit to people?

Rochelle, Colorado
August 30

★ ★ ★

Luis Carillo sat in his chair on a four-by-eight slab of plywood that lay next to the steps that led up to the back door of his cousin's small bungalow. It had just rained, and the air was clear and fresh. Anything was better than nostrils full of dust that reminded him of Afghanistan.

The house was not much better than many houses back in Galeana, and it was a far cry from the three-bedroom, four-bathroom gringo tract homes, but compared to what he had seen in Afghanistan, it was a palace. Compared to Afghanistan, anything with indoor plumbing and electricity—especially electricity that ran all day and all night—was a palace.

Ojo del Aguila had seen a lot of things in Afghanistan. He had seen things that the gringos could not see, and that was how his nickname had come about. He had seen things that he could not explain to the people at home and that had filled him with a confusing cloud of mixed emotions. He had left the world of Galeana

Poco and Rochelle, Colorado, and he had seen things that nobody here could understand. Now he was back.

Those with whom he had shared those things over there were effectively gone from his life. Sergeant Charlie Schlatter and most of the guys from Luis's steel rain battery were still in Afghanistan, their tours extended for another six months—and maybe longer. Buddy Sorrell was in a hospital somewhere. Both Ace and Deuce were dead, killed when the Mk 82 bomb came off the wing of the A-10 Warthog, killed in the same friendly-fire incident that tossed Luis more than twenty feet, crushing the base of his spine.

Amazingly, Luis suffered no other injuries. Not a scratch. He hadn't even been knocked unconscious. His first reaction was to think how lucky he was. His first instinct was to stand up and walk away, but the immediate and complete paralysis of his legs prevented this.

He had come home a hero, with a chest full of ribbons, but his tenure on the front page of the gringo newspaper had been short. Now he sat here, rolling back and forth on a sheet of plywood, filled with a confusing cloud of mixed emotions and nobody to share them with—or at least nobody who understood. He was eligible for physical therapy and psychological counseling at the VA Medical Center, but it was in Grand Junction, and he had no way of getting there. The VA had a Community Based Outpatient Clinic in Alamosa, but Luis knew that no amount of physical therapy could give him back his legs and that psychological counseling would probably make him more loco than he already was.

He and Roxanna had stopped talking about getting married. This was more just a lull in the conversation than a case of their beginning to articulate the idea of *not* getting married. They hadn't seen each other since that first night when he got back, but they were used to being apart. Since they first became involved on one of his occasional visits to Chihuahua, Luis had been in Colorado most of the time, and when she finally made it across the *frontera*, he was in Afghanistan.

Luis had gone to Afghanistan believing that his service to his adopted country would be a major stepping-stone to the *sueño Americano*. A big facet in that dream had been his conversation with Ben Meehan just before he shipped out. He had promised to get Luis a job as a carpenter's helper, working on one of the countless construction projects taking place around Rochelle. Such a job would have meant serious wages, not the minimum wage he received at Target or the few bucks a day that he netted doing casual labor. Luis had phoned Meehan when he got back. Meehan was sympathetic, but both men knew that nobody would ever hire a man in a wheelchair as a carpenter's helper.

So Luis sat in his chair on a four-by-eight slab of plywood that lay next to the steps that led up to the back door of his cousin's house. Later, he would lean down and shove the plywood back up in the steps so that he could use it as a ramp to get back into the house so that he could hoist his body onto the toilet.

This was his life now, day in and day out. At least the spinal cord injury had been low enough that he could still feel his bladder. Looking forward to a life without legs was bad enough. Living the rest of his life in a diaper would have been intolerable.

"Buenas tardes, Aguila."

Luis turned. Felipe was coming up the dusty street. Before he went overseas, Felipe had been less a friend than just one of the hombres with whom he worked occasionally on casual labor jobs. Luis used to look down on Felipe as a lazy slacker who would rather hang out at the cantina playing pool and swilling Corona than working to build a solid life. Now that Luis could no longer work, he had more in common with Felipe than he wanted to admit.

"Ready to go on down now to the cantina, amigo?" Felipe

asked in heavily accented Spanglish. Before Luis had gone away, he had hassled Felipe to learn English. He told Felipe that he couldn't form a decent life in America unless he did. When Luis returned, he discovered that Felipe was now trying, at least, to speak the gringo language.

"Yeah, I'm ready," Luis replied. "Not much happening here."

Felipe had actually proven himself as a friend. A lot of the guys around Galeana Poco had figured themselves as too macho to hang around with a guy in a wheelchair. Not Felipe. He had insisted on taking Luis down to Cantina Sinaloa, the local bar, so that he could hang out like the regular hombres. Felipe didn't mind being seen pushing Luis down the street in his chair. Luis could wheel it on his own, but Felipe was glad to push.

Felipe had even stood up to that certain crowd who referred to him as *Luis Lisiado*, meaning "Luis the Cripple." Felipe called him *Aguila*, using his old National Guard nickname, and told everyone else to do so as well.

By now, few people in the bar looked twice at the guy in the wheelchair drinking and laughing with everyone else. They even let him shoot pool from his chair, and he was starting to get pretty good at it. Luis liked going there. Before he lost his legs, Luis looked down his nose at people who hung out in the bar from early in the afternoon, but now he was one of those people.

Luis had grown to like being at Cantina Sinaloa. He liked it mainly for the human contact but also for the fact that it had a handicapped-accessible bathroom. It was a lot easier to use than the narrow room at his cousin's house. It was the little things that nobody else noticed.

Sometimes Felipe drank with Rafael, the man whom Felipe had always described as *"El Hombre,"* meaning *The* Man. El Hombre wore nice suits and always had plenty of cash to throw around. Often he was throwing it Felipe's way.

"You should get out from under Rafael," Luis said as they each sipped a cold Corona. He hated to see Felipe dependent on a low-life drug dealer.

"*Porqué?*" Felipe shrugged. "I make more gringo dollars delivering *pacquetes* for *El Hombre* than I do hustling pool. Like I told you before, you oughta try it. You ain't makin' no dollars sittin' around."

"I can't do much except sit around, amigo."

"So come on and work for *El Hombre*," Felipe insisted. "Ain't no cops gonna hassle a war hero in a wheelchair. You could make maybe *cinco cientos* a week clear."

"Not for me, Felipe."

"Leastways, talk to *El Hombre*. He's comin' in here later in the day."

Rafael's sporadic appearances at the little corner tavern were always predictably showy. He was, of course, *El Hombre*. He always arrived with his posse, who theatrically posed themselves around the doorway like bodyguards in a bad gangster movie. Younger men from the neighborhood who wanted to curry favor with the colorful Rafael always vied with one another to buy *El Hombre* a drink. He always ordered a shot of tequila, which he slammed in one gulp.

Felipe became starry-eyed around *El Hombre*, as though being seen with him was like being seen with an A-list movie star. The whole production disgusted Luis, although the thought of *cinco cientos* a week clear was growing on him.

"This is my friend," Felipe said as Rafael left the bar to sit at their table. "The one I told you 'bout."

"*Aguila*," Rafael said. "I heard about you, man. You're a big hero."

Luis reached out to shake *El Hombre*'s hand, but the big, well-dressed entrepreneur responded by touching his hand with his fist, gangsta-style.

"I was overseas with the National Guard," Luis said.

"Heard a lot about *Aguila*," Rafael said. "Even in gringo papers, man. I hear you wanna be makin' some extra dollars, man."

"I'm not so sure," Luis said hesitantly.

"Could use a man like you, man," *El Hombre* said.

Sitting across the table from this man in an expensive suit, Luis felt as though he were in a job interview. He was.

"To do what?"

"I got customers. They need to get the goods. "I need hombres to deliver the *pacquetes* and bring me the dollars. You bring me the dollars, I give you some dollars. Hombre like you, man, the cops wouldn't never stop you. I figure you could clear maybe *tres cientos* a week."

"Felipe said *cinquo cientos*," Luis said.

"Maybe *cinquo cientos*," Rafael shrugged. "We'll see. You in or not?"

"What's in these *pacquetes*?" Luis asked without answering *El Hombre*'s question.

"*Felicidad.*" El Hombre smiled with a wink. "Nothing but joy and happiness, amigo."

"I saw that kind of *felicidad* in Afghanistan, amigo," Luis began. "I saw a lot of people who lost their lives to that shit. Opium is everywhere. It's a big cash crop for the assholes who killed people that I knew. On my last day in that place, I watched a bunch of assholes get all loaded up on *felicidad* and run into a wall of bullets thinking that they were gonna be bulletproof or go to paradise of something."

"*Qué usted esta diciendo?*" Rafael asked. He was startled. Nobody spoke angrily to *El Hombre*. He was used to being sucked up to, not spoken down to.

Felipe just sat there with a terrified look on his face.

"I saw opium bringing no *felicidad* over there," Luis continued.

"I saw only hopeless misery and pain. I see the same thing around here with the people who buy these *pacquetes* of heroin or crack or ice or whatever shit you sell. I can't take dollars from people like them. I can't be part of their misery."

"Well, fuck you, *Aguila*," *El Hombre* said, standing up and staring down at Luis in his chair. "It seems that your righteousness has bought *you* only *miseria y dolor*. I heard they call you *Luis Lisiado* now. I didn't know your brain was part of what you got that's crippled."

Casting a glowering glance at Felipe, he said simply, "You should pick your friends more wisely, amigo."

"You fuckin' pissed off *El Hombre*," Felipe said, half in anger and half in horror, as the big man made an exit that was as contrived and showy as his entrance.

"So what? That shit only hurts. You saw it back in Chihuahua. So many people were laying around getting high. That turned our towns and our villages into the kinds of places that we wanted to escape from."

"He's right," Felipe replied. "I didn't know your brain was crippled, too, but it is. You pissed off *El Hombre*, and you got him pissed off at me. He didn't give me no dollars like he was supposed to. I need those dollars. You pissed off *El Hombre*. Now you better watch your ass!"

With that, Felipe stomped out of the room, leaving Luis alone at the chipped Formica table with two half-drunk Coronas and their bar tab.

Luis reached into his pocket and pulled out a wad of bills. At least he was still getting his money from the army. Maybe they didn't pay wounded veterans as well as *El Hombre* promised to pay his runners, but they were more dependable.

Luis paid the tab and ordered another.

Then he ordered another after that.

At the end of the bar, three girls stared at him. They looked so fine in tank tops and tight denim. They looked so fine, with long, dark hair and ruby lips. Luis stared back and waved, smiling broadly. Two of the girls looked away. The other continued to look in his direction. He thought he saw her smile, but maybe it was his imagination. In a moment, he lost sight of them as another group of people bellied up to the bar.

Luis longed for female companionship. He and Roxanna had not had sex since he had gotten back, even though the break in his spinal cord was low enough that the doctor said he could probably perform physically. He just hadn't been ready emotionally. Neither had Roxanna.

Ojo del Aguila sat in his chair at the chipped Formica table and took stock of his situation. It was pretty pathetic. Here he was, an hour after chastising *El Hombre* for what his drugs did to people, and Luis himself had sucked down enough Corona to make it hard to stand, even if he *could* stand.

When Luis began laughing, the people in the bar turned to stare.

"*Ironía grande*," he laughed, looking up from the chair at the people nearest to his table. "Here is the *lisiado* who is too crippled to stand, but who is now too drunk to stand, even if he could stand! Here is the drunk who scolds the big drug dealer and then gets himself smashed. *Ironía grande*, amigo, *ironía grande*."

Luis needed some air, so he left a wad of dollars on the table and pushed his chair out onto the narrow sidewalk. As he moved down the street away from Cantina Sinaloa, he looked up at the stars that were starting to gather in the darkening sky. He remembered that night in Afghanistan when he had looked up at the stars and thought about the corner of the American flag with all the stars, and about what he was doing to make *el sueño Americano* a reality for himself and Roxanna and for their future together.

He had to see her. He had to see her and to talk about their life together. They had avoided the topic long enough. It was time to talk about getting married and about the *niños*. Roxanna used to talk about the *niños* that they would have. She used to talk about the *niños* all the time, but she hadn't talked about them since he had been home.

Now was the time.

Cindy paused in front of the trophy case in the lobby of Jackson County High School. She stared with pride at the three that she helped put there, and she was determined to put another one—at least one—in there before she was through. When the bandages had come off three days ago, she had fallen into a bout of depression, but she was working her way out of it.

The first day had been the worst.

She had seen her damaged arm when the cast first came off and when they rewired her elbow. She saw it during the skin grafts. When she had seen that she had a thumb but no fingers, she had asked about her wedding ring. It must have been left behind, they told her, left behind with her finger on a dusty road somewhere half a world away.

She knew about her arm, because she had seen it, but she had not seen her face—or her lack of face—until the day before yesterday at the VA Med Center. On the left side, from her eyebrow to her chin, where there had once been a face, there was nothing but a concave bowl of reddish-purple scar tissue. She had no eye, no ear, and no cheekbone, just a sunken flap of grafted skin surrounded by jagged scars. The doctor had started to explain how they would reconstruct a cheekbone and eye socket, but Cindy told him to take away the mirror.

She started to cry.

When Jessie and Isabelle first saw their mother without the bandages, they had reacted with horror. Jessie, being older, sort of understood, but she still could not look at Cindy. Isabelle was genuinely frightened. She ran screaming to her father. She said something about "the witch" and demanded to know where her mommy was.

The first day had been the worst.

Cindy sat in the downstairs bathroom, sobbing for two hours. That night, she talked to the kids for long time with the lights out. She sat in their room and spoke to them quietly until they both fell asleep. When she went to the master bedroom, Peter, too, was asleep. She lay awake wondering whether he was just pretending to be asleep so he didn't have to look at her. She didn't blame him. She didn't want to look at herself, either.

The first day had been the worst, but the second wasn't much better. Cindy felt herself falling into a trough of depression without the energy to fight it. After Peter had gone off to his summer teaching job at the community college and Megan took the kids away to summer camp, Cindy found herself alone in the house. In the corner of the garage, she noticed her overseas duffel bag, dusty and dirty and out of place next to the brightly colored folding lawn chairs. When it was shipped back, she told Peter to "have them just put it in the garage. I don't want it in the house."

Now, she decided, was a good time to just throw it into the garbage can, push the can to the end of the driveway, and be done with all that it represented.

She started to do this but paused. Curiosity got the best of her, and she unzipped the bag, dumping the contents onto the floor of the garage. Both cars were gone. Peter had taken his, and she had insisted that he tell Megan to take the kids in the SUV.

The junk that spilled out represented everything that had been in or around her area in the barracks tent at Kandahar. When she was medevaced out to Germany, they had just shoved everything into the bag and shipped it home. It was a testament to army "efficiency" that it arrived in Iowa City a week after she finally got back.

The contents were mostly clothes. Mixed in among the camo-colored uniforms, she found her running shoes and cursed the bitter irony that she would never need these again. There were some odds and ends of underwear, some socks, and some pictures of her family. These, she set aside. She was scooping the rest back into the bag when something clunked onto the cement floor of the garage. It was her army-issue Beretta M9 semiautomatic pistol, wrapped up in its nylon holster with the spare clip Velcroed to the side. She had forgotten that she had decided not to take it with her on that last trip to Bayat. If she had, would she have pulled it and shot the guy with the grenade instead of tackling him?

She carefully unwrapped the pistol and examined it.

"Oh shit," she said under her breath. It had a clip in it, with a round in the magazine. This had been sitting there in the same house with the children! Cindy carefully unloaded it, wrapped it in a shirt, and shoved the pistol back into the bag along with the clip and zipped it back up. She thought about her plan to put the bag in the garbage but just pushed it into the corner instead. She figured that there was probably a law against dumping automatic weapons and live ammunition into the municipal garbage.

The first day had been the worst, but on the second, Cindy started to get better. She opened a bottle of merlot, sat down on the living room sofa, and turned on the television. She flicked around to the soap operas and settled on one of the typically sappy daytime talk shows. The guy that was on the show was a quadriplegic who had once been an up-and-coming NASCAR driver. She was going to change the channel again but got caught up in his story. At first it sounded corny, but soon she started to take it to heart. The guy had no usable arms and legs, but he was laughing and joking with the host.

By the end of the half hour, Cindy had decided if he could do it, she could damned well do it!

Now she was standing in the lobby at JCHS, headed for her first faculty meeting. The principal wanted her back, and she decided that, dammit, she would do it. She hadn't gotten her own trophy way back in her own days as a high school track star for being a slacker, so she would do it.

She looked at the woman reflected in the glass of the trophy case. For the first time since Germany, the woman in the reflection was exuding confidence. If the poor NASCAR guy could laugh about being stuck in a wheelchair, Cindy could laugh about being stuck with a cane. At least she didn't need help to go to the bathroom, like he did. The woman in the mirror even looked a little bit sassy with her large sunglasses. Cindy had discovered that with the shades to hide her lack of an eye, and her hair brushed over the place where her ear wasn't, a lot of passersby didn't even notice her. Someday, maybe she'd even be brazen enough to wear a tank top.

Last night, she told Peter that she was going to drive to the store—alone. Just as she suspected, the automatic transmission was easy with one good leg. This morning, it was Cindy, not Megan, who took the kids to camp. Then she drove herself here to JCHS. Her life was coming together.

Cindy was feeling a bit apprehensive walking into the meeting, but she soon fell into the familiar rhythm of these sessions.

One teacher had complaints about scheduling. Another wanted to extend the freshman lockers into the hall near the library. There were discussions of whether to move the senior study hall to the cafeteria, and Cindy threw out an opinion on that. Most of the people were old colleagues, with a couple of new teachers whom Cindy had not met before. Everyone knew her situation and seemed willing to accept the fact that she had a disability. That was until she removed her sunglasses. Several people seemed genuinely startled. Even the principal averted his eyes.

Was she really that horrible?

Was she the witch that her own daughter had seen?

By the end of the meeting, everyone seemed over the initial shock, but Cindy put her glasses back on so that they could look her in the face when they said good-bye.

She walked to her car alone, wondering how it would be when she faced students in the fall. What would they say? What would they do? What would be said in the notes that were passed?

At home that night, dinner conversation was still minimal.

"Windsor has PlayStation," Jessie announced abruptly during an especially long lull.

"Who's Windsor, dear?" Cindy asked.

"You know, Windsor Barstow, in my class."

"Oh yeah, I remember," Cindy said, pretending that she did remember everyone whom her children knew.

"I think I should have PlayStation, too."

"Well, that's something that we can sure think about," Peter said. "You do have a birthday coming up."

Cindy glanced at Isabelle, who looked away. She still had a hard time looking at her mother. Cindy still had a hard time looking at her daughter, too. Every time she did, she saw the little face from Afghanistan with blood trickling down her chin.

"In the place that your mommy went, kids don't have Play-

Station," Cindy began. "They don't have many toys at all. They don't have much of anything. They're lucky to have birthdays!"

"This isn't there; this is here," Jessie said.

"It's all the same world," Cindy said. "People can sit around here thinking that this is here and that is there, but people from over here are giving their lives so that people over there will have a chance!"

"Don't yell at me, Mommy," Jessie said with tears in her eyes. "I didn't mean nothing."

"Don't take it out on the kids," Peter said.

"Don't take *what* out on the kids?" Cindy shouted.

She looked around the table. Jessie was starting to cry. Peter was beginning to look angry. Isabelle just looked terrified.

"I'm sorry," Cindy said in disgust, standing up and carrying her half-empty dinner plate toward the kitchen. "Mommy's just too upset. Maybe...maybe Mommy is just too upsetting."

Angrily, Cindy threw the plate into the sink. It didn't break. She couldn't do anything right. She had just frightened the kids and angered her husband. Now she felt the frustration of being so inept that she couldn't even break a plate.

Peter told the kids that it was time to get ready for bed. They looked at him, took another look at their mother, and ran upstairs as fast as they could.

"I understand how upset you must feel," he said. "But this hasn't been easy on the rest of us, either."

"*You* understand?" Cindy said angrily. "How could you possibly understand what I'm going through? *You* didn't see what I had to see over there. *You* don't have to wake up every day for the rest of your life with half a face...or with a husband and children who have a hard time looking you in the face!"

Peter sheepishly left the room and walked toward the laundry room.

Cindy followed him, seeing that he hadn't touched the basket of laundry that she had asked him to wash several days earlier. With that, she went ballistic, telling him to get out of there, and she would do it herself.

Shaking his head angrily, he walked away in the middle of her tirade, poured himself a glass of chardonnay, and went into the living room.

Cindy heard the television come on as she struggled to get the laundry basket up where she could deal with it. Using her left thumb as a claw, she managed to figure out a way to move it. After that, it was easy. She went around the kitchen and downstairs bathroom, gathering up towels and dishrags and discarded children's socks. When she had everything consolidated, she started shoveling the smelly mess into the washing machine.

Suddenly, one of the objects stood out. At first glance, it looked like purple ribbon from a gift box. She picked it up. Thong underwear! It was a woman's thong. It certainly was not hers. She had never worn anything like this in her life. She could not imagine in a million years that it was Jessie's. Was it? Had Peter let her buy *this* while she was away?

Holding the underwear by one of its slender strings, Cindy limped into the living room.

"Do you know what this is?" Cindy demanded of her husband.

"Yes."

"What?"

"Underwear."

"*Whose* underwear?" Cindy demanded. "Did you let Jessie have something like this?"

"No," Peter answered. Cindy thought she detected a little nervousness.

"Then *whose*?" Cindy asked.

"It might be Megan's," Peter suggested.

Cindy was speechless. *Megan?* Megan, with her shorts and her perfectly shaped, unblemished legs. Pretty Megan, with her perfect body and her perfect smile.

Cindy felt faint, thinking about Megan and her perky attitude that made the children—Cindy's children—so happy. Cindy felt faint, imagining Megan's centerfold body in the same room with her husband. Cindy felt faint, imagining Megan's perfect centerfold body, smooth and naked, except for a purple thong—in the same room as Peter.

"What is Megan's underwear doing in the laundry at *our* house?" Cindy asked with a noticeable quaver in her voice.

"She must have left it," Peter said, still sitting on the sofa with a glass of wine in his hand. "She stayed here with the girls for two nights while I was at the Nineteenth-Century Authors Conference in Des Moines."

"*Megan* stayed with *our* girls in *our* home?"

"Yes, I told you that."

"When?"

"In an e-mail."

"Oh my God," Cindy said, throwing the thong at her husband as she retreated to the kitchen.

Had he told her? Was that part of the memory that had been burned out of her brain? How could she know? She thought of the way the children bubbled excitedly when Megan was in the room and how they seemed afraid of their mother and the way she looked. She remembered the day when Megan called her Mrs. Hunt and greeted her husband by his first name.

Cindy had felt like a stranger at JCHS. Now she felt like a stranger in her own home.

She and Peter had not had sex since she had come home. It wasn't that this was something Cindy was craving just now, but it had started to bother her that Peter seemed disinterested. With the discovery of the thong, pieces of the picture were coming together in her mind. Pretty, perky Megan had that perfect body and youthful smile that men craved. Was she? Were she and Peter...? Cindy didn't want to think about it.

Slowly and methodically, Cindy washed and folded every piece of laundry in the house—except the thong, which still lay on the couch in the living room where she had thrown it—cleaning the kitchen between loads. She had to do something to occupy her mind. It was nearly midnight when the last warm batch of towels was folded.

Rochelle, Colorado
August 30

★ ★ ★

He had to see Roxanna and see her now.

Luis Carillo would have liked to have flown on the wings of an *aguila*, or at least on the strong legs of a soldier, but he moved slowly and haltingly in his chair. Luis moved not like an eagle, but like a man in a wheelchair fueled by an afternoon and evening's worth of Corona and tequila shots. Luis had been drinking since around noon.

There were few sidewalks in Galeana Poco, and those that did exist were cracked and chipped. More often than not, the former *Ojo del Aguila* found himself on city streets, dodging oncoming cars as well as potholes and mud puddles that could tip over the rickety wheelchair and leave him floundering.

It would be great to have an electric wheelchair, but the waiting list at the VA stretched out for years, and the electric chairs usually were reserved for men—and women—whose upper bodies were far more impaired than Luis's.

* * *

The van dropped Roxanna Huerta at her cousin's house and rumbled away into the darkness to drop off the others. She was coming home late—again—after a long day's work in the gringo homes. She was tired and dirty, but she had a pocket full of dollars. Since she had been in Colorado, she had saved more money than she had ever even seen back in Chihuahua. She saved to make *el sueño Americano* a reality, but she was still not clear what *el sueño Americano* really was. Luis had seemed to have a very clear idea, and she had followed his lead. But now the tables were turned. The man who once worked a regular job, doing contract labor on the side, was doing nothing while Roxanna worked ten hours a day.

"Buenas noches, Roxanna!"

She turned at the sound of Luis's voice. She watched as he put extra effort into rolling the wheelchair up the inclined driveway, dodging the old pickup that belonged to her cousin's husband.

"I've been thinking," he said, speaking haltingly as he caught his breath. He looked awful. His shirt was stained with the sweat of having pushed the chair for nearly two dozen blocks, and he smelled of stale Corona. His hair was mussed, and his face was covered with a week's growth of black whiskers, too long to be attractive and too short to be a beard. He appeared to be very drunk, more drunk than she had ever seen him.

"About what?" Roxanna asked, using English. The gringos preferred it, and, like Luis, she had come to realize that it was the necessary language of *el sueño Americano.*

"I've been thinking about us," he said, looking up at her. "I've been thinking that we should start thinking about talking about us."

She watched as he struggled in the chair. He grabbed the edge of the porch railing, dragging himself with great difficulty to a standing position.

"I need to look at you in the eyes," he said, explaining himself. It was the first time that she had looked at him standing since long ago in Chihuahua, and she had forgotten how tall he was.

"I need to look at you in the eyes and talk to you about us, and about the getting married, and about the *niños*. Before, you used to talk about the *niños* all the time. We need to get married and have the *niños*."

Roxanna was speechless. She stared into the face that reminded her a little of the Luis Carillo whom she had once loved so desperately. She stared into the greenish-hued face eerily lit by the fluorescent porch light and saw a terribly disheveled man who stank of sweat and stale beer. She wondered what had become of the Luis Carillo she had once loved.

He reached toward her with a trembling hand, using the other to support his weight.

"I want you, I'm ready," he said with a loco expression on his face, his speech slurred drunkenly. It was José Cuervo speaking, not Luis Carillo. "Let's start to make the *niños* tonight… right now….the doctors said my parts will probably work. Let's do it now. I wanna get it in there."

She wondered what had become of the Luis Carillo she had once loved. He had gone away, only to be replaced by a stinking drunk, crudely propositioning her under the fluorescent lights that put huge, ugly shadows beneath his eyes.

Before she could speak, he lost his balance and fell backward. A man with useless legs has a hard time breaking a fall, and Luis had no practice. He grabbed awkwardly for his chair but only succeeded in knocking it over.

Luckily, he fell not on the asphalt driveway, but on the rain-soaked mud adjacent to the patchy lawn. His landing was soft, but the sticky mud was slippery. Luis lay flat on his back, trying to turn himself to get into a position where he could raise himself on his arms, but he slipped again.

Since that terrible day when she first saw the chair, Roxanna had wondered and worried, avoiding the necessity of accepting that the Luis Carillo she had once loved had been replaced by a different Luis Carillo, one whose life had been permanently and drastically altered. So, too, had his dreams and aspirations been altered, along with his ability to fulfill them. So, too, had his ability to be the man that she needed and of whom she had dreamed.

Roxanna wondered what had become of the Luis Carillo she had once loved. The man she watched, squirming and slithering in the mud, looked barely human in the greenish light.

"Help me," he begged pathetically as he twisted in the mud. "I want you. I need your body."

The thought of her body next to the body she watched squirming and slithering in the mud was revolting to her. The thought of surrendering her life—at the age of twenty—to a man who could barely go to the bathroom unaided was more than she wanted to handle.

Maybe she was young and selfish. Maybe she still lived in a little girl's fantasy world when it came to dreams of the love of her life, but she didn't care; it was her life, and this insulting, vulgar drunk was not the man she loved and definitely not the man she wished to be the father of her *niños*.

"*Usted no es un aguila*," Roxanna said disgustedly as she opened the front door of her cousin's home. "*Usted es un gusano!*"

Luis was stunned. The woman he loved, the woman for whom he had longed under the stars in distant Afghanistan, had said that he was an earthworm, not an eagle.

Almost immediately, Roxanna felt sorry about her choice of words, but she was tired and angry, and she needed to forcefully articulate her feelings. Roxanna felt sorry about her choice of words, but she felt the need to be as emphatic as possible. She was a twenty-year-old cleaning woman, not an orator. She had a point that she needed to get across. Whatever there had been between herself and who this man had once been, it was over—and she felt the need to use strong language to underscore that fact in an unambiguous way.

"Mi deseo es no ser la esposa de un gusano," she said as she pulled the door shut with a slam.

There. She had said it.

She had said what had been on her mind since Luis had come home without legs. Maybe it was a juvenile way to express it, but she felt that it needed to be said as forcefully as possible. Roxanna Huerta did not want to spend her life as the wife of a worm.

Waycross, Georgia
August 30

★ ★ ★

Lennie Cahner had gone on a fishing trip to someplace over in Alabama.

Lennie Cahner, the asshole, redneck son of the owner of Cahner's Quick Lube, had gone fishing. He really didn't want to be around when Jimmy Ray Flood came back to work. Partly, it was that the "shiftless nigra" whom he once constantly derided had come home from Afghanistan as a hero. He had become a hero in a war that Lennie boisterously promoted, but in which he had carefully avoided risking his own strawberry red neck.

The other part was the other night in the pool hall. Word was circulating all over town that Jimmy had beat a punk half to death for grabbing the ass of a cocktail waitress. Lennie felt that fishing was preferable to confrontation, and he wanted to put off facing Jimmy Ray Flood for as long as possible.

Jimmy's mother had lost five years off her life that morning when she had to miss work to go down to Oak Street to get her only son out of the Waycross city jail. Jimmy had stood up to the punk from Florida in the Marlins cap, but he stood silent for the nastiest scolding that she had dealt out since he was in school.

Drinking and fighting. Jail. What was her son coming to?

However, just as Jimmy had stood up to the punk in the Marlins cap, the other people in the bar stood up for Jimmy. They told the cops that the other guy threw the first punch. Jimmy didn't remember that this was true, but he didn't argue.

It turned out that the punk had outstanding warrants, and he was in no position to press charges. Since Jimmy was technically defending himself, the Waycross DA let him go without charges but with a stern warning to keep out of trouble.

Jimmy called old man Cahner the next day.

★ ★ ★

"Jimmy, have you had a chance to get to the distributer on Mr. Brewster's Toyota?"

Old man Cahner was a helluva lot nicer to Jimmy than Lennie was. He was an old-school, states' rights southerner who would have gladly voted for Jefferson Davis again if he had the chance, but he was also the kind of old-school southerner who believed in gentility, fairness, and human dignity. He treated Jimmy with respect, and Jimmy responded in kind.

"Yes sir, Mr. Cahner," Jimmy said. "Got it changed out and runnin'."

"Great, thanks."

Lennie never thanked anyone for anything, especially Jimmy.

"Jimmy, didn't y'all come in early yesterday?"

"Yeah, I had that transmission to finish up."

"Well, since you're at a convenient stopping point, why don't y'all take the rest of the day, and I'll clock y'all out when I leave."

"Great, thanks a lot."

"Don't mention it."

Jimmy wriggled out of his coveralls and headed for home. It was a perfect day to get off early. Kadeefa was driving down from Atlanta. She was, as she put it, "bringing Cathy to visit her grandmother." Of course, Cathy's father also lived in the house, but Kadeefa would be damned if she'd characterize her drive down to Waycross as "bringing Cathy to visit her father."

Big D bounded to meet Jimmy as he approached his mother's neat little bungalow. Jimmy knew that he had to find a place of his own again—and soon. Staying with his mother for a week or two was okay, but now that he was working again, it was time to move out. Of course, it might necessitate getting another car. His nephew Lamar had gotten used to using Jimmy's old Ford, and since Cahner's Quick Lube was walking distance, this had not presented a problem. If Jimmy moved, that would be a different story.

Jimmy scratched Big D good and hard as the dog lolled happily on the ground outside the screen door. Big D whined loudly when Jimmy dashed inside to catch the phone. He instinctively thought that it was probably one of his mother's church friends. They were the only people who seemed to ever phone on the landline anymore.

"Hello, Jimmy," the voice said when he answered. He recognized the voice immediately. It was Kadeefa.

"Listen, Jimmy, I gotta favor to ask. Y'know all that construction on the interstate? Well, it hung us up. Can you meet us out at the truck stop?"

"Why?" Jimmy asked. "Why can't you drive another dozen miles to my mother's place?"

"We're gonna be late."

"That doesn't matter. Ma will hold dinner for y'all."

"I can't stay for dinner," Kadeefa explained. "Gotta get back to Atlanta."

"Whenever I get caught in the construction along the inter-state, you never cut me no slack."

"Listen, Jimmy. I don't wanna argue 'bout this. Y'know, we gotta get back to Atlanta. We're late."

"Who's we?"

"Me an' DeVawn."

"Who's DeVawn?"

"Friend o' mine."

Jimmy seethed for a moment. Kadeefa had gotten herself another new boyfriend, and the bastard was riding in the car with Jimmy's daughter all the way from Atlanta.

"What time?" Jimmy asked through gritted teeth. Driving up the interstate to the truck stop would be inconvenient, but it would mean that the time he'd have to spend with Kadeefa would be much less than if she had stayed for dinner, as originally planned.

"About six or so?" Kadeefa said, sounding relieved. She, too, was pleased to avoid an extended confrontation.

When Jimmy's mother drove into the carport at five-forty, he explained the situation, told her that Lamar wasn't back from the bait and tackle, and asked to borrow her Buick.

"The chicken's been defrosted," she said cheerfully, handing Jimmy the keys. Her anticipation of seeing her granddaughter had her in an extremely good mood. "I'll have dinner on the table when you and Cathy get back."

Rush-hour traffic around Waycross was in a snarl, and it took Jimmy until almost a quarter past six to reach the truck stop. If Kadeefa yelled at him for being late, he could just yell back that he was going out his way so that she and what's-his-name wouldn't be inconvenienced. In any case, he and Cathy would be gone in less than five minutes, and they'd be eating fried chicken in less than an hour.

Jimmy recognized Kadeefa's Nissan as he pulled off the inter-state, and he recognized Kadeefa and Cathy as he drove closer. They were at the opened trunk, pulling out Cathy's suitcase.

As soon as Jimmy stepped out of the Buick to grab the suit-case, a man climbed out of the driver's seat of the Nissan. He was about Jimmy's height, and he was wearing a red and white Atlanta Hawks jersey. A cluster of gold chains hung from his neck to his generously rounded stomach. *Chains.* Just like the punk in the pool hall. He hated this bastard already.

"You late," he said, fixing his eyes on Jimmy.

"DeVawn," Kadeefa scolded. "Get back in the car. We don't want no trouble."

Jimmy opened the Buick's trunk and was about to put Cathy's suitcase in it, when the man approached him, deliberately ignor-ing Kadeefa.

"I said you was late," DeVawn repeated in a loud voice.

"Tough," Jimmy said. "I came outa my way to meet y'all up here. You ain't gonna be that late gettin' back to Atlanta."

"We got 'portant shit up in Atlanta," DeVawn insisted. "You made us late, and all you gotta say is 'Tough'?"

"DeVawn, why don' you just shuddup and let's get outa here," Kadeefa shouted impatiently.

"Gotta get me some respect out this muh'fuck," DeVawn explained.

That did it for Jimmy. DeVawn had pushed too far.

Jimmy's fist connected with a loud crack.

DeVawn staggered back slightly, having been taken by surprise.

Kadeefa screamed. Cathy recoiled in horror.

DeVawn's attempt to land his fist on Jimmy failed, and Jimmy struck again.

From that nasty hidden place deep inside him where anger

simmered constantly like a brew in a witch's cauldron, Jimmy's fury exploded. It was no longer predicated on his deep feelings of wanting to avenge the old dude in Sherishk or the honor of a pool hall waitress. It was just his sense of outrage at perceived wrongs and the instinct to simply annihilate perpetrators of wrongs.

Despite his arrogance and his willingness to pick a fight, DeVawn was in no shape physically to handle the situation in which he found himself. He was no match for a National Guardsman in nearly peak physical condition.

Despite DeVawn's squeals and Kadeefa's screams, Jimmy continued hitting the man. He went down, and Jimmy followed him down. It was just like the scene in the pool hall, except there was no crowd of strong men to pull the two antagonists apart.

Suddenly, Jimmy felt a hand on his ankle, and he turned, already swinging his clenched fist.

All Jimmy saw when he turned was Cathy, holding his ankle and looking at him with an expression of total and paralyzing fear on her face.

Jimmy, caught himself, stopping his fist barely ten inches from his precious daughter, whom he loved more than anything in the world.

His ears were filled with the scream of police sirens and the sound of running feet.

Oh God, what have I done?

Iowa City, Iowa
August 31

★ ★ ★

A man with a beard came in from the living room. He said something in a language that Cindy recognized from having heard it before in Afghanistan, although she did not understand the words. The knife in his hand flashed brightly as it reflected the track lighting above the stovetop. Cindy realized that she was lying on the kitchen table. She had a sense that Megan was also in the room, but she couldn't see her.

The bearded man grabbed her injured leg. The pain was horrible. She tried to scream, but she could not make a sound.

Cindy awoke from her nightmare in a cold sweat. The man was no longer in the room, but the wrenching pain in her leg was real. She found herself sitting at the kitchen table, where she had fallen asleep with her leg extended too far for the delicate, grafted tendons to support. She grabbed her knee with her right hand and bent the leg straight. The pain lessened considerably, and Cindy breathed easier.

It was dark outside, and the digital clock on the microwave

told her that it was 4:07. She was wide awake and felt as though she had slept much longer than four hours. She took a shower in the downstairs bathroom so she wouldn't wake the kids and made herself a cup of instant coffee. As she sipped her coffee, Cindy absentmindedly poked through the stack of papers on the table that she had asked Peter to clean up. Among them were several sheets of paper with drawings done by the kids. Her anger at Peter for not cleaning up the mess turned to guilt at having been so impatient with Jessie last night.

One by one, Cindy leafed through the pictures. They were typical of the crayon and marker sketches found in every home in America with small children, but which are each individually special for the families living in those homes. At last, she came to one of two girls, one large and one small, but dressed alike. Beneath them, Isabelle had labeled the smaller girl with her own name and the larger one with the name Megan.

Cindy put her cup on the table and her right hand over her face. She sobbed until she started to hiccup. What had happened to her? What had happened to her life?

She realized that ever since she had returned from Afghanistan, everything once familiar was becoming more and more alien. Instead of reimmersion into her old life, she felt herself drifting farther and farther from the old Cindy and the people whom the old Cindy had known and loved. It was harder and harder to find, much less hold on to, her former reality. Was she going crazy? Should she try to get counseling? The army had programs. Should she find one?

No. She just had to get away.

Cindy decided that she'd get dressed and go take a drive. She'd just slip out before anyone got up and leave a note. As she was dressing, the idea of going for a drive rolled around inside her head. Where should she go? The mall wasn't open yet. As she was picking through the laundry for a pair of jeans, she thought that maybe she would go up to Cedar Rapids. She could be back by dinner. Then she thought maybe she should drive over to Moline to her brother's place for a couple of days. She had not been very close with him for a number of years, but maybe that would be something to do. That's it. She'd throw a few things into a bag and take a couple of days to clear her head.

The more that Cindy thought about it, the longer the couple of days to clear her head became. It was just as easy to throw four shirts into a pile to take as two.

Cindy had started hobbling toward the stairs to go get a suitcase when she stopped herself. That would wake everybody. She couldn't do that. She thought about paper grocery bags. That was an inefficient way to pack clothes for a trip, but who cared? Then she remembered her military duffel bag. It was in the garage, just outside the door from the laundry room.

She pulled the bag into the house and started pulling everything out. Impulsively, she started throwing all her uniforms and stray socks crusted with Afghan mud into the washing machine. She might as well run a load.

The Beretta tumbled out and thudded onto the floor.

Oh, that!

What could she do with it? She couldn't leave it in the house, so she just threw it into the bag along with her clothes. The clothes that she had set aside hardly filled the bag, so she added more. Maybe she'd be gone longer than a few days. The idea seemed liberating. She was feeling better already.

Cindy remembered the can under the sink where she had always squirreled away money for emergencies. It was still there. She pulled it out and counted it. There were more than forty twenty-dollar bills, a couple of fifties, and an odd assortment of fives and tens. She jammed it all into her purse. This would keep her from overdoing it on credit cards when she needed gas money.

She zipped the bag and dragged it back into the garage. She reached for her keys and was about to unlock the Xterra. No, Peter—or *Megan*, damn her—would need that to carry the kids. She decided to take Peter's—actually *their*—Honda. Besides, the SUV was parked in the garage, and the Honda was in the driveway. She wouldn't have to risk waking her family with the clatter of the metal garage door. Peter was a big boy. He could figure out how to get over to the junior college without the Honda. Maybe he could drive Megan's Jetta.

With her bag in the Honda's trunk, Cindy went back into the house to grab her purse. She'd also better write a note. She wouldn't want to have them think she'd been kidnapped. Grabbing a sheet of paper out of the drawer where the kids kept their art supplies, she sat down at the table.

Dear Family,

I took the Honda, and I'm going to go away for a few days to clear my head. I know that I've been on edge a lot lately. I know this upsets you. It upsets me, too. I need to have some time to myself. I've been either on the army's time or JCHS's time, somebody else's time, forever it seems, and sometimes you just need to have some time alone. It's like taking a deep breath for your mind. I'm not sure where I'm going to go, but I'll tell you all about it when I get back.

Love, Mommy

P.S. Have lots of fun at summer camp.

With that, Cindy turned off her cell phone and set it on the table next to the note. It was her way of adding a postscript that said, *Don't try to call me.*

She grabbed a couple of boxes of granola bars on her way out the door. Passing the bank, she decided to get a little more money. She got three hundred dollars on her ATM card and decided to get another three hundred dollars on each of her credit cards for good measure. Why not? She could always put it back. This way, she wouldn't have to use her credit cards—at least for a while. She knew that if she used her credit cards, people would be able to tell where she was and when she was there. How could she be alone if they knew where she was going?

Heading north on First Avenue toward the interstate, she decided to top off the Honda's gas tank. That way, she wouldn't have to stop for a long time. Instinctively, she plugged her credit card into the pay point rather than using cash. She'd try to remember next time.

It felt good, she thought, to be up early in the cool morning air while at least half of Iowa City was still asleep. She relished the freedom of being on the road to somewhere and being on nobody's schedule but her own. Back in the car, she turned on the radio. The clock said 5:32, and the woman on KXIC was reading the first traffic report of the day.

"Expect long delays on eastbound Interstate 80," she said. "A jackknifed big rig has all lanes blocked near Exit 254…"

Just as Cindy had thrilled at the freedom of the open road, she faced the prospect of being stuck in traffic five miles outside the city limits. Her drive to Moline would be a bumper-to-bumper ordeal. Up ahead, she saw the interstate. The eastbound traffic was already starting to bunch up. The big green signs with the red and blue shields said 80 East, and 80 West.

West?

West!

Cindy realized that she didn't *have* to go east. Nobody had *told* her to go east. That had been *her* idea. She could go west. She hadn't been west in a long time, and she had never driven west of Omaha in her life. Except for a conference in Seattle once, she had never been west of Omaha at all. She and Peter had talked off and on about taking the kids to Disneyland, but they never had gone.

As the Honda passed under the interstate, she thought of all those people up there who would spend their morning stuck in traffic because they *had* to go east. As Cindy turned left onto the on-ramp and merged into very light westbound traffic, she smiled.

Mommy was getting away from it all for a while.

CHAPTER SIX

To the Edges
of Their Worlds

Helmand Province, Afghanistan
September 2

★ ★ ★

When Justin Anderson first came to Afghanistan so many months ago, one of the things that the old hands warned him about was to "Watch out for the guys with beards."

As Justin had looked around him, such a warning seemed like a joke. All of the Afghan men had beards, or at least ninety-nine out of a hundred. It was no joke, though. It was hard for Americans to tell the good guys from the bad guys.

Justin glanced across the rear compartment of the jostling Humvee at the man in the gray coat and cap. With his fearsome black beard, this Afghan National Police guy might just as easily have been one of the countless Talibangers with whom Justin had exchanged small-arms fire. He might have been, but he wasn't. Justin knew he wasn't, because the guy had saved his ass and probably the rest of him as well.

It was one of those split-second things that Justin had experienced in this crazy, violent place. It was one of those split-second things that Justin knew happened in wartime where the course of his life could have taken a very different turn. In this case, things turned his way. They were on patrol near a place called Garmsir when they stopped a car for bypassing a checkpoint. As Justin leaned into the vehicle to check something that was on the seat under an overcoat, he had noticed the flicker of movement as one of the clowns in the car reached under his coat.

Justin saw the gun in one of those flash-of-cold-steel moments. The way that Justin was awkwardly leaning, there was no way that he could get to his own weapon.

However, the Afghan cop had also seen that flash-of-cold-steel moment, and he had his own such flash-of-cold-steel moment. From an awkward angle, he put a round directly into the Talibanger's forehead.

He was a good guy, this Zalmai Nawsadi. Beneath the dour expression and that beard, flecked here and there with snowflakes of white, he was a regular guy. As the Humvee bumped along the mountain road, Justin watched the Afghan cop doze off, just like a regular guy. Toons could be regular guys.

He used to think about all the people he met in the Cal Guard and how they were so unlike the people he crossed paths with at UCLA or at the beach in Venice. Being at UCLA, he imagined that he had met and hung out with a pretty broad spectrum of people, but the Cal Guard had broadened his horizons farther than he might have imagined. Then there was Jimmy and the rest of the Georgia guys. You didn't run into many working-class southerners at UCLA.

Nor did you run into many working-class Afghans at UCLA. He knew a couple of Afghans there, but they were rich kids who had grown up in London. Besides, they were in the engineering school, and that was a pretty alien world for Justin when he was still at UCLA.

Today, all of UCLA and his life there was an alien world. He had worried when he felt that reality slipping away, but he didn't care anymore. In his mind, he had given up on UCLA. He didn't think he could go back to that.

His tour had been extended by another six months. He would not be home for Christmas this year. Some guys had been here for more than a year. Justin had worried for a long time that he might be here for more than a year, but no longer. He didn't care anymore.

As the Humvee bumped through a pothole, Zalmai Nawsadi awoke suddenly. He looked around at the three Americans, with their weird pink faces and their expensive gear. He had grown up believing that they were infidels, that anyone with a pink face was an infidel. He no longer believed this. How could people who had everything come halfway around the world to help rid Afghanistan of the Taliban be *infidels*?

He had grown fond of these men as he had gotten to know them. He had even learned a few of their words, and he was starting to understand their bizarre sense of humor. Most of all, he discovered that they had his back. Just as Keith Mackenzie, the Canadian infidel, had come looking for him that day near Garmsir, these American infidels had his back.

Not long after that day that the car bomb killed all those Canadians, Zalmai's Afghan National Police patrol had been ambushed by Taliban about forty kilometers from town. The American Cal Guard had shot their way in to save the Afghans.

A few days later, Zalmai was able to return the favor for the man whom the Americans called Dude, a name that sounded like Daoud. Zalmai had an uncle on his mother's side with that name. Zalmai had shot a Taliban as he pulled a gun on Daoud. It was easy. The muzzle of Zalmai's weapon was only a few centimeters from the enemy's head.

As Zalmai had gotten to know the Americans, he learned of

their fear of bearded men. To this, Zalmai had replied, through a man who spoke both Pashto and English, "If I have a beard, the coalition distrusts me and *may* kill me, but if I shave my beard, the Taliban *will* kill me."

The Americans got the picture.

Afghan men slept with one eye open, and such was the case today. It was not that he feared the Americans around him nor even a roadside bomb that might kill them all. It was the ghosts.

Zalmai never spoke of the year that he was imprisoned in Khadwal-i-Barakzayi. He put those memories away in a remote corner of his memory and constructed a wall around them. He didn't have to think about Khadwal-i-Barakzayi. The physical place was far away, and the memories were locked away.

Now he was going back to Khadwal-i-Barakzayi. Every bounce and bump the Humvee plowed through took them closer.

When Khadwal-i-Barakzayi was not in Taliban hands—although it *was* all too often—it was low-hanging fruit for the Taliban. It was also fertile ground for the ghosts that Zalmai tried to forget.

For Justin, Khadwal-i-Barakzayi was like déjà vu all over again. It was like so many of the forlorn little towns in Afghanistan, with its single-story buildings, a few cars on the single paved street, and its stench. So, too, was Lieutenant Sloan's message like what he had heard so many times before in part-time Taliban strongholds like this. The place reminded him of Sherishk, and Sloan's pep talk reminded him of Sherishk.

"I want the people here to know we're here and see us on foot patrol," Sloan, the platoon commander, explained. "It's real important that they see us."

It was the same story, again. See and be seen, again. As long as the locals could see the presence of the Americans—or someone from NATO or ISAF or some other infidel place—they would have confidence that the Taliban was being beaten and that the Taliban would keep its head down.

It was the same story for Zalmai, as well. It was why he wore his uniform: to let the people know, and to let the Taliban know that they were not alone. Someday, Zalmai knew, the Americans and ISAF and NATO and all the foreigners would be gone, but the Afghans would remain. Zalmai wanted them to see his gray uniform and know that the Afghan National Police was here to stay. Even in Khadwal-i-Barakzayi they had to know this.

As at Sherishk and countless other places, the platoon circled the Humvees and set up a command post. Lieutenant Sloan and the Afghan National Police officer who was traveling with them went to consult with the local officials, and the patrols went out.

Justin was one of four Cal Guard guys in his patrol. Sergeant Norm Briggs was in charge. A construction foreman from Santa Barbara County, he was a good leader but a lot more low-key than Alvarez had been. Justin still missed Ricky Alvarez, but he had learned not to make attachments or friendships. Two Afghan cops, Zalmai and an interpreter, went with the patrol. It was hard not to start liking Zalmai Nawsadi, but Justin was fighting the urge to call the bearded man a friend.

As they walked the streets, people watched them cautiously from a distance. Zalmai suggested that they sling their weapons, so that the patrol would seem less threatening, and he started speaking with the people in Pashto. Gradually, they began warming up. First it was the kids. The kids responded well to the bearded man who rarely smiled, because when he *did* smile, it was infectious.

Everywhere the patrol went, people responded well to Zalmai. This, Justin decided, was the future of Afghanistan. For nearly an hour, the smile never left the bearded face of this Afghan cop; then, suddenly, his demeanor changed. They had come around a corner and were staring down the street at a large gray blockhouse of a building. At the sight of this, Zalmai recoiled slightly. Justin watched his convivial expression change to one of dread.

"What's that place?" Justin asked the Afghan interpreter.

"That was the Taliban prison," the man replied quietly, as though the place still held remnants of the dreaded sect. "They imprisoned many people there in the 1990s. It has been empty for years, though."

"We should check it out," Sergeant Briggs said. "Just to make sure it ain't being used to stash weapons."

Justin noticed the two Afghan National Policemen glance nervously at one another. Briggs noticed it, too.

"Do you think there still may be Taliban in there?" Briggs asked the interpreter.

"No, but there are bad memories in there."

"I still think we had better give it a once-over," Briggs said hesitantly.

The two Afghans exchanged words in Pashto, shrugged, and nodded toward the ugly, hated building.

As they took a quick walk around the perimeter of the building, Justin could see that it was really no larger than a big house. It was a lot larger than his bungalow in Venice but about the same size as some of the bigger houses up in the Hollywood Hills. Though bounded by very narrow streets, it was self-contained and unattached to other structures, as were many buildings in Afghan villages.

The building's single entrance was covered with a stack of rust-covered, corrugated metal sheeting. Beneath this, the door consisted of a grille of iron bars over which some flat sheet steel had been welded. This contraption was sealed with a padlocked chain.

As it took them about five minutes to break the chain, Justin wondered whether this was a good idea. At the moment, the only entrance to the place was secure, and they were breaking the lock. After they left the place like this, there was no telling who would get into it. He thought about mentioning these fears to Sergeant Briggs but decided to keep his mouth shut.

As the doorway finally stood open, and they could feel the cold dampness from within against their faces, it seemed to Justin that they had just opened Pandora's box. He could tell by the expression on Zalmai's face that he was not alone.

Inside, the smell of the place was unbelievable. Most Americans find Afghan towns olfactorily challenging, but this place was off the charts. One of the guys, a new kid from Pomona who had just arrived two days before, lost his breakfast, but the smell of that was hardly noticeable. There was small animal shit everywhere: cats and rats, to name a couple of the vertebrate species. The men could hear the rustling of these creatures who used the place as a latrine as they move cautiously from room to room, weapons ready.

Justin could almost hear the evil spirits hooting and jeering in this place. Zalmai heard more than Justin. He heard the voices of the dead. He heard the voices of friends, of family members. He heard the voices of his long months in this very building under entirely different circumstances. He heard them talking, singing, crying, and screaming.

Zalmai felt the cold dampness on his face and despair in his heart. He felt the pain of steel cables slapping his back and of sharp objects mutilating his body. He felt most of all the hopelessness of believing he would never leave.

For so many years, he had built walls around these memories. Now the walls of the memories surrounded him.

Justin was amazed at the size of the cells. He had heard about places like this where there was barely enough room to stand and where it was nearly impossible to lie down. Room after room was like that. They were just concrete cubicles with a hole in the middle of the floor. The steel doors of some seemed rusted shut.

They passed a room with hooks on the walls. It took no stretch of the imagination to know what had happened here. It was at this moment that Justin started noticing the dark stains spattered on the walls. After all these years, the blood had turned nearly black. Having noticed these black stains once amid all the other crud and clutter in this hellhole, he started seeing them everywhere.

Justin could start to feel the evil spirits, the same evil spirits that Zalmai felt within himself today.

Zalmai had stopped at one of the cells and was staring into it. As Justin approached, he entered. Justin found him crouching in one corner, brushing the dirt and dried blood from a section of the wall.

At last, a small area was brushed clean, except for the filth that had settled into lines scratched into the crumbling concrete.

Justin recognized the scratching as letters from the Pashto alphabet. Someone, a long time ago, had carved his name here.

By the expression on Zalmai's face as he looked up at Justin, there was no doubt who that someone had been.

Somewhere West of Battle Mountain, Nevada
September 2

★ ★ ★

Cindy Hunt stared at the gas gauge and glanced nervously at the darkening sky. She wished that she had stopped for gas in Battle Mountain, but she was not willing to halt her westward journey long enough to turn back. She could probably make it the forty-one miles to Winnemucca. She hoped so. She hoped that a place with a name so bizarre as Winnemucca would have a gas station. At least it would have a casino. Every town in the state seemed to have a casino, even those that had little else.

Cindy had made her first stop for gas in Omaha. Before this road trip, it was the farthest west she had ever driven, and it wasn't even noon. She had started her trip by thinking modestly that she might drive over to Moline, but she had gone west instead. The farther Cindy went, the more she had liked the idea of going west. It was all new, places where the old Cindy had never gone. "West" became her mantra, her goal. She continued on Interstate 80 because all the signs said West.

She spent her first night at a Motel 6 in North Platte, Nebraska, and reached Evanston, Wyoming, the next night. She was enjoying the open road. She went hours without having to have anyone stare nervously or disgustedly at her missing face.

The only people with whom she had any contact were desk clerks at the motels or cash register jockeys at the truck stop minimarts where she bought coffee or junk food—and she would see each of them exactly *once* in her whole life. She didn't care what *they* thought. The woman at the minimart in Rawlins was so stoned that she probably thought Cindy's disfigurement was a hallucination. Cindy didn't care. She had cared so deeply what the teachers at JCHS thought that she had been on the verge of tears. She cared nothing about the opinion of the woman in Rawlins and all the others. She liked not caring. It was a relief not to care.

Since Cindy left Salt Lake City and crossed into Nevada, towns had been fewer and much farther between. In the vast emptiness of the Great Basin desert, there is not much reason for people to want to stay long or build any kind of civilization. It reminded Cindy a lot of Afghanistan—if Afghanistan had been crossed by an interstate highway.

Up ahead she saw some lights at the side of the road and an exit sign. As the Honda was nearly to the off-ramp, she saw a big sign that said Last Chance for Gas. It was as though the message were speaking only to her.

Other than a few dilapidated mobile homes and a couple of shacks, there were exactly two businesses in this godforsaken place: a combination bar and casino, and roadhouse café with two gas pumps out front. The sign on the gas pumps said Pump and Pay Inside. Cindy pumped, parked the Honda, and stepped inside. There were cheeseburgers on the grill, so Cindy took a seat at the counter.

"How you doin'?" asked the cheerful woman about her age

who was working the register. She reminded Cindy of a cowgirl, the kind of person whom Cindy could imagine living out West. "What can I do you for?"

"Well," Cindy said, looking at the woman and watching nervously for the mixed emotions that she usually saw in people's faces when she removed her sunglasses, "I owe you forty dollars for gas, and I'd like a burger and coffee."

"You want fries or slaw? Comes with. I'd recommend the slaw. She makes it with dry-roasted peanuts."

"Oh, I guess I'll have the slaw, then." Cindy smiled. The woman seemed not the least bit unnerved by her appearance, and her recommendation was great.

Cindy had finished her dinner and nodded for a second refill on coffee, when the woman spoke.

"You have a really nasty scar there, if you don't mind me prying into something that's none of my business. How'd it happen?"

Cindy did mind, but she answered anyway.

"Afghanistan."

"Oh my God, you were over *there*?"

"Yes, I was with the 3313th Communications Company of the Iowa Guard," Cindy answered, staring at her coffee.

"Are they taking care of you? The VA, I mean."

"Yeah, I guess so," Cindy said. "I'm supposed to go to the VA Med Center in Iowa City, where I live…for them to do reconstructive surgery."

"My husband was in the 'Ghan," the woman said with a matter-of-fact tone.

"Is he back?" Cindy asked, sensing that she was close to a kindred spirit.

"He came back," she said. "He came back without his legs."

"Is the VA taking care of *him*?" Cindy asked, looking the woman in the eye.

"The wounds got infected, and he passed away about a year ago," the woman said with a shrug. She had obviously passed through her grieving process. Maybe there really was an end to all this emotional pain.

"I'm sorry," Cindy said, standing up and handing the woman three twenty-dollar bills for the gas and the dinner.

"Can't take that," the woman said with a shrug.

"What? Why?"

"We can't take money from vets that gave of themselves over there," she said with a shrug. "It's a small, tiny way of saying thanks to heroes. It's on the house."

"Thank you...so much," Cindy said, shoving one of the bills into the tip jar.

"No, ma'am, thank *you*," the woman said. Her eyes were sad, but there was a smile on her face.

Cindy stepped into the cold night air, crossing to the place where she had parked the Honda. As she got away from the lights of the café, she looked up. The stars were certainly bright out here. That was another thing that reminded her of Afghanistan. A lot of things reminded her of Afghanistan. Was there really an end to all this emotional pain?

Two men stumbled out of the casino and started meandering toward their pickup. Both of them had consumed enough cheap tequila to put a whole basketball team over the legal limit, but they planned to drive home anyway. Of course, it didn't matter. Except for the interstate, nobody patrolled the back roads out here in Humboldt County.

As they neared their truck, they saw a youngish—thirties, maybe—woman staring up at the stars. They saw her in profile, from her right side. She was slender, with long hair that hung to her shoulders and a cute little nose. They had their fill of cheap tequila, and they had wrestled the one-armed bandit to a draw.

Partaking of one more of nature's pleasures would make their evening a success.

"You thinkin' what I'm thinkin'?" asked the first man of the second.

"Nice tits," was the only answer required.

"Hey, good-lookin'," the first man said, greeting the woman. "You wanna party? Let's have some *fun*!"

"What kind of fun?" she asked in disgust.

The men just laughed, imaging their kind of fun playing out sequentially in the back of their pickup on one of those lonely roads that nobody patrols.

They had almost reached her when she turned.

They stopped in their tracks.

An arm that ended only in a crooked claw reached up to brush back the long hair from the left side of what should have been a face. But there was no face—no eye and no ear—only an indescribable something that looked horrible and ghostly in the cold, white, flickering glow of the single mercury vapor streetlight.

"She turned into…it's a fuckin' monster!" the first man screamed in drunken horror.

"It's a fuckin' alien from a fuckin' UFO," the second man gasped.

To them, with their heads spinning from the tequila and their perception chemically distorted, the image of Cindy's face was like the unexpected scene in a horror move when the beautiful girl morphs into a zombie.

"It's a fuckin' *monster*!"

"Let's kill it!"

"Let's *not*," Cindy said. When she had turned her left cheek toward the two men, she was reaching into her purse for the Beretta M9. She had transferred it from her duffel bag that morning when there were some especially creepy bikers at Wendover.

They had smiled and waved when they rode off, and Cindy had felt a little foolish. She was not feeling foolish now about having the pistol in her purse.

She pointed the gun directly at the face of the bigger of the two and told him, as calmly as she could, "I have used this before on guys a lot scarier than you, and I have no qualms about using it again. Nothing would please me more right now than the opportunity to do to your face what I had done to mine."

The two men, rendered speechless by the sight of the gun, backed away slowly, then turned and ran.

Cindy's hands were shaking uncontrollably as she opened the car door and drove as quickly as she could toward the on-ramp marked 80 West.

As she drove into the darkness of the nearly deserted interstate, tears streamed down her right cheek, and her mind rewound and replayed the tape that repeated, over and over, "It's a fuckin' monster!"

Rochelle, Colorado
September 2

★ ★ ★

Luis Carillo wheeled himself through the automatic door at the *mercado* and made his way toward the produce aisle. His head no longer stung from the hangover he had nursed the day before yesterday, but that pain had been trivial compared to the pain that he still carried in his heart. The woman he loved, the woman for whom he had longed under the stars in distant Afghanistan, had said that he was an earthworm, not an eagle. After the inexcusable way that he had behaved the other night, maybe she was right.

"*Mi deseo es no ser la esposa de un gusano,*" she had said. In that one phrase, all of his hopes and dreams—at least all of those that had survived the loss of his legs—seemed to crumble into dust.

He awoke with a dry mouth begging for another beer, a beer that he knew he'd better not have. He sat in the shower, longing for the bath that he could not take because he could not get himself out of a tub. He shaved and drank most of a pot of coffee.

Luis had sat around the house for two days, but this morning, he woke up deciding to make himself useful. His cousin had said that he'd be picking up some groceries on his way home from work, but Luis phoned him to tell him not to bother. Luis said that he'd do it. Was he sure? Yes, Luis told him, he wasn't too crippled to carry a bag of groceries on his lap, and it was the least he could do. He put on his cleanest shirt and rolled his chair down to the *mercado*.

He had just picked out a head of lettuce and was examining the avocados when he felt the gentle touch of a hand on his shoulder.

"Excuse me," a soft voice said tentatively.

He turned and found himself looking up into the face of a young woman. Her face was familiar, and he fought to remember from where.

Damn the hangover.

Then he remembered. Wasn't she was one of the three girls who he had seen in the bar that night? It seemed so long ago already. Yes, she was the one who had continued looking at him after he had smiled and waved.

"I'm sorry to bother you," she said. She was definitely the same girl, but she had her hair tied back, and the tight jeans were superseded by a conservative-length black dress. "Are you Mr. Carillo...Luis Carillo?"

"Yes," Luis said. "That's me."

"My name is Rosa Calderon," she said, extending her hand. "I'm pleased to meet you."

"I'm pleased to meet you, too," Luis said, wondering why in the world she was introducing herself to him this way in the produce aisle. She was still attractive, but a lot more refined and studious-looking than he remembered. She spoke perfect, unaccented English, not like an immigrant but like a person who had grown up in the United States.

"I'm sorry to bother you," she repeated. "I've read about you in the papers, and I've seen your picture. I wasn't sure. Was that you in the Cantina Sinaloa the other night?"

"Yes," Luis said, wishing that he had denied it, letting her think it was some other drunk in a wheelchair.

"I heard what you said to *El Hombre*," she said. "I was shocked to hear someone say those things to him. He's a very powerful man in Galeana Poco. Nobody ever speaks up to *El Hombre* that way, and word is starting to get around."

"Well…" Luis started to say, assuming that she must have been sent to tell him that he was rolling on thin ice by mouthing off to Mr. Big. He felt his life becoming rapidly worthless. After what had happened with Roxanna, he had forgotten that he had also pissed off a man who would just as soon kill him as tell him to fuck off.

"Well, I can explain…"

Luis wanted to say that he was sorry and that he had not been as tactful as he should have been, when Rosa interrupted him.

"I thought that was one of the bravest things I had ever seen," she explained. "Then I realized that you were a war hero, and it made sense. Galeana Poco needs more people like you."

"Ummm thanks," Luis said, unsure what to think about going from earthworm to hero.

"There's something I wanted to ask you, Mr. Carillo," she said, putting her hand lightly on his shoulder again. "I'm the executive director down at El Centro de Comunidad. We sure could use someone like you to come down and speak to the kids…especially the preteen boys. A lot of them are getting caught up in this gang thing, you know, idolizing these punks like *El Hombre*. They need a better role model…they need a role model like you. That is, if you have the time to come down."

"I got all the time in the world," he told her. "You know, I got all the time in the world…but I don't think a guy in a chair is a very good role model for a bunch of kids."

"I'm sorry, Mr. Carillo, but I'd have to disagree with that. You're the war hero who stood up to *El Hombre*. Word spreads fast. The kids will know about you. You are a *perfect* role model."

"Yeah, I suppose I could," Luis said thoughtfully. "When?"

"What's your schedule like next week?" Rosa Calderon asked.

"I don't *have* a schedule," Luis said with a chuckle. "I can come in tomorrow if you want."

"You're free *any* day?" she asked, seeming surprised. "You're not working?"

"Well…" he said, slightly embarrassed. Not only was he a cripple, he was an unemployed cripple. "I'm sorta between jobs."

"I don't want to impose," she said. "And I don't know whether you'd be interested, but our senior counselor position is open. It's a federally funded position, you know, and they like to see veterans get hired. If you're interested?"

"That's real interesting," Luis said. "How would I apply?"

"If you're real interested, let's say you just did. I'm the executive director. I write the recommendations. Can you come in tomorrow?"

"I thought you said next week." He smiled.

"You were the one who said tomorrow." She smiled back. "I didn't know when I said next week that you'd be applying for the job. There's a lot of paperwork formalities to get through, and besides, I'm also real anxious to have you start meeting our kids."

Luis noticed that she hadn't stopped touching his shoulder.

Mendocino, California
September 3

★ ★ ★

The drive through the vineyard country north of Cloverdale was beautiful in the late afternoon light. The view of the Pacific Ocean at Navarro Head was unlike anything Cindy Hunt had ever seen. The crashing waves and the fog bank lingering out at sea were so marvelously unlike anything you could see in Iowa. Back home, the only seas were of cornstalks.

She took a deep breath, climbed back into the Honda, and looked again at the road map that she had picked up when she stopped for gas west of Auburn. Less than ten miles to Mendocino, California. Long ago, she had seen something on the food channel about Mendocino. It seemed like a magical and wonderful place, an ancient whaling village perched on the cliffs above the sea. As with most things you see on television, Cindy had forgotten about it until she happened to see a postcard when she stopped for gas.

Mendocino. Magic Mendocino.

When Cindy had left Iowa City, her only plan had been to

go west, and so she did. She woke up in Auburn knowing that she had reached nearly to the end of Interstate 80. She would be in San Francisco in a few hours. She was almost to the end of the continent. Where would she go next? She had no idea until she saw the Mendocino postcard. Now she had a new plan. She bought a road map, found Mendocino on it, and headed west.

Cindy hadn't stopped to spend last night in Winnemucca as she had planned. She just wanted to get as far away from the two men as possible. One minute, a stranger was buying her dinner for being a hero, and the next minute, she was "a fuckin' monster!"

She crossed Donner Pass in darkness and woke up a motel clerk outside of Auburn. She slept later than she had since she began her road trip, but she made good time on Interstate 80 and was in San Francisco before noon. She had read about the Golden Gate Bridge all her life, and now she could say that she had driven across it.

If she did say that, who would she say it to?

It was not until now, as she was driving up the hill north of the big orange bridge, that she wished she had brought her cell phone. She had left home deliberately not wanting to be in touch. Now she was starting to wonder. Should she phone Peter? Was she ready for that? Was he ready?

She missed her kids so much that it hurt, but what hurt more was the image of the two girls dressed alike, one labeled Isabelle and the other Megan. Pretty, perky Megan, whose underwear had been casually cast into the clothes hamper at Cindy's home. Pretty, perky Megan, who had become more of a mother—and certainly more of a friend—to Isabelle and Jessie than Cindy was. Pretty, perky Megan, who Cindy imagined was more of a special friend to Peter than Cindy could be. What man wants to make love to "a fuckin' monster!"?

With Cindy gone, they would make a happy family. Peter

was too old for Megan, but she apparently didn't care. They were obviously comfortable enough with their relationship for her to casually leave her sexy little purple underwear at his house—*and* the kids liked her a lot.

No, she was *not* ready to phone Peter.

Cindy arrived in Mendocino at dusk. With the vivid orange horizon and the light of a rising full moon, her first look at the place transcended the magic that she remembered from the food channel program. As she drove into town, she could see the lights of fishing boats twinkling out in the ocean.

Cindy wished that she could remember the name of that restaurant that was profiled on the food channel, but she spotted one that looked informal and cute. She guessed that she would have some seafood and then try to find one of those bed-and-breakfast places that she knew were so popular around here.

The young waiter glanced, but did not stare, at Cindy's shortage of face. He was friendly and polite and even recommended some merlot from a local vineyard that she might like.

Cindy was feeling relaxed and happy as she ate a cup of chowder, and she paid little attention as a group of people sat down at the booth off to her left—until she heard a bit of a ruckus.

She glanced over. It was two women about her age with four children more or less Jessie's age. The women were casually dressed but obviously wearing very expensive casual clothing. This must be what Californians called "chic." They each had very large diamonds glistening on their ears, and other diamonds on their ring fingers. Cindy thought about her own rings, left in the dust so far away, and wondered who was wearing them tonight.

From their behavior, Cindy could tell that the children were strangers to the kind of parental discipline that prevents them from being spoiled. They came from homes where discipline was imparted by nannies rather than parents. The kids were all wearing identical, brand-new, never-washed T-shirts that spoke of a fund-raiser for an ecology organization. They had all apparently been in Mendocino "raising awareness" and raising money to save the whales or something.

Cindy had paid little more attention and was finishing her chowder, when she detected the shadow of someone approaching from her left. She turned her head so that she could see who it was with her eye and found herself facing one of the women who had come in with the kids. At first glance, Cindy admired her perfect nails and her perfect makeup. Who had time to spend on such things?

"Excuse me," the woman said with an impatient expression. "Would you mind very much turning the other way? You're frightening the children."

She impatiently made a little circular gesture with a long, slender finger, indicating that Cindy should sit on the opposite side of her table so that children would not have to look at her scarred face.

Cindy was stupefied. She glanced over at their booth. The second woman was frowning, two little girls were hiding their eyes, and a boy in the group mouthed the word "freak" as she looked at him.

"And *that*," the woman said, pointing at Cindy's shirt. "*That*...something like that...promoting violence...is *very* inappropriate to be wearing around children. This is Mendocino!"

Cindy looked down. She remembered that this morning it was pretty warm, so she put on a T-shirt. It carried the legend "U.S. Army, Camp Kandahar." What a contrast it was to the designer clothing that the two women were wearing.

Cindy stood up very slowly and stared after the woman as she returned to the booth.

"I'm very sorry," Cindy said, leaning forward so that she was almost face-to-face with the woman. "I'm so very sorry that you are offended by my face and by my shirt. I got them both in Afghanistan. I don't know whether these 'frightened' children have heard of it. It's a place a long way from here where a lot of very wonderful young men and women are losing lives and body parts to serve their country."

Cindy stood up straight, looking at the flabbergasted expressions of the two women.

"I will wake up every morning for the rest of my life wishing that I could choose not to wear this face," Cindy told them, gesturing with her left, clawlike, thumb. "But I'm *proud* to wear this shirt."

With that, she scooped up her purse and jacket with her left arm, handed a wad of bills to the stunned waiter, and walked out.

The door closed before she heard the people at two other tables stand to applaud her speech.

As she started the car, all she heard was that voice from last night in her head.

"It's a fuckin' *monster*!"

As she meandered through Mendocino's darkened streets looking for Highway 1, she wondered again about calling Peter. Maybe it *was* time.

She pulled into a gas station, and in the light of its illuminated sign, she scratched around in her purse for some coins. Armed with nearly four dollars in dimes and quarters, she went to the pay phone and dialed 1 and then 319, the area code for Iowa City. She paused, took a deep breath, dialed the last seven numbers, and listened to it ring three times. The duration between rings seemed like a minute or more. Her hand was shaking, her heart pounding.

"Hello," a woman's voice—a *young* woman's voice—answered.

Damn you, Megan, thought Cindy.

"Hello, is somebody there?"

In the background, Cindy heard Peter's voice asking, "Who is it? Is it her? Let me have the phone…"

There was a scraping sound as the receiver was passed.

"Hello," Peter said. "Who's this? Is that you, Cindy? Hello. Hel—"

Cindy just hung up. What man wants to love "a fuckin' monster" when he has pretty, perky Megan in his home?

She didn't know what to say. She didn't know what to do. She didn't know where to go. Like that morning in Iowa City so long ago, she just got in the car and drove, leaving Mendocino on the road that had brought her there.

About a dozen or so miles north of Mendocino, Cindy saw a turnout at the side of the road toward the ocean, and she pulled over. The vivid clarity of the waves illuminated in the brilliant white of the full moon was beautiful. It was the edge of the continent, but it seemed like the edge of the earth. The steep cliff dropping toward the crags of rock around which the waves were crashing seemed dramatically final. There was nothing but darkness beyond the waves.

Cindy had driven nearly two thousand miles through cornfields, through deserts, and across two ranges of mountains unlike anything she had ever seen in the Midwest. The smell of the ocean was unlike anything she could have imagined. She had driven through redwood forests and vineyards to reach this place. It seemed like the edge of the earth. There was nothing but darkness beyond the waves.

Once she had been a wife and mother, but then there was Megan. Once she had been a teacher and track coach, but if the principal found it hard to look at her, what about the teenagers? Once she had been a soldier, but that had ended badly, too.

What was left? Her own daughter called her a witch. A little kid called her a freak. A stranger thought of her as "a fuckin' monster!"

It seemed like the edge of the earth. There was nothing but darkness beyond the waves.

Cindy took the Beretta 9 mm from her purse and examined it in the moonlight.

She felt herself at the edge of the earth. There was nothing but darkness beyond the waves.

She put the muzzle to the side of her head and felt the cold against her temple. Then she touched the muzzle to her lips. She wrapped her lips around its cold roundness, touching the metallic circle lightly with her tongue. She wondered why some people do it in the head, and some people put it in their mouth. The result is the same. What does it feel like? Does it feel different in the mouth than in the side of the skull?

She looked out at the rocks and felt herself at the edge of the everything. There was nothing but darkness beyond the waves.

She thought of the quadriplegic NASCAR driver and wondered what he had gone through. He never had—and never would have—the choice of whether to put the muzzle to his head or into his mouth, but she was sure that he had wanted to. She looked down at the waves and went through the motion of throwing the gun into the frothy sea. She didn't let go. It remained, heavy and cold in her hand.

Her eyes were growing accustomed to the darkness now, and she noticed that she was parked next to a trailhead. She looked closer and saw in the moonlight that the trail snaked all the way down to the base of the cliffs.

She slid the gun into the waistband of her jeans and started down the trail.

Somewhere down there was the edge, but beyond, there was nothing but darkness.

Waycross, Georgia
September 7

★ ★ ★

The last time that Jimmy Ray Flood stood in the Greyhound bus depot on Forsyth Street in Atlanta, he had tears in his eyes. The last time *and* this time.

The last time, he had just said good-bye to Cathy to go off to Afghanistan for at least six months and probably more. He didn't know when he'd be coming back.

This time, he knew that he might soon be looking into the eyes of the little girl he loved and hugging her for the last time—ever. He was probably going away for a very long time. He didn't know when he'd be coming back.

By the time he returned, she would no longer be a little girl.

If Jimmy got fifteen years for aggravated assault, the best he could hope for would be getting released on parole when Cathy was in her early twenties.

Jimmy's life had changed in an instant, and he had only himself to blame. Had he not slugged DeVawn Petrie, he and Cathy would have been happily eating fried chicken less than an hour later. Had he not slugged DeVawn Petrie, he and his mother would have shared a happy week with Cathy.

His mother had taken three days off from her job at the insurance agency, and it would have been a most wonderful week. But she never got to see Cathy at all. He had let his mother down, but most of all, he had let Cathy down. In an instant, he had let her see the monster that he thought had been tamed.

Had he not slugged DeVawn Petrie, Jimmy would not have spent a week in jail waiting for his arraignment. They had not let Cathy see him in jail. This had hurt Jimmy deeply, but now he was glad that she had not seen him that way. How would it be when he was in the Georgia State Prison at Reidsville? How would it be for her to see him in that place? How would it be for her to spend her high school years visiting her father in Reidsville instead of having him come to her basketball games and see her in her prom dress?

How would it be for him to watch her grow up in two-week increments through a two-inch plate glass window?

No wonder he had tears in his eyes.

Today, at least, she would see him standing in the air, *almost* as though nothing had happened. He had four days of freedom before the trial started. His brief breath of liberty came when bail was finally granted, and it was paid for with his mother's life savings sitting in the county's bank account to guarantee that he would not try to run. His bail took every penny his mother could scrape together.

Today, Cathy would see him standing in the air, but it was not as though nothing had happened. They both knew something had happened—something very bad.

"Hello, Ma," Jimmy said, recognizing his mother's phone number on his cell phone. He stepped away from the entrance to the MARTA platform, glad that he caught the call before he got inside, where he would not have cell reception.

"Ma, I'm steppin' outside here where I can hear you," he said. He could barely hear her voice. She was breaking up—in more ways than one. She was sobbing.

His heart stood still.

"Can you hear me, Ma? Why you crying?"

"Just got off the phone with Mr. Moore," she sobbed.

This took his breath away. It couldn't be good. She was crying, and Mr. Moore was his lawyer. He was one of the best criminal defense attorneys in Waycross. He would not have even looked at Jimmy were it not for the fact that he was a longtime personal friend of one of the partners in the insurance agency where Jimmy's mother worked.

"Wha'd he say, Ma?"

"He said he talked to the judge this morning. He said the judge'll accept a lesser plea 'cause of your service with the National Guard."

"What does that mean?"

"It means parole, Jimmy," she sobbed. "It means time served. It means no goin' to Reidsville."

Jimmy practically passed out.

"So why you cryin', Mama?" Jimmy asked when he had finally caught his breath.

"I'm sittin' down here in Waycross bawling my head off 'cause I'm so relieved that my only son is not going to prison after beatin' two men half to death. I'm bawling because the good Lord has handed you a second chance that you probably don't deserve, and you had better make the most of this. The good Lord don't go around handin' out second chances like this every day."

"I understand, Ma."

All the way to Kadeefa's apartment, Jimmy thought about what he'd say to Cathy. She had been through hell, too. No girl her age should have to see what she had seen and know that her father was in jail and about to go away for a long time. No girl any age should have to endure the pain and humiliation that Cathy had experienced. Jimmy even wondered for a moment whether or not his parole was the best thing for Cathy. If he really *was* that man she saw in the parking lot at the truck stop, maybe it was good that he *not* be in her life.

After what had gone down, Jimmy was surprised that Kadeefa was allowing Jimmy to see Cathy at all.

It was supposed to be their final good-bye before Jimmy's trial, their last true face-to-face good-bye before Jimmy went away for what would be a virtual eternity in Cathy's life.

Kadeefa answered the door more subdued than he had seen her in a very long time. She even invited him in and told him to sit down on the sofa. On nearly every other visit to this apartment, he had been left standing in an open doorway. Cathy was not there, but Kadeefa told him that she was at a friend's apartment and would be back shortly.

When Jimmy explained the news that he had just gotten from his mother, Kadeefa was speechless. Like Jimmy, she sat in stunned disbelief. Her jaw dropped, and she just stared at Jimmy. Finally, she started to sob. She was behaving very unlike the angry bitch whom Jimmy had come to know and despise.

"That's good," she said at last, wiping her eyes with a tissue. "That's very good for Cathy. Even after all this shit, she needs a daddy."

As Kadeefa wiped beneath her eyes, a layer of makeup came off, revealing a patch of purple.

"What happened to your eye?" Jimmy asked.

Kadeefa looked startled, as though he had seen something she was trying to hide.

He had.

"Oh, nothing," she said. "It's really nothing."

"It's really something," Jimmy countered. "Who did that to you? DeVawn?"

"I just have a helluva time with men," Kadeefa sobbed.

Jimmy tensed, and Kadeefa looked horrified.

"Don't even think about it!" Kadeefa said, sensing that the anger and violence were about to boil over. She could easily imagine a dead DeVawn and Jimmy in Reidsville for the rest of his life.

"I won't," Jimmy promised, releasing his clenched fists and closing his eyes. "I have been thinking about almost nothing else except *not* to be thinking about that kinda shit. When I saw that look on Cathy's face that day and knew how bad I'd fucked up, I knew I couldn't never do that, or even think about that shit, ever again. Never."

Kadeefa relaxed.

"He had it comin', though," Kadeefa admitted through the tears. "He had it comin'. That DeVawn was an infantile asshole and a bully. He had it comin' to tangle with somebody like you who wouldn't take shit from him."

"You had a lotta trouble with him?"

"Yeah, I guess so," Kadeefa said. "Like I said, I haven't had very good luck with men."

"Why you tellin' me this?"

"Because you are the only man I've ever been with that didn't hit me," she said, breaking into tears.

Jimmy reached out and took the hand of his sobbing ex-wife.

"Ever since we split up, I've been getting myself in with men that ain't like you...men that are so far different from you that they don't remind me of you...and I've fucked up every time. I've fucked up so bad tryin' to get away from you."

Jimmy just squeezed her hand a little tighter.

"I just wish all of this shit had never happened," she sobbed.

"None of it. I just wish that we hadn't gotten so far off track. I wish things were like that night that Cathy came home from the hospital. When we were, y'know, so happy."

Jimmy wished that someone, somewhere, sometime would explain to him the thought processes of women.

"I just miss that so much," she said, putting her arms around his neck and hugging him.

Jimmy, too, started to feel tears welling up inside.

At that moment, the front door swung open, and Cathy came into the apartment.

As she beheld her mother sobbing, she froze. Cathy had seen so much over the past few years. She had learned the hard way that seeing her mother in tears meant only one thing—and it was never a good thing.

"Come here, baby," Kadeefa said, motioning toward Cathy.

Hesitantly, Cathy moved toward her embracing parents, trying to size up the situation.

They were both crying, but the expressions on their faces were not those of anger or pain. They were both smiling. Their expressions were inviting. Their eyes filled not with hate but with love.

Nevertheless, she approached them with great trepidation. She had learned the hard way that seeing her mother in tears meant only one thing—and it was never a good thing.

As she got within a couple of feet of the two adults, they both reached out and pulled her into their embrace. For a moment, she felt as though she had stepped back in time. For a moment, she felt the way she had felt when she was a little girl.

If only for a moment, Cathy felt as she had during the happiest years of her life.

Epilogue

★

Helmand Province, Afghanistan
September 7

★ ★ ★

The hills were engulfed in flames. The village of Khadwal-i-Barakzayi lay at the base of a burning ridge. The sheets of flame and the billowing pillars of black that were creeping ever closer to the structures reminded Justin of Juniper Ridge. It seemed like a lifetime since Juniper Ridge.

It had been.

"Here they come!"

As Justin turned, the ripping sound of automatic weapons filled the air. A large number of armed men in turbans were rushing the narrow defensive line where the men of the 3rd Battalion of the 184th Regiment of the California Army National Guard were dug in.

This day had started like any other day in the endless succession of days.

It involved a patrol into the dry, brushy hills above Khadwal-i-Barakzayi. It was supposed to be routine. It was so routine that Lieutenant Sloan allowed a camera crew from some cable news network to join his men. Actually, they were stringers for a cable news network. Almost nobody sent their regular people outside Kabul anymore, but they were always happy to accept feeds—especially live feeds—from freelance camera crews. There were always more than a few freelance camera crews roaming around and anxious to provide live feeds. The money was good—really good. Sometimes they took the same chances as the soldiers—but they could leave any time they wanted to, and they got paid *a lot* better.

Today, the camera guys got more than they had bargained for. The patrol had been ambushed two miles from town, and they were pinned down on a lonely ridge. Justin had been in a place like this before. The camera guys had not.

Through the haze, it was hard to tell how many bad guys there were. They were like blue-black shadows materializing out of the smoky air. They looked like ghosts, except for the bright yellow-orange muzzle flashes of their AK-47s.

The muzzle flashes were the same color as the flames that burned on the hillside above the Afghan village.

Justin felt no fear, only numbness.

His fearlessness was not that of great heroism but rather the fearlessness that comes from surrendering one's emotions to that which has become automatic. In the army they have a saying that when a well-trained soldier is in a firefight, the training takes over. It becomes the guiding principle that steers his action. The training, beyond reason and intuition, is the guiding force. For an experienced soldier, though, it is the experience that takes over.

There was nothing to do but return fire. His experience told him that. He had been here before.

As two Taliban slowed to navigate a cluster of boulders, Justin carefully aimed his M16A4 and squeezed the trigger. One man went down instantly, but the other managed to survive a few moments before he, too, crumpled to the ground.

Raymond "Spider" Rhead screamed angrily, and he squeezed the trigger of his M240 machine gun. He always screamed angrily at the Taliban. He wanted to kill them all. Ever since that experience on the hill, he had been a one-man killing machine.

For the first few weeks after the hill, Justin had wondered how a man like that could ever reintegrate into society back home. Justin didn't think about that anymore, especially after he found himself growing more and more like Spider than like the cheerful surfer dude that he had been when he was given the nickname he still carried. Justin wondered how a man like himself could ever reintegrate into society back home. Having given up on UCLA, he wondered what he would do.

Mainly, however, he had learned that there was a point while a man was in combat that he just stopped thinking about the rest of his life and concentrated on the Taliban in front of him.

"Way to *fuckin'* go," Spider screamed.

A cluster of Taliban, coming off the hill in a line, had gotten into his sights, and he had mowed them down.

"There! Get the damned 240 on *there*," Sergeant Briggs shouted, slapping Spider on the shoulder. "We got 'em over *there*, too!"

The camera guys had hunkered down so low that their backs were nearly flush with the red dirt in the bottom of the narrow drainage ditch where the Americans had taken cover. It was almost comical—but not quite. They had left their camera propped up and pointed toward the town. Justin imagined that they weren't getting very good pictures through all the haze.

Justin hunkered down himself. His throat was dry, but instead of reaching for water, he reached for another clip for his M16A4. He pulled out the spent clip, slammed in the new one, and looked out in the direction opposite from where Spider was shooting.

Things did not look so good.

Zalmai was firing his AK-47 at the advancing enemy. Justin saw his shoulders jerk each time he squeezed off a shot, but he could barely hear the shots. The wall of sound was so loud that individual sounds were absorbed in it like water into a cloth—like blood into a bandage.

The other Afghan guy who usually traveled with the patrol was down. He was lying on his back. There was a lot of blood. Someone had put a compress on one of his wounds, but it was just sitting there now. It was probably too late. Poor guy. Tough luck.

Justin glanced the other way.

Briggs was on the radio. Justin could hear enough to know that someone had just told him that air support was impossible because of all the smoke.

Spider was screaming obscenities and banging a bloody fist against the breach of the M240 machine gun. It was jammed, and he was trying to clear it. Justin knew—as Spider knew—that the M240 was a vital piece of equipment for beating off the Taliban. Without it, the Cal Guard boys and the Afghan cop were in big trouble.

The Taliban still looked like blue-black shadows materializing out of the smoky air. They still looked like ghosts, and their muzzle flashes like the flames that burned on the hillside above the Afghan village.

Justin felt no fear, only numbness.

"Daoud!"

The wall of sound was torn by the urgency of the call.

Justin turned as he heard Zalmai scream his nickname.

Three more Taliban were materializing out of the smoke, and were nearly on top of them.

How could these bastards have gotten this close?

Los Angeles
September 7

★ ★ ★

Laurie Hall closed her laptop and stared out the window of the Starbucks. She watched the traffic passing on Wilshire Boulevard without really seeing it.

She didn't recognize him anymore. For weeks, even months, she had thought she was in love with Justin Anderson. That night beneath the stars on the beach at Malibu was magic, as magic as any moment in her life. As time had gone on, the magic of that moment took on a life of its own, magnified in Laurie's mind into a turning point.

She had gone so far as to admit to a friend that it was the happiest moment of her life.

Then he had sent her that e-mail that he signed with "Love, Justin."

Her life had changed. She was in love, and he was in love with her. It was silly, but the next few weeks were filled with happy, delicious fantasies about being with him—forever.

Gradually, the tone of his e-mails had begun to change. He

became absorbed with death, with the death of friends and people he knew. She had felt for him, and she wanted to hold him in her arms and comfort him. She told him this, but he did not respond to the comment.

The e-mails became fewer and farther between. He said that they were on patrol a lot, and that he didn't have Internet access. She believed him.

She had tried to imagine what his world was like in Afghanistan, but it was so abstract. Nobody she talked with had any experience with it. They only knew—and she only knew—what they saw on television, and this was invariably bad. Nobody she talked with really wanted to talk about it. They always changed the subject.

Afghanistan was another world, but it was Justin's world. She read a few blogs, but they were depressing. Maybe that was why Justin seemed so depressed. That, and the fact that he would not be home for Christmas. That thought hadn't even entered into her mind when he left. He was going for six months. Christmas was longer than that. What happened?

Last week, Laurie had met Travis Mathers, and things had started to change. He was a grad student in finance. His father owned a chain of copy shops over in the San Fernando Valley around Mission Hills, and up into Glendale and Pasadena. He was tall, cheerful, and easy on the eyes. Laurie had blushed when they talked, and she knew it. She knew it, and he *saw* it.

Yesterday, she had seen him again over by Kaufman Hall. He had asked her out. She had asked for a rain check. She was still in love with Justin. Someday—if not for Christmas, then someday—Justin would be back, and they would recapture the magic of the night on the beach at Malibu.

But, she had asked for a rain check. She hadn't told Travis no. She had blushed. She couldn't help it. It wasn't rocket science that guys could figure out that blushing meant "Please ask me again, *soon*."

Last night, she sent Justin an e-mail, just to prove to herself that she was still in love with him. She had told herself that she loved him, and she felt the need to prove it—as much to herself as to Justin.

Much to her surprise, he answered almost immediately!

She discovered his response as she logged on at the Starbucks this morning.

Already!

She was relieved that he was in a place with Internet access. That, in her mind, meant that he was someplace safe.

His mind, however, seemed to be anywhere but in a safe place. He told her of having seen a prison, and he told her how horrible it smelled and how there was blood all over the walls.

He told her that he had "popped a Talibanger" last week. He said it as casually as he might have told her about getting his Porsche detailed. She knew that "popped a Talibanger" meant that he had killed a human being with a gun. Laurie had never even touched a gun in her life. She knew from his past e-mails that he had taken other lives, but she had ignored his comments. She read them but did not think about them.

It was not so much the killing; that, like everything about Afghanistan, was still abstract for Laurie. It was the casual way that he killed and talked about killing. Even if they were his enemy and it were self-defense, how could he refer to inflicting mortal injuries as having "popped" another human being?

It was the last paragraph that made her hands turn clammy.

Any time that a man begins a sentence with "I've been thinking," you know that it is a rare look into how they really feel. For women, who are typically unused to hearing men share their feelings, this is unnerving.

"I've been thinking," he wrote. "When I get back to LA, I'm not going back to UCLA. It's just too weird to think about going back there with all that stuff that goes on. It's like when you get out of high school and you know that part of your life is over, and you couldn't ever go through that again. I don't belong there. I've changed too much, I think. That's another world, just like this place is another world, and there is nothing in common between the two worlds except that I used to be in that one, and now I'm in this one, and I don't want to be in either one. I don't belong there. Maybe I belong here. I could stay. Ha-ha. They are giving bonuses if you stay and kill bad guys. When I get back, I really don't know what I'll do. My dad will be pissed off that I don't go back to UCLA, but I can't. I don't know what I'll do. See ya, Justin."

Laurie stared out the window at the traffic passing on Wilshire Boulevard without really seeing it.

She didn't recognize Justin.

The impulses to hug him and comfort him were gone.

She didn't know who he was.

She shed a couple of tears at the thought of the magic night at Malibu being lost, consigned forever to the dark recesses of her memory. She wiped her eyes and tried not to cry. She always thought it pathetic to see people sitting alone in public places and crying. She did not want to be one of those.

The television on the wall was tuned to one of the cable news channels. The caption on the bottom said something about breaking news. In smaller letters, she could make out the word "Afghanistan." There was another word, but the television was too far away for her to read it. She knew that Justin was over there somewhere, but it still seemed so abstract.

Laurie looked around. She was the only person in the room who was watching the screen. Several people were working on laptops. Three well-dressed people were having a business meeting. There was a Hispanic nanny with a pink-cheeked baby in a stroller.

Laurie felt really alone in the midst of all this, alone with the silent, flickering images of that place so far away. There were flickering images of flames, of columns of smoke and of a town. There were flickering images of people running. They were running into the fire.

Bill Yenne is the author of numerous works of both fiction and non-fiction, including the Raptor Force fiction trilogy, also published by Berkley. Gary Sheffield, Professor of War Studies at the University of Birmingham in England wrote that another of his earlier Berkley novels, *A Damned Fine War*, "succeeds triumphantly....It is an excellent read." *The New Yorker* wrote of Yenne's recent biography of Sitting Bull that it "excels as a study in leadership." *Publishers Weekly* has described his work as "eloquent," while the *Wall Street Journal* recently called one of his military histories "splendid" and went on to say that he writes with "cinematic vividness."